Saxon Fall: Rise of the Warlord

Book 8 in the
Wolf Warrior Series
By
Griff Hosker

Published by Sword Books Ltd 2014
Copyright © Griff Hosker First Edition

The author has asserted their moral right under the Copyright, Designs and Patents Act, 1988, to be identified as the author of this work.
All Rights reserved. No part of this publication may be reproduced, copied, stored in a retrieval system, or transmitted, in any form or by any means, without the prior written consent of the copyright holder, nor be otherwise circulated in any form of binding or cover other than that in which it is published and without a similar condition being imposed on the subsequent purchaser.
A CIP catalogue record for this title is available from the British Library.

Chapter 1

Caer Gybi 626

I had been named Hogan Lann, son of the Bane of the Saxons, Lord Lann of Rheged. The moment my father was buried beneath the snowy tops of Wyddfa I became Warlord: The Warlord. Until the day my earthly life ended I would be Warlord. I would lead the armies of the lands of Rheged and Gwynedd and fight to defeat the Saxons. I had been entrusted with halting the seemingly endless waves of Saxons who looted and pillaged their way across the old Roman province of Britannia. We had stopped them up to now. With the aid of King Cadwallon, king of Gwynedd, we had drawn a line across the land. The invaders were halted. We had had to compromise and ally ourselves with some Saxons to do so and that did not sit well. The Mercians fought alongside us. Myrddyn, my father's closest friend and adviser, had persuaded me that we had to be pragmatic. He was a wise old man and he could see into the future.

One cold and bone freezing day, just a month after Yule I was with my warriors at the fort close to the port of Caer Gybi. It was on Ynys Mon. We were at the very edge of Britannia and we could see Hibernia, the old land of Rheged and Wyddfa from the top of the mountain. Myrddyn had asked that we come here to speak with my father's brother, Aelle. He was the only uncle I had left and my father had been very close to him.

As I watched my household equites gathering in the great hall in the heart of the fortress, I reflected that we were much diminished since we had last defeated the Saxons. Back then we had fielded more than two hundred equites and squires. That was before the plague which devastated our fort beneath Wyddfa. I had lost all. My wife, my children and my stepmother were all taken by the illness which seemed to come from nowhere. Even old Oswald the priest had fallen foul of the insidious disease. The followers of the White Christ took great delight in telling us that it had been because we were pagans that God has visited the plague upon us. As Myrddyn, the wizard, said, "It took pagan and Christian alike; their God must not be able to tell the difference!"

We knew what it was, it was *wyrd*. I had abandoned the fort and invited King Cadwallon and his wife, my sister, to live there. It was a safer home than the one he used on the borders of Mercia. I could not live there for the memories were too painful. The men of Mercia were his friends now but we all knew the treachery of the Saxons. They could turn like a rabid dog at any moment.

The warriors who remained had all lost family. The exception was my brother, Gawan, whose son, daughter, and wife had been many miles from the disease. That too was *wyrd*. He was the dreamer and he was the one who went with Myrddyn to dream in the dream cave and to speak with the spirits of our ancestors. I did not resent the idea of his speaking with our father while I could not. He was the dreamer and I was the warrior; it was meant to be.

I knew why Myrddyn had summoned this meeting at the fort of Cam. He had dreamed in Wyddfa's heart and seen the future again. It was never a clear picture but it would tell us if it were to be good or ill. I was pleased to be here with my men away from the memories of my empty home beneath the brooding peaks of Wyddfa. Lann Aelle was also looking forward to being reunited with his father. One armed Aelle was the last of the three brothers and I had a lot of time for my uncle. As each visitor arrived he was welcomed by my equites. We were the guardians of Rheged still and we fought for all those who had been summoned. Myrddyn had been insistent about the guest list for this rare conclave. Every visitor would help us to defeat the Saxons. It was Gawan who spoke with Myrddyn and not me. I had inherited our father's skills as a warrior. Gawan was the wizard and the thinker but we made a good team.

Myrddyn finally made his appearance. We did not have our oval table here and we were forced to use one long table and three shorter ones to accommodate everyone. His appearance caused silence to descend on the hall. The slaves were dismissed and two guards stood at the doorway to prevent us being overheard. The ten nobles from the island and my uncle were seated on one table while my warriors occupied the others.

"It is four years since Lord Lann, the Warlord, was taken from us. His sacrifice has bought us time to prepare for the Northumbrians. Last week I dreamed and I dreamed alone. Lord Lann came to me in the tomb where he lies. He told me of the danger from the north. Already Edwin gathers his forces on the island of Manau. It is a matter of time before they will come here. Lord Lann's spirit told me that we must make a hard decision." His sharp eyes scanned the room. "The evil that killed so many has made us fewer but stronger. We cannot expect the new Warlord to defend this island and defeat King Edwin. The Warlord will need to take the war to Northumbria. Mona must look to itself from now on. The Warlord and his equites must travel the length of this land to fight the Northumbrians wherever they present themselves." He stared at the nobles from the island. "The farmers must become warriors too!"

He sat down. This was a speech most unlike Myrddyn. It was blunt and without the flowery language of the dream world. I would have to ask him later why but now was not the time. We had to present a common front. I had expected his words. They were no surprise to me but I could see that the nobles from Mona were most upset. The exception was my uncle. He looked calmly at me with a smile upon his face as the others railed and ranted against Myrddyn.

"You cannot abandon us! The only thing which stops the Northumbrians is the Warlord. It is his duty to protect us!"

"Lord Lann would not have abandoned us!"

"We grow the grain for our people. If you take away our defences then we will all starve."

"Who will protect us without the Warlord?"

Aelle stood. Such was his authority that all went silent. He glowered and glared at his fellow islanders. "It is many years since we travelled here to be protected by the Warlord's father, my brother, Lord Lann. Whenever we were threatened he came to our aid. He defeated all the predators that would have torn our world in two. Even when he was betrayed by my nephew, who came from this island, he never once thought of refusing to aid us." He allowed those words to sink in; especially the treachery of Morcar.

I could see that some of the nobles thought that Aelle was agreeing with them and they began to smile and applaud each statement.

Aelle shook his head, "We are not children. We are not helpless. I may only have one arm but I can still defend my home and my family. You should all be ashamed of your words. We should have defended ourselves before now! Myrddyn should not need to explain why we have to do this. We have a responsibility to protect ourselves." He turned and jabbed an accusing finger at the portly man seated next to him, "You, Garth, son of Griffith, look at you. You are half my age and twice my size. You could not even find a horse to carry you, let alone climb upon it and ride. You cannot fight because you choose not to. You have grown comfortable on the blood and sacrifice of others. And you," he spread his arm around the room, "have all grown rich with many slaves and that is because of the sacrifice of others. The disease on the mainland did not touch us but look at these equites. These are all that remain of those who laid down their lives for you all."

Garth ap Griffith looked suitably embarrassed and he spread his arms, apologetically, "You are right, Aelle son of Hogan but how can we fight? I have not picked up a weapon these last ten years."

"We make every boy and man practise with arms one day a week. We organise them into tens, as the Romans did. We make our homes like forts." He banged his good hand onto the table. "This fort can laugh away a siege. I will move here and I will defend this and the port. I say we each become responsible for one area of the island and look after that. What say you?"

His words had shamed them for they were all half of my uncle's age. They began to bang the table in time and chanted, "Aelle, Aelle, Aelle!" over and over.

I looked over at Myrddyn and saw a smug smile on his face. "You knew this would happen." I said quietly.

"Of course I did," he snorted. "What kind of wizard would I be if I could not see into the future? Besides they just needed a push. I have known Aelle since I first followed your father. There is steel in him. He has a mind as sharp as any. He will defend this island and when he dies he will join your father in the spirit world."

I had thought that we would have many hours of talk but it was not meant to be. It was *wyrd*. One of the sentries at the door burst in. "I am sorry for the intrusion, Warlord but there are Saxon ships on the southern side of the island. They are landing at Porthdafarch!" Our watch towers might have saved us again. They ringed the island of Ynys Mon.

There was little point in lamenting the fact that we had been surprised. We were warriors and we would deal with it. "Equites!

To horse. Uncle, you and Myrddyn command here. We will attack them on the beach." I had no idea how many there might be but I knew that the only chance would be to strike them quickly and horses were the best for that.

I was already in my mail. I donned my full helmet and took Saxon Slayer. It still inspired fear amongst the Saxons. My shield bore the image of a dragon and I slung it over my shoulder. Finally I picked up my spear which was taller than the tallest warrior. By the time I reached the stables my equites were there. We had just sixty now but all were the finest warriors in the whole of Britannia. I mounted my horse, Star. In times past, our horses had been as armoured as we were; now they just had mail about their heads.

Captain Tuanthal was the last of the warriors who had served with my father. He was a greybeard now but he was wise in the ways of war. "What say you, Tuanthal? What is our best defence?"

"Hit them before they have unloaded their boats. Do not give them time to organise."

"Wolf Brethren! Ride!"

We galloped across the open courtyard towards the south eastern gate. Already men were hauling it open. The advantage we had was that the beach they had chosen was not large. Had they chosen the next beach down, some two miles away at Trearrdur, then they could have spread out their forces. They had chosen badly, *wyrd*. The problem we would have was the steep slope leading down to the beach. Speed was of the essence and we covered the half a mile to the edge of the slope quickly. I could see just two Saxon ships drawn up on the beach but another six were approaching. I saw that just thirty men had disembarked from the two vessels. None of them wore armour save for their helmet.

Once we reached the sand and shingle our horses were able to power forward. I did not bother to unsling my shield. I leaned forward with my spear. As I saw the first Saxon brace himself for my blow I pulled back the shield. I timed my blow so that I punched the spear into the warrior at the perfect moment. It had taken years of practice to perfect the blow. He tried to brace the shield and protect himself. The force of the blow and the speed of my mount meant that the edge of the shield angled towards him and the spear ripped into his throat. I was already twisting it away as the white sand stained red with his blood.

Three warriors tried to make a small shield wall to protect each other. This time I raised the spear and, urging my horse to climb I soared over them. As I cleared them I stabbed down and the spear plunged into the shoulder of one. Pol and Bors were behind me and I heard two screams as the other two were slain.

I reined in Star to let him catch his breath and so that I could examine the beach. Two more ships were edging in to the sand, ready to disgorge their crews. The Saxons had not rowed in mail and until they put it on then we would have the advantage.

"Do not let them land!"

Some of my equites were armed with bows and half a dozen arrows flew into the air and struck warriors as they tried to climb down from the ships to the sea. I saw a knot of five warriors and they were trying to assemble a shield wall.

"Pol, Bors, Kay, follow me!"

The four of us thundered towards the knot of men which was growing larger as others struggled through the water to reach them. There were now eight of them with locked shields. When we were just ten paces from them we hurled our spears. Three of them were too slow raising their shields and they were transfixed by the heavy spears. The wall was broken. I drew my sword and sliced down, as we broke through the flimsy line. My sword hacked deeply into the unprotected back of one of the warriors. The surf turned red with their foaming blood. I sensed a warrior to my left and, as I tugged on the reins, slipped my foot from my stirrup and kicked him hard in the face. As he fell, Star kicked out with his hooves and I heard a crunch as his skull was cracked open.

I slowed down again and regained my stirrup. I took the opportunity of moving my shield around to protect me. There were eight equites with me now. "One more charge should do it!" I shouted. Turning around I rode back to pull my spear from the body of the dead Saxon. As I did so I saw, on the headland, Myrddyn and some men manhandling a bolt thrower into position. I saw the flicker of a torch and knew what he intended.

"Into them!"

I saw that Tuanthal was leading his equites into the men trying to disembark from the ship on the far side. There were just three ships on the beach now and the others were waiting for these three to off load so that they could land their warriors. As Myrddyn hurled his fire at the middle boat we charged the one nearest to us. The first warrior I tried to spear had more about him than the others had and he braced his shield so that my spear merely stuck into it. I released the spear and I grabbed the mace which hung from my saddle. I swung it with all of my might. The weight of my spear sticking in the shield caused it to lower slightly and the mace cracked into the warrior's helmet. I drove the nasal into his nose and part of the helmet into his head. He collapsed to the sand. I whipped Star's head around and swung the mace at the back of the next warrior's skull. It had the same effect.

I turned and saw the middle Saxon ship in flames and the warriors hurling themselves into the sea. I slung my mace, drew my sword and roared, "The Saxon Slayer bites! On, men of Rheged."

The effect of my words, the flames and, most importantly the sword, had a dramatic effect. The Saxons tried to get back to their ships. I was not allowing them to escape. They would pay. I galloped Star next to the Saxon ship and threw myself from the saddle. I ran through the surf. I stabbed one Saxon in the back as he tried to clamber aboard. They had thrown a rope for him and I slung my shield on my back and grabbed the rope. I began to climb up the strakes. The Saxon ships had a low freeboard. Suddenly a warrior grabbed an oar and tried to strike me with it. I sliced down with my sword and sheared it in two. Pulling myself on board I hefted my shield around to protect me from the attack which I knew would come.

There were ten warriors on the ship. I spoke in Saxon so that they would know who I was. "Saxon dogs, I am the Warlord and none of you will leave this ship alive."

Their leader was an overweight warrior. "You may be the Warlord but you are one man. Kill him and bring me his sword."

I did not wait for them to attack me. I ran at them. I punched one with my shield and he tumbled into the water. As I did so I sliced forward and felt my sword rip into the soft belly of the leader. A sword came out of nowhere and struck my mail. It merely broke a couple of links. I held my shield before me and swung the sword at shoulder height. I felt it bite into flesh. A spear punched towards me and although I caught it on my shield it twisted and scraped along my side.

I pulled my left arm back and the warrior who had been leaning against it overbalanced and fell to the deck. I raised the shield and brought the metal edge down sharply to break his neck. There were just five men left and they made the mistake of backing off. I feinted at the man on my right; he fell backwards and I twisted the sword in the air to hack the head from the next warrior. I stepped forward and punched the fallen warrior in the face with my hilt. The crosspiece ground into his eye and he fell overboard, screaming. The other two had had enough and they jumped over the side.

I began to bang my shield, "Saxon Slayer!"

The cry was taken up and I saw that we had won. The Saxons had either fled or were dead. There was the smell of burning flesh coming from the blackened Saxon ship struck by Myrddyn and my men were walking down the beach despatching wounded Saxons.

As I remounted Star I realised that this had been *wyrd*. We had given the nobles a lesson in how to defeat the Saxons, even when outnumbered. I wondered just how much Myrddyn had known of the surprise attack. The speed with which the thrower had been dragged into position suggested it had been readied before. That was the advantage of having a wizard. He saw things other men did not.

Clearing the battlefield was always a gruesome task. There was little mail to strip but we had the metals from the helmets and the swords which could be reused. This time we had gained a Saxon ship and part of the others could be reused. We wasted nothing.

It was after dark by the time I returned to the citadel. Aelle and Myrddyn were talking. "You need to take more care, nephew! Climbing aboard a Saxon ship when you are outnumbered eight to one is not a good idea."

Myrddyn sniffed, "His father learned how to be more prudent but it is something in the blood that makes them act this way." He smiled, "I have not yet dreamed your death, Warlord."

I shook my head and laughed, gently, "That was ever the cry before my father went to war."

"And so long as I live it shall be mine."

I caught something in his tone I did not like, "Have you dreamed your death?"

"I know how I shall die but not when. I do not think my death is close. But when I am in the spirit world you will have Gawan. His skills are improving."

I sat down and poured myself some of the heavy red wine we imported from Lusitania. I looked at my uncle. "You said you would defend the island. It is much to ask someone who is…." I struggled for the word.

"Old? Do not be shy, nephew. I am well aware that I have outlived my brothers and those I fought alongside. There are just two of the original warriors who remain: Tuanthal and Myrddyn. To answer your question I say yes, I will defend the island but there is much work to do. In a way I am pleased that the Northumbrians attempted the attack for it means they will not return soon." He took a drink of the wine. "It was Northumbrians I take it?"

Myrddyn nodded, "It was. We questioned a couple before we helped them to the Otherworld. They came from Manau."

"And that means that they must have a foothold on the west coast and that is worrying."

I detected an approving look from Myrddyn. "I am pleased that your brain is not addled Warlord. You are thinking as your father would. You are right. If we can cut off their supplies from the mainland then it might be we prevent their attacking us here."

I stood and walked to the window which looked south. I remembered my time in Constantinopolis. They were a sophisticated people. Their minds did not work in straight lines. I had lived, for a while with Pol and I had picked up some of the ideas and strategies.

"We need allies who will harass the Northumbrians on Manau."

Aelle looked interested while Myrddyn smiled enigmatically. "We have the men of Strathclyde. Who else is there?" Aelle looked at Myrddyn as though he might have the answer. I answered for him. "The men of Hibernia."

"You would ally with those bandits and murderers." It was a shocking thought for my uncle. He knew that the Hibernians had tried to enslave the island of Mona many times in the past.

"I would buy them. Their island is a poor one and they need money. We have gold. We are a rich people. We buy them and use them as mercenaries. The Emperor in Byzantium does the same with the Pechengs and the Arabs. He uses others to fight his battles for him. If we can destroy Edwin's base on the mainland the Hibernians will have an easier time assaulting the island."

"But that is dangerous is it not? Vortigern did much the same with the Angles and look what happened there."

"If the Hibernians take over Manau we will deal with that problem in the future. The problem we have now is with the Northumbrians and until we can build up both your strength and that of the army we need all the help that we can get."

Myrddyn clapped, "Well done strategos. Masterful."

"You approve?"

"Of course I do. You have thought it through well. We will bolster the defences here. I think more artillery and, perhaps some underwater defences at Porthdafarch." He looked at Aelle. "You will need to deal ruthlessly with your nobles. Make them train their men and ensure that they do maintain a watch. We need the towers again. There is little point being the breadbasket of the west if anyone can walk in and steal it."

I felt more settled. Myrddyn knew how to play me. I was like an Irish harp in his hands. I had worked out the best solution to the problem with just a few prompts. Byzantium showed us the way and we would copy the Empire which survived surrounded by a sea of enemies.

"I will leave on the morrow with my equites. I will visit with Cadwallon and then Gawan. They should know what we are about. Then I will take '*Gwynfor*' and visit Hibernia." I looked at Myrddyn, "I will need you with me."

"Of course you will. Do not worry, Warlord, by the time you have returned I shall be ready. I will help your uncle make this particular delicacy of Mona unpalatable to the greedy Saxons."

Chapter 2

We left the next day and headed towards the Narrows and the mainland. The mountain on which we had built our fort was visible behind us as we headed east. But our gaze was drawn ever to the mountain of Wyddfa and the fortress which nestled beneath. Until my family had been taken from me I had been happy there, It was secure from attack and protected by the spirits in the mountain; now I spent as short a time as possible within its walls. I did not sleep well there. I heard the cries of my children, my wife and my step mother. I longed to dream as my father and brother did but that was not my destiny. I was destined to suffer mortal nightmares which made me wake sweating and fearful. It was another reason for shunning the fortress; those weaknesses were not part of The Warlord.

King Cadwallon and I were of an age. We had trained together as youths along with Pol. The king had married my little sister, Nanna, and they were happy. He had served with my father before Lord Lann had helped to regain his throne. He was forever grateful.

He greeted me as a brother. "How goes it Warlord?"

"The Saxons came some days ago by sea to Ynys Mon and tried to take us by surprise."

He examined my face as he asked his next question. "Did they succeed? Have you been forced to flee?"

I shook my head, "If I had failed then my bones would lie bleaching on the beach at Porthdafarch. No, we drove them hence with many losses."

He led me to the hall my father had built with the large oval table. Our names were still carved upon it. Out of habit we both sat in our appointed places. I had sent the others hence for I wished conference with Cadwallon only.

"The Northumbrians on Manau are becoming more adventurous. We have not the manpower to invade and subdue them. I intend to travel to Hibernia and pay for the warriors of that land to attack Manau."

"Can you trust the Hibernians? Are you not substituting one bad neighbour for another?"

"Possibly but the plague and the war have decimated my men. It will be two years or more before we have enough men to replace the ones we lost." I shrugged and sat back, taking in the painted plaster which showed my father leading the men of Rheged to victory over the Saxons. It seemed a hollow victory now. "I will not be based on Mona any longer. My horsemen can inflict more damage harrying the Saxons. I intend to invade Northumbria."

Even my old friend was surprised by my words and my ambition. "How many men do you have?"

"Not many: sixty equites, twenty archers and twenty squires. But we will all be mounted."

"That seems to go against what you have said. Will you not wait until you have more men?"

"The small numbers mean that we shall be mobile and can strike and run. If I can draw Edwin's eye here it may prevent him invading Mona."

"Do you wish me to supply any men?"

"I want you to build up the strength of your army. Use Penda and King Cearl as allies too. I hope to irritate Edwin so that he comes south to punish us and we can draw him into battle."

"A risky strategy."

"Sitting behind walls is a safe strategy and it does no good. It merely invites tragedy."

"I am sorry for your family, Warlord."

I nodded, "But you cannot bring them back. If they had been taken by an enemy then I would have flayed the flesh from his body." I shrugged as my anger subsided, "as it is I am impotent."

"Will you see your sister and stay awhile?"

"No, we will push on to my brother. I will need his men and his support."

He nodded, "His wife and family are welcome here, you know."

"I am sorry King Cadwallon but this place has too many bad memories for me. I suspect that Gawan would prefer to stay at Deva. The plague did not touch them there. We will ensure that his wife and his family are well protected. All of my foot warriors will remain here. We take mounted men only. I will become a swift moving enemy who strikes like a ghost when the Northumbrians are least expecting it."

As he walked me back to my horse he said, "You have changed, Hogan Lann. There was a time when you laughed more and were gentler."

"And then I became Warlord and my family died." I tapped my chest. "Something died in here too. I have one purpose now, to defeat Edwin and rid the land of the Northumbrians. I cannot free Britannia but I can free Rheged."

My brother was at Deva which was the old Roman fortress guarding the Dee and the entrance to King Cadwallon's lands. He lived there with his wife, Gwyneth and his son Arturus. He had had another son and a daughter but they had both died young.

He greeted me warmly but I saw him examining my face carefully. He was a wizard and could read men through their eyes. I found it uncomfortable and I shifted my gaze to his son. Arturus was growing rapidly. He was at least ten summers old. "You are growing Arturus. Soon you will have your own armour and become a warrior."

I could see that I had pleased him. "I hope so uncle."

"Go and find your mother, my son. Tell her we have visitors." He ran off. "Brother," he warned, "let him have his childhood. The world is not just about war and fighting Edwin."

"It is for me," I realised that it had sounded cold and I shrugged and gave my little brother an apologetic smile.

"You need a woman. You are still young enough to father children."

"I may be but I am aware of the passing of time. We need to slow down the advance of the Northumbrians. The Northumbrians are flexing their muscles; they tried a sneak attack on Mona." We sat in his hall and I told him of the failed attack and my plans. "So I need some of your equites and, if possible, you."

"Of course I will join you but why do you need me? There are better equites than me."

I laughed, "Because you complete me. I need a wizard. Our father gave half of his skills to you and the other half to me. I can fight but I cannot dream."

"You have Myrddyn."

"Myrddyn is getting old. I need you, little brother. Even if your sword remained sheathed you would still be invaluable to me. You are the only one, save Pol, who can think as quickly as I do."

"What about Tuanthal?"

"I would take him too but he is old and I would that he protected Mona with Uncle Aelle. The two of them can protect our home."

"Very well. When do we leave? It is almost summer now."

"I will be in Hibernia until Midsummer's Eve at the latest but I warn you that I intend to winter in Northumbria."

That surprised even Gawan. "But you have horses and the winters are harsh."

"And we can punish the Northumbrians for they will not expect us. We will become a spectre. We will haunt them in the darkest and longest nights. I have plans for feeding the horses. Fear not."

And I did have plans but I told them to no one yet.

I took but twenty of my equites with me on my trip to Hibernia. Before I travelled I met with Aelle and Tuanthal. "I told King Cadwallon that I would be taking a hundred men with me to raid the Northumbrians but I want you two to train as many as you can. If any show prowess as riders then they will come with me. We need every boy as a slinger and the girls too."

"Girls?" Women did not fight.

"Yes Tuanthal. If the Saxons come they will not be spared will they? They can fight for their freedom as can the boys."

Myrddyn stood next to me as we set sail. "You may have ruffled feathers on Mona, Warlord, but I am pleased with this ruthless warrior I see before me. The land will need a firm and strong hand. Your father both trained and chose well in his successor."

"I am just sad that I cannot talk with him."

"*Wyrd*. But he talks to me and to your brother. I hide nothing from you, Warlord."

"But it is not the same."

"I know."

I had chosen Pol to accompany me and the rest were young equites who were yet to be blooded. I hoped that this expedition would not be dangerous but I needed to know my young warriors and how they would react to the unexpected. Pol and I had shared many experiences; from having been my father's squire to travelling to Constantinopolis. He was even closer to me, in many ways, than Gawan for I had spent almost every day with him since I had been a child. When I went to war he was on my right hand side and I never looked for him on the field of battle for he was always there.

While Myrddyn slept, he did much more of that these days, I went to the prow with Pol. We had sailed west and then north to avoid the Saxons on Manau. Once the captain turned north we would begin to see the coast of Hibernia. Pol pointed off to the horizon. "Where will we go to seek these mercenaries, Warlord? There are many on the island who would slit our throats for our helmets alone."

"They would have to be fine warriors to do that but I will go to the north of the island; to the land of Fiachnae mac Báetáin."

"He is in Strathclyde is he not? And, as I recall the Uí Néill are untrustworthy."

"True but Fiachnae had a brother, Fiachra, whom he left to rule in his name. I hope that he may know some men who may wish to earn our gold."

"This use of gold does not seem honourable, Warlord."

Pol was one of the few men who could speak to me as critically as he did. "I have learned that there is little honour these days from any. Look at my cousin, Morcar. He had no honour and my father did. Had my father been less honourable then he might still be alive." Morcar and his witch had killed my father with a poisoned blade. I had killed Morcar but I wished to kill him over and over again. One death was not enough.

Pol was silent for a while. "And yet even if he were that would not bring back your family, would it, Warlord?"

He was right of course and my silence was enough of an answer for him to contemplate the coastline which began to appear to our left. It took us two more days to reach the beach which was closest to the home of Fiachra. Last time we had been here my father had brought horses for he wished to impress the Hibernians. I had no need to impress them now for they were our allies and the journey would have been difficult for them. It meant, however, that we would need to walk. I wondered if Myrddyn was up to it.

Dawn had just broken when we clambered ashore and I told Daffydd ap Gwynfor to wait for us offshore. My ship was a tempting prize for any pirate and I wanted him to have sea room. It only took Pol and I a mile or so to regain the use of our legs, properly. Some of the younger ones marched as though they were drunk. They would learn- eventually. It amused Myrddyn. Despite his frequent naps the wizard seemed to be able to march as quickly as we did.

Perhaps someone had been watching us for, as we approached the coast, a group of armed warriors trotted down to meet us on the small hill ponies so favoured by the Hibernians. I had tried it once but my feet trailed along the ground and I could not see the point. My size went against me. The leader bowed, "Prince Fiachra saw you as you approached. He recognised your ship and sent us to escort you to the oppidum safely."

Something in his voice alerted me, "Safely? Is there trouble afoot?"

He nodded, "The Uí Néill has begun raiding for slaves. They came in the night. The king is away and they think we are weak." He spat into the grass. "We were less than vigilant, that is all. We will recover them."

"How many did they capture?"

"A whole village. They killed the old and the handful of warriors who were there. They have over thirty women and children."

Something in the bitter way he spoke told me that this was personal. "You lost family?"

"I did." He set his face in a look of stone. This was a warrior. He would get his family back.

I knew that in Hibernia slave trading was a lucrative business. Many would be sold to the Saxons. They knew better than to try to sell them to us or the men of Strathclyde. I wondered if I had come to the right place. It seemed unlikely that there would be spare men for me to hire as mercenaries.

I remembered the king's brother. Fiachra was a good and loyal brother to the king but he was no general. The king would have been better served appointing a trustworthy leader for his people and keeping Fiachra as the leader of his bodyguard. There were more sentries around the hill fort than the last time I had visited but the ditch had not been deepened nor had it been sown with traps. My plan looked to be faltering before I had even started.

He looked older than the last time I had seen him but that had been some years earlier. He gave a deferential bow as I approached. Like my father before me I was no king but many warriors were impressed by my armour, helmet and the trappings of an equite. They treated me as a king. The Hibernians fought without armour and most deigned a helmet. However they had seen my father fight in armour and knew the effect.

"It is good to see you, Warlord, and you come at a propitious moment."

"I heard about the raids. Does your brother know?"

His downcast eyes gave me my answer, "I have yet to tell him. The raids were less than two days ago."

"Have you tried to get the slaves back?"

He had a complete look of surprise upon his face. "Get them back?"

I sighed, "As I recall you do not have large armies here in Dál nAraidi. If you chose your men well and they went hard and fast after the raiders then you should be able to catch them. Slaves do not move swiftly."

The warrior who had brought us to the oppidum, Fergus, said, "Let me go after them, Prince. They have my mother and my sister."

I saw the doubt upon his face, "But if you fail?"

Fergus stood defiantly, "Then I will have died honourably and be able to face my father in the Otherworld."

Fergus was still a pagan. Many of the Irish had become followers of the White Christ. This man was a warrior who followed the old ways and I suddenly saw a way out of this dilemma as well as providing a solution to my own problem. "Give me twenty of your warriors, and Fergus here to lead them and we will try to get back your captives."

"You would go with them?" I nodded. Fiachra brightened, "With the Warlord leading them then there might be a chance."

"Then we must leave now and make haste." I almost ignored the Prince. "Fergus, gather your men and horses. If you have man sized horses then…."

He shrugged apologetically, "We have four only, but we have many ponies."

"Four will have to do. Fetch them." He ran off gathering his men as he went. "Myrddyn, you would only slow us down I suggest you stay here. You know the reason we came."

He nodded. He was a strange bird. Sometimes he would take offence at the slightest comment and at others he would ignore an obvious insult. "Very well Warlord. Do take care. We have greater worries than this to think on. I will seek to do what you wish of me."

Pol and I took two of the horses while Fergus had the third. I did not know my men and I asked Pol's advice. "Who would be the best on a horse?"

He pointed to a broad and muscular equite, "Garth son of Daffydd is a reliable warrior."

Thus mounted we headed south. The equites on the ponies did not look happy but travelling on four legs rather than two meant we would catch up with them sooner. The Hibernians, in contrast looked to be more than comfortable. They were however very lightly armed compared with my men. None had a helmet. Most went bare-chested and none had a shield. Their weapons were swords, axes and daggers. My father had always said he could conquer the whole island with just two hundred warriors if he so chose. I could see why.

Chapter 3

As we rode south east towards the stronghold of the Uí Néill, I quizzed Fergus, "You know where they will take them?"

He pointed to the east. "There is a slave market on the coast. It is three days hence."

"They will be half way there then?" He nodded glumly. "Do not worry. We can travel three times faster than men with slaves. You are worried about your sister?"

"I am. She was due to be married but her husband to be was killed at the village. She has a wicked temper on her and I fear that she may upset her captors and they would hurt her and leave her."

He had not voiced his true fears but I knew what he meant. "Then we will have to endeavour to catch them sooner."

After four hours of riding I held up my hand, "Dismount!"

"Why? Fergus almost screamed at me.

"We walk for an hour and then ride for four. We will get more from our mounts and we will still catch them. Fear not. We are horsemen and we know how to get the best from our beasts."

The men were exhausted when night fell. The horses were tiring too but they still had life left in them. "Does this track keep going in this direction?"

"It is the main way to the coast. Why?"

"We keep going in the dark but we walk now and save the horses completely." I turned to Garth. "Are you tired, Garth son of Daffydd?"

He grinned, "No Warlord."

"Good then give your horse to Pol here and see if you can find the camp of these slavers."

Fergus looked at me in surprise. "We will catch them this night?"

They were captured the day before yesterday?" He nodded. They will have walked for eight hours or so and then camped. They will not wish to sell slaves who look to be dead on their feet. Today they will have done the same. We marched for twelve hours. They will not be far ahead. Go and find them, Garth."

He loped off into the dark.

"How can you be so sure of yourself?"

"I study people. These are not the first slavers I have pursued. They will not wish to arrive at a slave auction with exhausted and weary slaves. They would have expected a pursuit immediately. Now they will think they have escaped."

"Those of us with family in the village wished to do so but Fiachra worried we might make ourselves vulnerable to another attack."

I saw that I would need to speak with the king about his brother. If he intended to leave his homeland in the hands of another then it should be a strong leader who could be decisive.

I was beginning to worry that perhaps they had pushed the captives harder than I expected when Garth loomed up out of the darkness. I held my hand up and the column halted.

"Warlord, they are three miles up the road. There is a hill with a small wood at the top and they are there."

"Good man. How many are there?"

"It is difficult to say. There are ten sentries watching the road and the captives and I would guess that there were another forty at least."

"Good. The track, it carries on beyond the hill?"

"It does."

"And the sentries are all around the hill and the camp?"

"No, Warlord. They have placed them in a half circle facing in this direction."

"Have they built a wall of brush?"

"No, Warlord."

"Perfect. Gather your men around too, Fergus." They all leaned in and I spoke quietly. I knew how sound travelled at night. "Pol, you will mount our men and take them on a sweep around the far side of the hill. I will go with Fergus and his men. We will attack as soon as we arrive. Their attention will already be upon us so that when you hear the noise then you attack from the other side."

"Yes, Warlord." Pol showed no surprise at my orders and I knew he would be there. We would be going on foot and would arrive after Pol and his men were in position. I didn't want any of the raiders fleeing with captives. This would only work if we captured them all. If any escaped then we would be caught by the rest of the warband. I needed to be with the Hibernians for they would be attacking twice their number. "Go, and may the Allfather be with you."

They disappeared in the dark. All of them were excellent horsemen and more than capable of riding without making too much noise. "Fergus, leave two men here to watch the horses." As he detailed them off I turned to the others, "We attack silently and without any war cries. We must eliminate the sentries and then begin to kill the sleeping warriors."

One of the younger warriors said, "There is no honour in that!"

I pointed to the horses, "Go and change places with him for I do not want you with me." He looked as though he would argue. "Obey me or the first blood I spill here will be yours!"

Fergus said, "Calum, do it!" When he had stormed off Fergus asked me, "Would you have killed him?"

I looked at the Hibernian and said, coldly "Without a second thought. Now we are wasting time. Draw your weapons now so that there is no sound when we get closer to the camp."

As we neared the wooded hill I could smell the wood smoke from their fires. They were not making a sound. This was a careful warband. There were twenty of us and ten sentries. The odds were in our favour but it takes a different kind of courage to stick a blade into a man's back or his throat. I hoped that these men had it in them. I waved my sword to the left and right and the men spread out. I was the only one with a shield. I would not necessarily need it but I felt more comfortable with one on my arm. Although my helmet was a full face helmet I had large enough eye holes so that my vision was not impaired.

The sentries were looking in the distance and not at the ground close up. As I crouched my way up I saw the first sentry who would die. He was looking to the north and staring intently. That was a mistake. A good sentry moves his head slowly and watches for movement. I was just two paces away when he glanced down. I saw disbelief on his face which allowed me to take one step forward and thrust Saxon Slayer into the man's throat. I caught him on my shield and lowered him to the ground. I moved to my right and there I saw one of the Hibernians sneaking up to the next sentry. A broken branch gave him away. As he shouted and swung his sword at the Hibernian. I slashed sideways and felt his backbone crack as my sword sliced through to his vitals. The game was up and it now depended upon Pol and my equites. The enemy knew we were there.

I leapt towards the sleeping forms. A warrior tried to rise to his feet. I buried my sword into his neck and he gurgled his life blood away. I heard Irish voices exhorting the warriors to fight us off. I glanced to my left and right and saw at least ten of the warriors I had brought up the hill. It would have to be enough. Fergus appeared at my side.

"We attack on my command!" I raised my sword and bellowed, "Saxon Slayer! Charge!" I wanted the slavers to believe that we were a large force and we were all to their fore.

A rough line of warriors approached me. Most were shieldless. I took an axe on my shield whilst stabbing the next warrior with my blade. I twisted my shield and the axe man overbalanced. I chopped down and almost severed his head from his body. Then I heard a roar as Pol brought the equites up and into the rear of the line. I have never seen the fight go out of men as quickly. They threw their weapons to the ground and shouted, "Mercy!"

I saw Fergus' men raise their weapons. "Hold! We take them prisoner!"

I looked first to my equites. All appeared to be unharmed. They had had the easier of the skirmish. Fergus looked to have lost four men; a small price for the recapture of the hostages. "Bind them."

As the prisoners had their hands bound behind their backs one of the freed slaves suddenly sprang at one of the prisoners and tried to gouge out his eyes. Fergus put his arms around her and picked her up. "Let me go I will kill him!"

Fergus turned her away from the Hibernian and she saw me. I became the subject of her vitriol. "Who are you to say these men should be spared? Kill them all! You know not what they have done!"

"I can imagine what they have done and yet they will still be taken back with us. I have spoken. I am the Warlord!"

"You are not Warlord here!"

"Hush Aileen! It is because of the Warlord that you are saved." He lowered her to the ground. "I am sorry, Warlord, this is my sister. I said that she might be upset."

"I can see that. We have no time for petulance. We must hurry back. When these men do not return with the slaves then the Uí

Néill will come with revenge in their hearts. I want to be within the walls of Fiachra's oppidum by then. Put the old and infirm on horses."

The prisoners were encouraged to run by my men with blades held close to them. I allowed a one hour stop at noon the next day. We drank from a nearby stream. I took the opportunity of speaking with the fifteen prisoners we had captured. The leader of the ones who remained was obvious. He wore many warrior bands upon his wrist and the scars to his front had been gained in combat.

"What is your name?" He gave me a sullen look. "You are defeated and I could have you killed out of hand. Just tell me your name. At the very least it will be recorded after your death if you continue to annoy me."

"You are the Warlord? The one who wields the sword, Saxon Slayer?"

"I am."

"Then why do you not bear the wolf shield?"

"That was the sign of my father. I am the son of that warrior."

"Then you should bear his shield or are you ashamed of him?"

I began to become angry and I put my hand on my sword. Even as I did so I knew that he was right. Except that the shame was for me. I had not stopped his death. "You may be right. Now you know my name and my origins. What is your name?"

"Aengus Finn mac Fergus Dubdétach."

"And you serve the Uí Néill?"

He laughed, "I serve no man! We were hired to attack the village and bring back slaves."

"You are swords for hire, you are gallóglaigh." I now knew who they were. They were mercenaries. Wyrd.

"We are now. We had a dispute with our own king and were banished from our lands far to the west. The pay from the Uí Néill would have bought better weapons so that I could have gone home and regained the throne of my people."

"Would you fight for me?"

For the first time I had surprised him. "You? Does the Warlord need slaves? Would you have me go on a Táin Bó?"

I laughed, "No, I need neither slaves nor cattle. But I can pay more than the Uí Néill. And you would not be hurting Hibernians."

I rose to my feet, "Think on it Aengus Finn mac Fergus Dubdétach and I will ask again when we reach the fort."

"And if I refuse your offer, will you have me killed?"

I shook my head, "If you refuse I will hand you over to Fiachra. I am doing this as a favour to him."

He nodded, "You are not what I expected, Warlord. I will think on your words."

As we ran again Fergus came over to me. "Why were you speaking to the slaver?" I had taken my helmet off and carried it so that Fergus was able to see my face clearly. I said not a word but I knew he he was frightened by my look. "I meant no offence, Warlord, I am curious for he looked less belligerent when you had finished."

"I offered to pay him and his men to fight for me."

Realisation dawned, "That is why you are here."

I laughed, "You thought I came here to rescue your people."

He nodded, "I thought that Myrddyn the wizard had seen it and brought you across the seas to our aid."

He looked slightly disappointed. "No, I came here to pay warriors to fight for me and to conquer their own lands."

He went quiet as we continued to head north and safety. When he did speak I could see that he had been considering my words. "I know warriors who would fight for you, Warlord; I for one."

"And how would Fiachra view that?"

"The Prince only wishes to protect his brother's land. He is loyal."

"As he should be. Does that mean that you are disloyal?"

"No, Warlord but a man must look to his own family first and our land is a poor land." He pointed at my armour. "That is why you fight in armour and we do not even own a helmet. That is why we are the prey of every warrior who wishes to take from us. If I fight for you I will have the coin to buy weapons and defend my family."

"We will speak more when we reach your fort."

It was late in the night when we reached the oppidum. Some of us had run for a whole day and a night. Many of Fergus' men looked ready to collapse but we made the safety of the fort.

When Fiachra saw the freed slaves and the prisoners he was delighted. "We will hang these men on the morrow."

"No, Prince Fiachra, you will not for they are my prisoners and I will decide what is done with them."

He looked at me in surprise. "This is my land!"

"It is the land of your brother and you are its steward. If I had wanted them dead I would not have wasted my time returning here with them." I was weary and I did not choose my words wisely, "I am tired but my warriors and I will spill blood here if you dispute my decision. It matters not to me!"

Fergus spoke, "Prince Fiachra we have our people back. The prisoners are payment to the Warlord."

I was grateful to Fergus. He had given me a diplomatic way out of the dilemma. Had Myrddyn been awake he might have counselled me but we had let the old man sleep on.

"Very well, Warlord, but we will speak more of this in the morning."

"I would have your guards be vigilant, Prince Fiachra. The Uí Néill may be hot on our heels. I do not believe this is over yet."

He looked at me in surprise which confirmed my opinion of him that he was not the cleverest of leaders.

It was Myrddyn who woke me the next morning. He was shaking his head as he handed me the warm beaker of honeyed beer. "I can see that either Gawan or I must be with you at all times. You are a warrior and a good one but you know not how to control your words!"

I smiled. Myrddyn was as close to a grandfather as I had and he was right. "In my defence I was tired."

"I know but you are Warlord think on that. You have a greater responsibility than just to yourself. Now tell me all." When I had finished telling him of the pursuit, the fight and the conversations I had had he nodded. "Had you not upset the Prince then I might be praising you for doing so well." He turned to leave, "I will now go and speak with the Prince and use my honeyed tongue. You need to speak with the prisoners. We shall need them sooner rather than later."

He was still enigmatic but I was pleased that he was on my side. I went to the prisoners who were still bound. I took out my dagger and slit the bonds of Aengus. "Come we will walk and we will talk."

I saw that it was almost noon and a bright blue sky greeted us as we stepped out into the light. Aengus shielded his eyes from the sun's glare.

"Well Aengus, have you thought on my words?"

"I have but I have questions for you."

I gave him a thin smile, "And you are in a position to make bargains?"

He shrugged, "If it is my time to die then so be it but I would know all before I answer you."

"Very well ask away. My wizard has mellowed me."

He nodded, "He spoke with us when he brought us drink this morning. Is it true he once flew into a castle and killed a king?"

"Is that one of your questions?"

"No, but I am curious."

"He and my father did go to Din Guardi and slew King Morcant Bulc but they did not tell me how they did it. He is a powerful wizard."

"What is it you wish me and my men to do? There are but a handful of us."

"I have more than just your band in mind. I intend to hire two boat loads."

"Then we will not be fighting in Hibernia?"

"No, you will be fighting Saxons."

That seemed to please him. "Already I am more inclined to serve you. And what would we be paid?"

"I will arm you and your men, give you a boat and pay twenty gold pieces."

"In return for?"

"That I will tell you when you have agreed and when I have all the warriors I need."

He seemed satisfied. "Then I am your man." He held his hand out and I clasped it.

"You speak for all of your men?"

"I do."

"Then let us go back and speak with them for I fear we may need your skills before the day is out." When we returned to the Hibernian prisoners I slit the bonds binding them. They looked from me to Aengus. "Your chief has pledged his word that you will work for me. I will now take an oath from him but all of you will be bound by this oath. Is that clear?" They all looked to Aengus who nodded. They stood and inclined their heads. I took out Saxon Slayer and held the blade towards Aengus. "Swear an oath on this blade to be my man and not to take up arms against me or my people."

I saw him hesitate when he saw the gleaming blade but he put his hands upon it and said, "I so swear and we are your men unto death."

Pol and my men had appeared during this. "Give them some arms Pol. I must speak with the Prince."

I found Myrddyn and Fergus with the Prince. They all looked up when I came in. The two Hibernians had the guilty look of someone caught talking about another. I took the bull by the horns. "I have just hired the prisoners and armed them. They will fight for me."

Myrddyn shook his head and rolled his eyes at the sky. Fiachra said, "The wizard has told us of your plan. Why did you not explain that to me, Warlord?"

"I would have done but you needed me to recapture your people did you not?"

"I did. Fergus tells me that the Uí Néill will come here."

"I believe so. If they do not then it is a sign of weakness. The fact that they hired these men to make war is evidence that all is not well. I believe that they will come and if we can defeat them then you will have peace for some time."

Fergus nodded, "And you will be able to pay for more of us to fight for you?" I inclined my head. Myrddyn nodded his approval. He turned to Fiachra. "Then, Prince Fiachra, when we have defeated the Uí Néill I would serve the Warlord."

Fiachra nodded his agreement.

"But you know not what I ask."

"From what I have seen Warlord it will be something worthwhile and it will be away from Hibernia. I am your man."

"Then swear on the sword." He did as Aengus had done. "You will be swearing for your men. How many do you bring?"

"The ones who followed you and recaptured our families."

"Good. And now I will get cleaned up, eat and prepare to fight." Fiachra said, "You know they are coming?"

I pointed to Myrddyn, "Tell them, wizard."

"The Warlord is correct. They will be here this night. You had best have your men clear the ditches and lay traps. Water and food should be gathered for we know not their numbers and they may lay siege to this oppidum."

As the fort was prepared for war and I washed I worked out that I had one boatful of warriors. I now needed a second. It was *wyrd*. If we fought I would see the mettle of the Hibernians I was going to buy. Myrddyn was so far seeing; what would I do without him?

I took Myrddyn and joined Pol and Prince Fiachra. "I will use two of my men as scouts to warn us of the arrival of these men."

Fiachra asked, "Can you be so sure they will come tonight? They might not have missed the prisoners yet."

"Firstly Myrddyn is never wrong." The wizard had his normal smug and self satisfied face. "Secondly we found them but half a day from the coast. They would be missed. We did not bury the bodies. They will come."

We had much to do. The walls were not the strongest I had ever seen and the ditch had been full of rubbish discarded from the oppidum. It was now clear of the spoil of the fort and the sides were steeper. Pol and my men had managed to embed a few stakes on the south facing side. It was not ideal but it was better than nothing. I told Fiachra that all of the men who had been on the raid needed sleep and that included our new allies. I had had to use Pol and my men to protect Aengus and the others from the wrath of their captives. The fact that there had been a chief of the Uí Néill leading the raid seemed to have escaped their notice. They wanted vengeance on the survivors even though they were hired swords.

Although all of the recaptured Hibernians were less than happy with me it was Fergus' sister, Aileen, who kept giving me the blackest glances. She would be no friend to me.

Chapter 4

I needed no waking. I was up before night fell. I washed, dressed and then ate. Pol and the others woke while I was eating. Myrddyn appeared. He had a happy smile upon his face. I knew what it meant. "You have been busy wizard?"

"I have prepared a few surprises for our nocturnal visitors."

"How are the Hibernians?"

"Worried. They are more used to cattle raids than assaults on their oppidum. That is why they had let the ditch fall into disrepair."

I nodded and strapped on Saxon Slayer. "Come let us go to the walls."

Myrddyn shook his head. "No, Warlord, leave the men of the village to do that. We do not want our attackers to know that we have almost forty men that they know nothing about. They will know the number of warriors within these walls. If they see helmets and armour on the ramparts then they will be suspicious. We want them confident and eager to punish Fiachra and his warriors."

It made sense but I could not see how it helped us. "What do we do then?"

"I will wait upon the walls. When they come, you and our new allies will wait by the gate. It is not a well made obstruction and they will easily break it down. I have prepared the ditches to discourage their use. When they come through the gates then you can kill them."

I saw Pol nodding his approval. It made perfect sense. They would burst through thinking that they had won. There would be no order to them and we would have the advantage. My men were better than any three Hibernians who often fought without a shield and always without armour.

"Very well. Pol, bring Aengus here with his men so that I can show them how we fight."

Fergus and his warriors joined Myrddyn and became the sentries on the wall; they waited. I noticed that Myrddyn had two torches on the gate tower. I shook my head. That was a mistake a warrior would not have made. It ruined night vision. I contemplated removing them and then I realised that I would be seen if I did so and the enemy would be watching us. It probably did not matter as we just needed the raiders to break through the gate.

We lay down to conserve our strength but none of us slept. I watched the moon rise and wondered if they would come this night or wait until dawn. Would we have had a lost night's sleep for no reason? A short while later my question was answered when one of Fergus' men plunged from the ramparts transfixed by an arrow. We rose silently and I led my men towards the gate. We made a wedge with me at the centre. Aengus' men were just behind us. I saw Fiachra ordering his warriors to throw spears and rocks. Fergus did the same on the other side of the gate. Suddenly I saw Myrddyn hurl a torch to the left and then one to the right. A wall of flame erupted along both sides of the gate and I heard the screams of burning warriors. Fergus and his men cheered.

Aengus came to me, "Is it over, Warlord?"

"No, Aengus. That is just one of my wizard's tricks. He has driven them from the ditches and the only way left to them is the gate. They will enter soon enough."

I heard the axes as they began to hack a way through the poorly maintained gates. The men of the village continued to harass the attackers. It would infuriate them all the more and make them desperate to get at us. That all worked in our favour. I saw cracks appearing in the wood of the gate. Had it been daylight I would have seen the attackers on the other side.

"Ready your weapons but wait for my command!"

My men chorused, "Aye, Warlord!"

Suddenly an axe severed the retaining bar and the wooden gates crashed open. The warriors swinging their weapons to break in had tumbled to the floor. When the ones rushing from behind tripped over them, I shouted, "Charge!"

I held Saxon Slayer just behind me. One of the warriors was just struggling to his feet when I swung it sideways. He had a helmet but no protection for his neck and the blade sliced through it and decapitated him. So powerful was the blow that his head flew through the air. I smashed the edge of my shield on the head of the man who was to my left and stabbed forward with Saxon Slayer at the same time. Another warrior, who had just risen, took the sword in his unprotected middle. My men slew the ones in the gateway and I ran on to the bridge over the ditch. I had time to see men writhing in the ditch; they were covered in flames. Myrddyn had used one of his tricks. The shocked warriors who were left were gathering on the far side of the ditch; now was not the time of self congratulation.

I held Saxon Slayer aloft and shouted, "Rheged!" My men surged after me. I recognised a chief by his helmet, long hair and fine cloak. He too had a shield but I gambled that it was not as good as mine. I swung my sword overhand as I braced my shield for the strike of his blade. I heard a crack as his sword struck my shield. My sword travelled the full length of my swing and when it struck the shield it smashed it in two and continued to sever his left arm. He looked in shock at his arm and I plunged my sword into his chest.

When he fell the heart went from the raiders. The rest turned and ran. "Aengus, Fergus after them!"

The Hibernians were better suited to a foot race. We went around the wounded raiders despatching them. Fiachra came to join me. His face was filled with both joy and amazement. "There were over eighty warriors and yet you went through them as though they were grass."

I tapped my shield with my sword, "A good shield and armour make all the difference. Look at the shield where the chief struck it." He examined it in the light from the flaming ditch. "The leather is ripped and that is all. When I return home I will refit a new leather cover. Make good shields. They cost little and save lives."

He nodded. "What did your wizard conjure in the ditch?"

I shrugged, "I do not know nor do I need to know. That is why I have a wizard so that he can do such things."

Dawn began to break and we had the gruesome task of removing the charred, burned bodies from the ditch. We piled them together away from the ditch. The villagers could dispose of them later. We salvaged all the weapons that we could. There were some helmets which Aengus and Fergus could use. One or two of the swords and axes were usable too but most of them were only fit for melting down and using for arrow heads or sling shot.

The warriors returned during the morning. One or two sported wounds but they had not lost any. A fleeing man is always easier to kill; he has his back to you. In their arms they carried the captured weapons from the raiders they had despatched. I was pleased to note that they now spoke to each other as they returned. They had fought on the same side and they had won. That helps to build bonds.

When they reached us I pointed to the captured weapons and helmets. "Divide those amongst yourselves. I am going now for your ships. I may be away for almost a month. Be ready when I return. I need the same number as you are again and so if you can recruit any warriors into your bands then they can have the same terms."

Aengus nodded. "I will go to the villages close to my home. Many of those bear no love for the new king there. I may be able to get more."

"And I will find the young warriors close by here, Warlord. They will be keen for glory, combat and coin."

I returned to the oppidum and spoke with Fiachra. "I have my warriors now. My two new captains will be recruiting more men. If I were you I would repair the gates. You should not have any trouble from the raiders; at least not for this year. Their chiefs have been killed and they have marked the road home with their dead. They may come again but you should have more warriors trained by then." I pointed south. "You need to have eyes and ears there to watch for danger."

"Thank you, Warlord."

As I passed my new mercenaries, still dividing the booty and haggling over the better pieces I said, "Any more warriors will be sworn to me as you are."

"Yes Warlord."

We marched back to the beach. I had done what I intended and I had the beginnings of a mercenary army. This was like the game with wooden pieces we had played in Constantinopolis, zatrikion. You moved one piece to disguise the move of another. I would relieve the pressure on my island by threatening Manau. I would then use the distraction to attack deep into the Northumbrian heartland. I was taking the war to the Saxons.

With the recently captured Saxon ship we had two vessels for the mercenaries to use. Daffydd had two young captains for them. Both were keen to become masters and this would be the start. I had no doubt that neither Fergus nor Aengus would have any experience of sailing. My own captains, Tuanthal, Gawan and Lann Aelle had not been idle either. We now had a bigger force than when I had left. We could field sixty equites, twenty five squires and thirty mounted archers. The squires were a mixture: formerly they had been those young men who had shown skill in riding and would spend some years training with an equite and learning how to fight. Latterly they were a mixture of some of the older squires and youths of just fifteen summers. What they all had in common were skills in riding and with weapons. When we found them armour then the older ones would join the ranks of the equites. They were the weapon our enemies feared. As well as those fighting men we also had the last three scouts who were left from Aedh's elite. Felan, Dai and Aed would have to do the job of ten men until we acquired more skilled scouts.

I left my men to head north. I took Lann Aelle's eldest son, Pelas. He was just fourteen summers old but he could ride and he was desperate to be a warrior. We sailed aboard the *'Gwynfor'* with Myrddyn and accompanied the two Saxon ships. We also carried spare arrows and fodder. I aimed to make a cache of supplies closer to home than Deva. I had brought with me my father's shield and gave my dragon shield to Pelas. The time at sea had given me the time to think and plan.

As we headed towards the north eastern coast of Hibernia he asked me why. "I am honoured that you give me the shield which you bore into so many battles but I would know why." He hesitated. "Does it have bad luck?"

I laughed, "No, just the opposite but when I last used it someone said that the Warlord was associated with the wolf. They were right. I have my dragon standard. By using my father's shield I keep his memory alive. Besides I use his sword. Do not worry Pelas, the shield will protect you."

He nodded. After glancing at Myrddyn who appeared to be asleep he said, "Why does not Myrddyn fly and save the voyage across the waters?"

I saw the smile on Myrddyn's face and knew he was not asleep. He allowed me to answer, "So that he can watch over the two of us. A wizard should not waste his powers but use them judiciously." I pointed to the coastline which was just appearing over the horizon. "And now, Pelas son of Lann Aelle., you need to learn your duties. As well as keeping Saxon Slayer sharp, cleaning my armour and watching over Star I would have you keep your eyes and ears open whenever we are with those you do not know. Sometimes young eyes and ears can pick up things which I miss. Just because you are standing in the shadows does not mean that you are not serving me. Understand?"

"Yes Warlord, my father told me what to do. He impressed upon me that I must not let you down," he hesitated, "as Morcar did your father."

"Do not worry, Pelas that was as much my fault as it was Morcar. I should have been more aware of his heart. That will not happen again."

When we reached the beach we manhandled the two horses ashore. Myrddyn decided to explore the beach and see what he could find. He managed to unearth treasures wherever he went. What to me was a strange type of grass would prove to be an herb of inestimable value.

We rode to the oppidum and reached it far quicker than the first time we had come. It was a well sited hill fort and Fiachra had heeded my words; it had been repaired and improved. He would not be caught as easily a second time. He and my new warriors came down to meet with me. Their ranks had swollen to fifty. They also had their women with them. I was not certain how they would fare. The ruthless side of me did not care. So long as they occupied the Northumbrians on Manau then my plan would have succeeded. However, no matter how much I tried to be totally ruthless once I had fought with someone and they had sworn an oath to me I felt bound to protect them. I wanted these warriors and their families to win.

I clasped hands with Fiachra who had a huge smile upon his face. "It is good to see you, Warlord."

"And you, Prince Fiachra. What has made you happy?"

"The Uí Néill came to sue for peace. It seems they feared our wrath and thought that you were intent upon conquest."

"You did not tell them that I had no interest in their lands?"

He smiled, he was gaining guile. "The question never came up and I am not to blame for another's thoughts am I?"

I clapped him about the shoulders. "Your brother would be proud of you." I pointed to Fergus and Aengus who were waiting with the men. "These are now my oathsworn but when they have finished my task they may return to their home." I was warning him, as diplomatically as I could that they would be much more powerful as warriors once they had been equipped by me and had gained skill in war. If they failed then it would be a different matter but I needed Fiachra to know that there might be a time when he had forty hardened warriors roaming his land.

"I know but I know Fergus and I have discovered that Aengus is more honourable than I first thought."

"If you need to send a message to me, then send it to Caer Gybi on Mona. My uncle rules there in my stead. Farewell Fiachra."

As we approached the small band I smiled to myself for Aileen now had a short sword in her hand. She saw my look and said, proudly, "Needs must I will defend myself Warlord, should anyone try to take me against my will." She threw a black look in the direction of Aengus who rolled his eyes to the heavens.

I nodded, "That would be a brave man indeed." I turned to her brother. "If you will follow me, your ships are here and your supplies."

Pelas and I walked our horses, the better to speak with Aengus and Fergus. I asked them about the volunteers and how they were getting on as a war band.

Fergus answered. "We found we have much in common. It is *wyrd*."

"And can you work together without one leader?"

Aengus answered, "We have one; it is you, Warlord. But we would know precisely what you wish of us."

"That is a fair question. Your gold is on the ships. I will pay you before you do as I command. It is yours to keep. The ships are yours to use until you have either succeeded or given up."

Fergus looked at me quizzically, "Given up?"

"I would not have you throw your lives, or those of your families away. If you can succeed then I will be happy but if not then live long and prosper."

"What is it you wish?"

"I wish you to try to take Manau from the Saxons." They both nodded. I had not surprised them yet. "I know not how many men they have but we destroyed three boat loads and only five escaped. You will be outnumbered but I believe you can strike at the smaller places. There will be slaves, weapons and food. Prince Fiachra is more than happy for you to return there between raids."

"That is what you are suggesting is it not, Warlord? That we do not try to take the island all at once."

"I am. Even I would not try that with my whole army but you can learn to be better warriors and you will be able to attract others who will fight alongside you. Take what you can from the Saxons. The more food you take for the winter the less there will be for them. You stop the Saxons from raiding my home."

They asked me many more questions before we reached my ship. Once there they were like children as my men distributed helmets, spears and other weapons. I gave the gold to the two chiefs knowing that they would distribute it fairly. Myrddyn trudged along the beach having collected his herbs and greenery. I noticed Aileen watching him. As he laid them out, to dry, she wandered over and began to talk to him. It was the first time I had not seen her scowling. Pelas and I used the time to load our horses back aboard '***Gwynfor***'. Once they were settled I felt happier.

We camped and ate on the beach that night. Sailing at night time was never a good idea. The precocious gods could play cruel tricks on mortals. Myrddyn pointed over to Aileen. "She is a bright young thing. She has a keen interest in magic and some knowledge too."

I shook my head, "Remember Morgause, Myrddyn? You were taken in by her." Morgause and Morcar had poisoned both Myrddyn and my father before Morcar slew him.

"This one is not a spæwīfe. She is more like your stepmother, Myfanwy. She has an interest in herbs."

"I am just being careful wizard! Gawan is not here should she poison you."

He laughed, "You are a little young to be my mother, Hogan Lann. I will be careful."

Fergus and Aengus joined me when Myrddyn climbed aboard the boat to sleep. "One last piece of advice; curb your natural Hibernian nature. Do not rush into things wildly. I beg you to use your heads. If you can conquer Manau then so much the better but even if you just make them look inward you will have earned your gold."

Fergus nodded, seriously, "Our King conquered a whole land because he took your father's advice. We will do the same, Warlord."

"And if you need us to come and fight for you on the mainland we will do." Aengus held up his new helmet and mail aventail. "My warriors feel like heroes already."

We left them the next day. They were already planning on scouting out the island and choosing a good target. I was happier already.

Chapter 5

We sailed east. There were two rivers which we had selected: one was the Lune and the other the Belisama. We would visit the Belisama. If it was unguarded we would await our men there. If there were enemies then we would head north. The first part of this assault had to be performed in secret. We wanted to appear like wraiths in the heart of Northumbria. I wanted the Northumbrians looking over their shoulder and wondering where we would strike next. I had once done this, albeit on a smaller scale, for my father. I knew how to succeed. The last time we had run out of supplies. That would not happen this time. I had had time to think and to prepare.

The estuary was quiet when we approached it. The land to the north and the south was gentle and undulating. It was not the high peaks of the land of the lakes or around the Narrows. We knew that there were two old Roman watchtowers. They were both deserted or they appeared to be. With just a crew of sailors and the three of us we were in no position to fight any defenders. Daffydd took us in under the smallest canvas he could. We wanted stealth. We sailed further up the river. I wanted to be hidden by the banks. In the bow was a man with a lead tipped with wax. He would warn the captain of rocks. Suddenly Myrddyn shouted. "Captain, stop here."

Daffydd took in his sail and dropped an anchor. The ship swung around to face the sea and we were in the middle of the river. It was not wide at this point but we had been able to turn.

Myrddyn pointed to the northern bank. There were walls which looked Roman. Myrddyn was the keeper of Osric and Oswald's maps. They were not with us for he had embedded them in his mind. "That is the place. We have secure Roman walls. We wait now for those sluggards to make their way here."

I shook my head. I knew that Pol and Lann Aelle would be heading north just as fast as they could. They would, however, be careful and avoid any Saxons. "Captain, take us closer to the shore. Pelas and I will investigate this fort."

"Aye, Warlord. Do you want some of my men as guards?"

"No Daffydd. I think we can manage, eh Pelas?"

"Of course. Should we take armour?"

"No, just our swords and our bows." I smiled, "Perhaps we may find some food to hunt."

We jumped into the water and sank a little in the river mud. Then we made our way up the gentle slope. As I had expected, the old Roman fort had had a ditch at one time but it had gradually been filled by the passage of time. Leaves had fallen in the bottom and rotted. Soil had dropped in from ramparts which were no longer maintained. The gates had long gone and some of the stones had been taken. The Saxons were not great builders in stone and had concentrated on stealing the wood. The fort looked like every Roman fort we had found. It had two long sides and two shorter ones. There was a parade ground and a Praetorium. That was the building we sought. Some of the roof tiles had gone but it was still reasonably sound and dry. That would be important. We could use it for shelter. There were signs that animals and birds had used it but men had stolen everything of value and then left it alone. The Saxons feared the ghosts of the Romans. They did not understand building in stone. That suited us for it meant that they would be unlikely to return. We scouted the whole of the outside of the old fort. We found no evidence that men had been there for some time. The tracks were made by animals and it was their spoor we saw and not that of man. We returned to the ship.

When he heard our news Daffydd had his sailors build a fire so that we could cook some of the fish his men had caught. We would sleep on the boat, for safety, but we would eat a hot meal and that was always welcome.

The scouts from the column appeared the next morning. Aed waved and turned around to ride south to the rest of the column. The other two forded the river and joined us. "Did you have any problems, Dai son of Llewellyn?"

"No, Warlord, we saw no sign of the Northumbrians and only met our people." He shook his head sadly. "There are not many of them and they told us that small bands of Saxons come raiding them, especially around harvest time."

I pointed to the east. "Scout to the east and find what there is within ten miles of this estuary." They rode off. Myrddyn wandered over. "It seems we have chosen a good time to make war on the Northumbrians. They will be coming in the next month to steal from our people. We are here before them."

"It was meant to be, Warlord. You have spent enough time grieving over your father and berating yourself for things which were out of your control." He saw me start and laughed, "Your father could never come to terms with my skill at reading men's thoughts. Get used to it!"

I laughed, "Captain Daffydd we will bring the cargo up and my men will be able to move it."

He gave his orders and then turned to me. "When should I return?"

"Every two moons come here and wait two days. You need not leave your ship if there is danger close by. If we are here then we will find you. Each time you come bring fodder, food and arrows; unless, of course there are problems on Mona and then they have the priority. Have the other captains keep an eye on Manau. I would know what our neighbours are doing."

"We do not trade with Byzantium?"

"Until we have dealt with Manau, Northumbria and Edwin we keep our entire surplus for us. Besides the last message we had was that the Emperor was being beset by the Arabs. I suspect they will be preoccupied at the moment."

Pelas and I mounted our horses as the fodder and weapons were brought ashore. "Come we will see if there is a better crossing for the column further along."

We did not have far to travel before we found a usable ford with gentle banks. "Ride across, Pelas, and find the column. Bring them here and I will wait."

He splashed across the river and I rode along the bank and towards a distant clearing. I saw the remains of a house. It was a house of Rheged, or had been before it had been destroyed. The burnt timbers and stone foundations were blackened by fire. The ditch still remained but it was full of water and leaves. Star whinnied as we crossed the ditch. I could see the burnt decomposing bodies within. The roof had fallen in and covered them but there were the marks and signs of animals having disturbed the dead. This was the work of the Northumbrians. I suspected this had happened in the spring. The fields round about looked to have been tended and were not totally full of weeds and tares. The farmer had been industrious. All had been taken by the voracious Northumbrians. This had been the reason my father had begun his fight all those years ago and it was my duty to continue it. It was a sombre reminder of why I did what I did.

The column was just crossing the river by the time I returned. I rode back to the ship with Pol, Gawan and Lann Aelle. I told them of Fergus and Aengus. Lann Aelle counselled caution, "I am still worried, Warlord. We have brought the wolf into our home. Who is to say it will not bite us?"

I patted the shield hanging from my saddle. "Have you not noticed, Lann Aelle, that I now bear the wolf shield of my father? It is we who are the wolves."

Pol pointed behind at Geraint, "And we still retain the dragon standard of Rheged. The beasts that men fear are the warriors of Rheged, us!"

Myrddyn was in the fort when we reached him. He had had the sailors lift the stone which marked the legionaries' repository for valuables. It lay beneath the floor of the Praetorium. We would use it for the arrows and weapons we would store. It took us an hour to transfer our precious weaponry. Once it was inside and safe then Myrddyn replaced the stone and disguised the entrance with dirt and broken stone. The fodder we placed in the granary. We could not hide this but it was only of use to men on horses. The Saxons went afoot.

We bade farewell to Daffydd who sailed south and awaited our two scouts. Their news was not unexpected. "We found just one small settlement tucked in a small valley off the main one. They hid when we approached."

"Myrddyn, you have the map in your head, which way should we journey?"

"If we head up the valley your scouts found there is a narrow, little used pass over the hills. There is a Roman Road over the top but, in places, it is in need of repair." I looked at him in amazement. "It was Brother Oswald's doing not mine. There is no magic here. He merely updated the maps each time someone returned from the area. He was not idle." He shook his head, "I miss the old priest."

We all did.

"And where does it bring us out?"

He smiled, "The home of the Wolf Warrior, Stanwyck."

"*Wyrd.*"

"*Wyrd*, indeed."

We set off, even though there were just four or five hours of good daylight left. We would use each moment the Allfather gave us. It was truly *wyrd*, for we would come out in the heart of Edwin's land. We could go north, south or east. I would choose the route when we reached my father's old home. I needed no map to tell me that we would reach there by the following day. It was another reason for leaving promptly. But it was like all journeys, it was best started quickly.

We passed through the small village. The smoke told us that there were people there but they hid. It was nestling in a small valley just a short distance from the Belisama. Once through we found the Roman Road and made better time. We pushed on until dark began to fall. Our scouts rode in. "There is another village. They did not see us. They are our people."

"We will use this village for I would have information. Daffydd, take the archers and go around the far side. They will flee but I would have them in the village tonight, so be gentle with them."

"Aye, Warlord."

The road descended through a wood which must have been cut further back in Roman times but had since encroached across the old ditch. This looked to be a bigger place than we had seen for some time. I wondered why the Saxons had left it alone. My scouts were rarely wrong about the identification of people and I knew that they would not have made a mistake. I did not try to hide and we rode towards the village. There was a ditch and there was a wall which was intended to keep out animals only. I heard the sound of consternation as the villagers tried to flee. There was little point in trying to talk to them. I would wait until they had run into Daffydd.

"Bors, secure the walls."

Gawan and I dismounted and I handed my reins to Pelas. I smiled as I saw my father's former squire, Lann Aelle, watching his son. He had done this too.

Gawan spread his arm around the village. "This looks prosperous and yet it is close to the Northumbrians."

"It is still on the west of the divide and the road is little used. We have seen that for ourselves."

"The ones we passed south of the Belisama were even further west of the divide and they had been attacked and pillaged."

"You may be right brother." I waved over one of the equites who had been in Hibernia with me. He had impressed me. "Osgar, I want you to take ten equites. Camp, tonight, upstream from the village. Watch and restrain anyone who tries to leave."

"Aye, Warlord."

I saw him choosing others who had been in Hibernia too. As we waited for Daffydd to return with the villagers I went into the largest hut I could see. It looked comfortable. I saw fine pots. They looked to be of the same quality as our own. The village did well. I left when I heard the sound of the villagers returning. They were herded together and Daffydd and his mounted archers kept them penned.

"Who is your headman?"

A tall man stepped forward. "I am Aedh, son of Osric."

"I am the Warlord of Rheged. We would stay close by your water for the night."

He nodded. "And why does the Warlord of Rheged visit our peaceful valley?"

I did not like the man and his attitude. It seemed to me he was telling us we had no right to be there. I looked around and saw that the people had divided into two distinct groups. There were four or five men with Aedh who looked as though they were warriors. They had fine brooches on their cloaks as well as good swords. There were another eight men who, by comparison, almost looked like slaves. There was something not right in this village. I did not answer him straight away. Instead I glanced around the village. The hut I had looked in was well made and had a good position. There were four others in the same area and they were all well spaced. The rest were huddled by the water. The mud close by told me that they would be hard to keep clean. I decided I would not speak until I had had the chance to seek the advice of Myrddyn and Gawan. My immediate reaction was to take out my sword and to use the power of my equites to cow him. However Myrddyn's words from Hibernia still rang in my ears.

I smiled, "We are passing through on our way to Civitas Carvetiorum."

He scoffed, "There are ghosts there and that is all!"

"Aye, you are right. They are the ghosts of the kings of Rheged, and the brave warriors, who held back the Saxon onslaught for so many years." I noticed that Aedh and his party did not like those comments. "We will not impose upon you, save to use your water." He gave me a smug smile. "Pol, we will camp downstream from the village I would not have us polluting their water."

I led Star and followed Pol. I noticed the looks the small group exchanged with each other. I needed to speak with my brother and my wizard. There was something going on here and I needed those who could read men's bodies and faces.

We did not use tents. I knew not how we would cope in winter but that was a bridge we would cross when we had to.

Pelas took Star away and I led my leaders off to a rock by the stream. My men organised our camp.

"Well, Myrddyn, what do you make of it?"

"They are hiding something."

"There are two distinct groups of men in the village, brother."

"I noticed that and yet they are all of our people and they are not slaves."

"Not all slaves wear a yoke, Warlord."

"These were not slaves but they were the poorer elements." I looked at the waters flowing past the village. "We need to keep our eyes and ears open tonight. I did not expect this."

We lit fires and the scouts brought some small game for us to cook. It augmented the cereal we used as our basic food. We were just settling down for the night when Daffydd and two of his archers came in with a slumped body.

"We found this one trying to leave the village. He tried to run. Tadgh had to subdue him." Tadgh was a powerfully built archer. One blow from his ham like fists would have felled a bull.

I rolled him on his back. It was the headman. Myrddyn felt his neck. "He will live."

"Pol, go and fetch his wife and son but do it quietly. I do not want the village arousing." As I stood I noticed a face peering at me from behind one of the huts lower down the stream. "Pelas come with me. Gawan, you take charge here."

We moved down the bank. As we neared the hut the face appeared again. I waved Pelas to the left and I went to the hut. I saw the figure disappearing into the village. When I reached the end of the hut there was Pelas with the man pinned to the floor. It was one of the poorer villagers. I smiled, "Well done, Pelas. You know how to wrestle but you can let him up now."

The man looked terrified and stood cowering. Had I become such an ogre that I could terrify a villager of Rheged? He almost sobbed, "Please do not tell Thegn Aedh that you caught me spying. I will be punished."

I went closer to him, "Thegn Aedh?" Thegn was a Saxon title.

"Yes, Warlord."

"Who made him Thegn?" He looked even more afraid as he realised he had said what he should not. "I promise you my protection." He began shaking and seemed incapable of coherent speech. He was terrified. . "Pelas, stay with him and see if you can calm him. Do not let anyone else speak with him. Shout if you are in danger."

"I will Warlord."

I went back to my men. Aedh had been revived and his wife and son were with him. His son was a little younger than Pelas while his wife was as well dressed as Gawan's.

"Which Saxon made you Thegn? Was it Oswiu or Oswald?"

The looks on their faces told me all that I needed to know. It had been a guess, an educated one but a guess nonetheless. I saw Myrddyn and Gawan nod their approval.

"Well, which one?"

The three of them remained mute. I could see that they were frightened but not frightened enough. I pulled Saxon Slayer from its scabbard and held it close to Aedh's face. "This is the sword that men call Saxon Slayer. If you are not the Saxon's man then you will swear an oath upon it." I saw the look on his face; his hand came towards it. "It you do not speak true then the sword will punish you." His hand recoiled as though he had been burned. I stuck it in the ground; I was well aware that it looked like the cross of the White Christ. It was another test for this Saxon puppet.

I stood and pointed to Myrddyn. Out of all of us he looked the most nondescript, lacking armour and weapons he could have been taken for a clerk. "Do you know who this is?" Aedh seemed to see him for the first time and he warily shook his head. "This is Myrddyn the wizard. Their religion was confirmed when the woman made the sign of the cross. Aedh and his son looked terrified. "You have heard of him then. You can hide nothing from the wizard. You cannot flee the wizard. King Morcant Bulc hid in his mighty fortress behind his whole army and the wizard found him." I let the silence hang like a dagger in the air and then I barked, "Who paid you?"

Even some of my men jumped at my voice. The man spoke and it was like a dam bursting. "It was Oswald. He was my master and he brought me here and told me that I had to pay a quarter of all that the village produced and send all the young men to fight in his warband."

That explained why there were only older men in the village, save Aedh's son. I now had the picture. This had been a freed slave. I could not blame him for his choices. I took the torch held by Lann Aelle and pulled down his tunic. There were the tell tale marks of the yoke on his shoulders. He had been a slave. It explained his treatment of some of the other villagers.

"Bind him, and his wife." I stood. I would need to know when Oswald or his men were coming back. I had no doubt that someone would tell him of our presence. My plans to appear like a wraith would come to nought if word got out.

Suddenly I heard, "Warlord!"

I turned and saw Aedh's son with a dagger in his hand, raised to stab me. An arrow head stuck from the front of his head and his body crumpled to the ground. Daffydd said, "I had no choice, Warlord. He moved so quickly."

"It was *wyrd*, Daffydd." The bound woman was weeping. "This is the punishment from the Gods for your treachery." I shouted, "Pelas bring him here."

The villager came fearfully, led by my squire.

"Bors take these two to their hut and guard them until I decide what to do with them." When they were gone I turned to the villager, "What is your name?"

"Scanlan, Warlord."

"I know of this man's loyalties but now I need answers from you." He seemed to notice the dead boy and he recoiled. "He tried to kill me. Fear not Scanlan you will not be harmed. Now tell me when will the Saxons be here again?"

He pointed to the skies. "When the new moon comes."

"Two days." Kay nodded.

"And why did you and the others not stop Aedh. He treated you badly did he not?"

"Any who opposed him had their sons selected to be warriors and taken by the Saxons or their girls were made into slaves."

Now it made sense. "Thank you Scanlan. We will change the way things are here. You can trust me."

"Will the Warlord stay this time?"

"The Warlord is here to stay. Go back to your hut." After he had gone I said, "We need guards on Aed's confederates. It may be that they were opportunists or perhaps the treachery goes deeper."

"What do we do, brother?"

"We ambush Oswald's men and we make sure that this village becomes Rheged once more."

"And the headman?"

"I do not know."

Myrddyn said, quietly, "He should die."

"Many men should die but I will think on this. For the moment we need to guard the village and then tomorrow find out where the Saxons come from."

Gawan came to me as I lay down in my blanket. "I will ask again, brother, now that no one can overhear. What do you intend?" I remained silent. "I know that your mind is troubled. You do not want to have this man and his wife killed and yet you cannot let them resume their rule and their work for the Saxons."

"You are becoming like Myrddyn and you see inside my mind."

"Let us rather say that I know you well. You are much like father was and he would have had the same dilemma. The gods and the spirits work in strange ways. Sleep and let the spirit world come to your aid."

"But you are the dreamer and not I."

"Who knows?" He smiled as he left me. What did he know that I did not?

I slept but I did not remember any dreams. I was not visited at all. However I felt better the next day. We gathered the villagers around us and I brought out Aedh and his wife.

"These two have done you all a disservice. They have sold your daughters into slavery and sent your sons to fight for King Edwin." I pointed an accusing finger at Aedh's confederates. "Others have aided them. I will pass judgement before we leave but first I intend to stop these Northumbrians. You are all the people of Rheged and I am the Warlord. Had you told me of Aedh and his tyranny, I would have dealt with him. Keep silent no longer. How many Saxons come?" Before they could answer I pointed at one of the well dressed men. "You! How many?"

"Sometimes twenty and sometimes forty."

The man we had spoken to the night before jabbed an accusing finger at him. "You lie. There are never less than fifty!"

The liar dropped to his knees. "I am sorry, Warlord. I have a son and I do not wish to lose him."

I lifted him to his feet. "Then be a man and make your son proud of you. We will fight these Saxons even if there were a thousand of them. You all have a choice; you fight or you die! We can end this Northumbrian tyranny. So think and answer freedom or slavery? Which will it be?"

Even those who had been Aedh's confederates jumped up and shouted, "We will fight!"

Chapter 6

Aed and his scouts headed east. The villagers had told us where the warband came from. It was the old capital of Elmet, Loidis. I was fairly certain, after speaking with the villagers, that this was the work Oswald and Oswiu. They were playing a treacherous game with Edwin. They were being their own warlords. This was their land to rob and to rule. I had helped them as had Cadwallon by attacking Edwin in the south. They had built up their strength. It did not need Myrddyn to tell me that I could stand back for they would eventually fight each other. I could not do that. There would be more villages like this one and more people being terrorised. I would stop Oswald and Oswiu. I would stop Edwin. That was my purpose.

We had ample warning of the arrival of the warband. There were sixty of them. They came on foot although their chief rode. From the description of my scouts it was neither Oswald nor Oswiu. That was a pity. I would have liked to rid the world of one of them. They would be coming down the Roman Road. Leaving our horses in the village with a third of my men and the villagers I took the rest to the rock strewn pass through which the Saxons would have to approach. The road ran along one side of the gorge like valley. By hiding in the rocks to the south we would be able to fall upon them with only one exit for them; down the rocky filled valley to the stream below.

I deliberately left our horses in the village. This was partly to save them for the hardship which would come eventually but mainly to hide our identity from any of the Saxons who might escape. Daffydd ap Miach and his archers were at the eastern end of the pass. The rest of us were spread out along the southern side. The archers would close the trap and then we would attack. All of my equites had a bow and many of the young squires still had their slings. A sudden onslaught would, hopefully, take the fight from them.

They came as Aed had predicted. The horseman led. I saw his shield had a design like four running legs painted in red. He had a long byrnie and a full faced helmet. In his hand he carried an axe. His oathsworn came behind him. There were ten of those in byrnies: some long and some to the waist. The other fifty had helmets and shields but no armour.

We waited patiently for Daffydd to release his arrows. Once he did so then we would all join in. The arrows soared high. My captain of archers had cleverly waited until they had passed him. The Northumbrians did not see the arrows and none defended themselves. The battle was won in that instant. I sent my arrow high into the air then I dropped my bow, unsheathed my sword and hefted my shield. A second flight had left the bows of my men as we tumbled down the slope to attack the shocked Northumbrians.

I led the equites towards those with the byrnies. My squires and archers could dispose of the rest. Two of the oathsworn were down but the rest locked their shields. Luck was with me that day. I ran down the slope and managed to avoid all the hazards which might have tripped me. As Kay had to move to his left so I adjusted my feet and I leapt on to a large rock. I sprang in the air from the rock and almost flew at the Saxons. Falling I swung my sword. My feet crashed on to one warrior cracking his skull like an egg whilst my sword sliced down, through the mail and into the shoulder of a second. As I tumbled to the ground Kay slashed his sword at the Saxon who tried to stab me in the side. As I stood I saw Lann Aelle slicing upward to kill the leader of the warband. And then it was over. The speed and ferocity of our attack allied to the skill of our archers had won the day for us. We had had the element of surprise and used it well. The wounded were sent to the Otherworld.

Daffydd and his men joined me, "Well done my captain of archers. Did any escape?"

He shook his head, "They all fell."

"Take their armour, helmets and weapons. Throw the bodies into the valley."

It had all gone far better than I might have dreamed. We returned to the village. The armour came in handy for the squires who had none yet. The helmets, shields and swords went to the villagers. The spare horse joined our string of remounts.

Myrddyn, who had stayed in the village, came over to me. "You have a decision to make."

"I know and I have made it." The men in the village were gathered around me and then the two prisoners brought out. "Tomorrow my men and I will leave this village and head away from here. We will return at some point in the future. You will hold this village for Rheged. You will all share in the bounty of this valley and you will all fight the Northumbrians." I glared at them all. "How do you say?" They all nodded. I pointed to Myrddyn, "And remember, I have a wizard. You all know of Myrddyn's power." I smiled, "Even those who are now Christians."

I took out my sword and I saw the two prisoners brace themselves. "I am Warlord, and I answer to no man! I have the lives of these two in my hands." They both closed their eyes and awaited the slice of my sword. "It is not, however, me whom they have betrayed, it is you. I give their lives to you. Do they live or do they die? The decision is yours." Out of the corner of my eye I saw a smug smile on Myrddyn's face. I had done what he had hoped.

They looked at each other and then back at me as though this was some sort of trick. I stood patiently waiting. This decision had to be theirs. When they made it I would know that I could trust them. It was Scanlan who spoke. "I say they should live. Even though my children have both been taken from me Aedh, too, has also lost his only child. I say they live." He paused. "So long as they live with us and not over us." He turned to the former headman.

"I will. I have learned my lesson and my wife…" he put his arm around his wife who still looked as though she was in shock following the death of her only son.

The other men then nodded, in turn. I sheathed my sword. "Good. Then this afternoon we deepen your ditch and raise your walls. The next time the Saxons come you will show them that the men of Rheged still have fight in them. If you submit then you will be slaves once more. Fight and you will earn your freedom."

We left the village early the next morning and headed along the Roman Road. Already the bodies of the dead Saxons had been ravaged by the beasts and the birds. Nature always won in the battles between men.

Gawan rode next to me. "Loidis then, brother?"

"Not at first. I intend to sweep to the east of the fortress and raid about the old Roman settlement of Eboracum. It is rich farmland. I would make the Saxons starve this winter. Loidis is also easier to defend than some of the places we will attack."

"You know them well?"

"I know them. I campaigned with father. Uncle Raibeart was married to the daughter of the last King of Elmet and Rheged joined the last alliance against the Saxons. We failed."

"That is why you fight as you do."

"I will make alliances and use them but I will not rely on them in battle. This band of warriors, brother, can defeat anything which is thrown at us, so long as we choose the field and we choose the time."

We saw isolated farmsteads as we passed along the road. I dare say there would have been Saxons we could have raided but, in my head, I had a plan and I wanted to stay with it. We had three months before the autumn weather would make movement difficult. Until then I wanted to fly from one end of the land to the other. When we struck it would be in the heart of Northumbria.

My scouts reported that there were Saxons at Stanwyck and they had refortified it. We gave it a wide berth. It would be visited, but not yet. Once we had passed the hill fort we made much faster time. This was horse country and the flat vale was crossed in half a day. We may have been seen but it was a risk we had to take. It was important that we disappeared. We climbed the hills which protected the northern side of the old capital of Northern Britannia, Eboracum. There we found shallow valleys and high moors both afforded us protection from prying eyes.

Aed and Dai returned to our camp by the fast flowing river which bubbled through a valley which was steeper than the others. I hoped we could use it for a couple of days. They had been to the settlement to the south while Felan was away to the east.

"Warlord, there is a Saxon hall and village to the south."

"Do we know its name?"

Myrddyn, whom we had thought to be asleep said, "It is called Elmeslac."

"Are there any warriors?"

"Not that we saw and there is no wall either."

"Lann Aelle, take twenty equites and twenty archers. Burn their hall, kill their men and drive the women and children hence. Take what you can to feed us and destroy the rest."

He hesitated before nodding and saying, "Aye, Warlord."

"Pol I want all but ten squires to be ready to ride as soon as Felan returns. The ten can stay here to watch the camp and Myrddyn."

"I need no watching."

"I know wizard but the remounts do."

Felan rode in a short time later. "There are many farms between here and the sea. They have a fort at the end of the valley by the coast. They have warriors there."

"Mount up and we will ride."

As we rode Gawan and Pol placed themselves close to me. Gawan was my brother and he could tell me what others could not. "This destruction of Saxon farms does not sit well with the men. They do not mind fighting warriors but not making war on women and children."

I bit back the retort which sprang into my head. They were questioning me for the right reasons. "The Saxon is like a bear in a cave. We need to make him come from the cave so that we can destroy him. He is big and he is slow but once he gathers himself he will come after us. We are goading him and making him weak at the same time. I intend to capture this fort and the warriors. We will then return to our camp and then destroy the farms on the way back. In two days time we will be north of here. The Saxons will begin to gather their forces. I know that my men are honourable and do not like to make war on women and children but there is no other way to make the bear angry."

I had explained it to them so that they would be able to answer my warriors' doubts. I need not have. They were oathsworn and I was Warlord but my father had taught me well. What I did not say was that this pressure would make their families back in our land, safer. It would make the people of Rheged to the west safer. Edwin had many warriors but he depended upon the food that he grew to feed them. Therein lay his weakness.

It was a rich vale through which we passed. The farmers hid as we galloped through. We rode horses and they knew that we were enemies. I suspect they wondered why we did not attack them. We reached the fort on the headland by the afternoon. There was a Roman fort atop the cliff and they had re-used it. That suited us for we were familiar with the layout of the forts. We spied upon it from a spot a mile inland. We rested before dark and then rode, silently, towards the stone structure.

Although the Saxons used the Roman forts they did not understand them. They never maintained the ditches and they never used traps within them. Although they watched the walls they rarely used enough warriors to keep an effective watch. At night time they were vulnerable. We would exploit that weakness.

We left the squires to guard the horses. I estimated that there were fifty or so warriors within the walls. There would be a thegn there who would be responsible to Edwin, or possibly one of Aethelfrith's sons. It allowed the king to control a large area.

Daffydd and his archers watched the walls; they were ready to strike down any sentry alert enough to see us. The younger equites were thrust up on shields to scale the walls. Kay led them. I waited with Pol, Gawan and the more experience equites by the main gate. I thought that we had managed to eliminate the sentries silently but a sudden cry told me that the alarm had been sounded. The gate groaned open and we raced inside.

I saw three bodies lying on the ground. A light from an opening door revealed the Saxons racing out to meet us. Some had donned armour but most had not. I used my shield to deflect the spear which was thrust at me from the side and I slashed the sword across his unprotected middle. I saw one of my younger equites as a huge warrior swung his axe and took his head. I ran towards the giant. He was a little taller than me and he had put on his byrnie. Leaving my men to deal with the rest I faced him. It was a two handed axe he swung. He had a shield on his left arm and he was strong enough to wield the long weapon with his right only.

He grinned, his teeth showing in the light from the open door of the hall. "You have come here to die, Welshman!"

"I have come here to snuff out your candle, Saxon!"

He whirled the axe expertly and it came towards me at an angle designed to take off my leg at the knee. I lowered my shield and braced myself. This was not an Hibernian axe; this was a powerful weapon used by an expert axe man. It bit into the shield. As he pulled it away I saw a chip of wood fly off. He saw the wolf design. He snarled, "So the Wolf Warrior has returned!"

"Aye Saxon and I have teeth which bite." Instead of swinging my sword, which he would expect, I stabbed forward at his face.

He had a shield which protected his eyes but he recoiled as the wickedly sharp tip lunged at his throat. It meant he could not swing his axe and I punched forward with my shield. He was already off balance and the blow sent him tumbling to the ground. For a big man he was quick and he scrambled to his feet and swung his axe in an arc to give himself breathing space.

My little flurry had damaged his confidence. Around us his warriors were being slaughtered but it was as though we were in our own world. He took a leaf out of my book and punched at me with his shield. I pivoted and spun around. His punch took him into the space I had occupied and I brought Saxon Slayer around to smash into his back. He had a good byrnie but I felt and heard the crack as the rings on his mail shirt were severed. The sword ripped through the leather byrnie and he grunted as the iron propelled him forward.

He tried to turn quickly but I stabbed down with Saxon Slayer and the tip burned into his knee. This time he roared in pain but he had the strength and the presence of mind to bring his axe down in a steep swing overhand. I used the shield to angle the axe head down and I stabbed forward with all of my might. Saxon Slayer sliced through the mail and the leather. I saw his eyes widen as it tore through his stomach and when the hilt was stopped by the mail I twisted and pulled it out. Intestines were wound like wriggling worms around the red blade. The axe fell to the floor and he stood there looking surprised. He used a hand to try to hold the blood and his knees gave way. He sat on the floor holding himself in the middle.

"You are the Warlord."

"I am."

"Then I have been slain by the bane of the Northumbrians, Saxon Slayer. Give me my sword and send me to the Otherworld I beg of you; one warrior to another."

The man was not a Christian. I took his sword from his scabbard and he smiled. "First, who are you and whom do you serve?"

He scowled but knew he could do nothing about it. "I am Aelfraed of Scar and I serve Oswald."

I nodded and gave him his sword. "Go to the Otherworld and meet your oathsworn." I stabbed him cleanly in the throat and he sighed his way to the afterlife.

I sheathed my sword and walked around the fort to make sure that all were dead. "Pol, collect any armour and weapons which you can find. Give the armour to the squires. See if there are any horses."

"Warlord!"

I turned to see Osgar. "What is it?"

"We have found two cattle!"

"Excellent" Slaughter them. We will stay here tonight and return to our camp in the morning."

The Saxons had done nothing to make the fort more habitable save repairing the gate. They had used the barracks which had a roof remaining. That would have to be our bed too. After setting sentries we ate in the open courtyard. We hacked off the cooked meat and left the carcasses of both beasts to cook overnight. The meat would last three or four days. This was a gift from the gods.

Pol and Gawan sat with me. "Was he Edwin's man?"

"No, he served our enemy, Oswald." It had been the two brothers Oswald and Oswiu who had suborned and seduced Morcar and Morgause. I smiled, "That makes me happier."

"Why, brother?"

Pol knew me as well as any man, "Because, Gawan, it means it is more likely that Oswald will come here to give battle and that is what the Warlord wishes."

I nodded, "I will sleep easier when those snakes are dead."

Gawan looked thoughtful. "It still makes me wonder where King Edwin is. We know that he campaigns in the summer and collects both slaves and tribute."

"He has the whole of Northumbria to visit, brother. He could be in the south."

"I would be happier knowing where he is."

Gawan never spoke for the sake of filling a silence. "Speak your thoughts, brother. You know that Pol is of our mind too."

"If he is not in the north then perhaps he is threatening Cadwallon and Deva."

Now I understood. He was worried, naturally about his family. "Have you not dreamed, as Myrddyn might have?"

He shook his head, "I need to be in a holy place for that." He looked apologetic, "I am sorry brother. I am not Myrddyn."

"Perhaps not yet but you will be one day." I threw the rib I had been gnawing into the fire where it sizzled. "I had planned on raiding north, along the Dunum to aid King Fiachnae mac Báetáin and perhaps wrest more of the north from King Edwin's greedy fingers but we can head south towards Loidis and thence to the lands closer to Mercia."

There was a look of relief on Gawan's face. "Thank you, brother."

"And we will speak with Myrddyn. Perhaps he has dreamed."

The next morning we rose at dawn and placed the bodies of the Saxons in the barracks. The men gathered kindling and we set fire to the fort. We would never use it and I wanted the Saxons to know that we had been here. The pall of smoke rose high in the sky.

There had been just two horses in the fort and we took those with the hunks of meat we had cooked. As we passed along the fertile vale I sent parties of men to burn the farms and take what we could. Our funeral pyre had alerted them and the farmers and their families fled while their land burned. We could have hunted them down, as slaves, but that would have slowed us down. I wanted to strike swiftly.

It was early evening when we rode into the camp by the river. Lann Aelle was there and he had three horses and some cooked pork. We would still be eating well.

While the spare armour and weapons were distributed I spoke with Lann Aelle, Pol, Gawan and Myrddyn. "Have you dreamed of Edwin, Myrddyn?"

"He is hidden from me." I sighed. He smiled and said, "However, if I were to make a guess I would say he is not far from here at Eboracum."

"Why?"

"When we were in the village I spoke with those men who supported Aedh. They told me that the King was to be wed and it would be in Eboracum." He paused and then delivered a statement which set us all thinking. "It may well be that he is becoming Christian. They believed that a priest sent by the Pope in Rome was coming."

"You may be right then."

"Warlord, we have not enough men to assault Eboracum."

"I know but if this is a wedding then he will have many nobles and warriors there. We all know that they like to hunt. We may have an opportunity to damage their leaders and that, in the long run, may be crucial."

Gawan nodded, "And Oswald and Oswiu may be there too."

"Then I am decided, we will head for Eboracum." I tapped the wolf shield of my father. "We shall become the hunters."

The next day we went south east, towards the old Roman fortress. I knew that, just south of the city, there were many forests which teemed with game. The Saxons hunted them on the eastern side of the river. The Romans had used it and I could see Edwin regarding it as a royal hunting ground. We left the farms we saw and avoided contact. We could resume our raiding after we had found the nobles.

I divided my warriors into four columns. Each had equal numbers of equites, archers and squires. Pol, Lann Aelle and Gawan led three of them. We arranged to meet some ten miles from the fortress and south of the forest in two days time. We were gambling and if it did not pay off then we would resume our raid. I hoped that one of us would come across Northumbrian nobles. An attack in the heart of their homeland would be demoralising. We did not need large numbers in each column. If there were hunters then they would only have a handful of retainers. We were strong enough to deal with them. I took the younger equites and Osgar. He had proved himself to be dependable and it would allow the others to have the more experienced warriors. As night fell and we drifted into the eaves of the forest some of the younger equites were disappointed that we had not seen any Saxons.

Myrddyn, who had decided to cook for us, waggled his ladle in their direction. "When you go fishing you do not expect a fish each time you cast. Learn patience."

The next morning we left Myrddyn and half a dozen squires in the camp we had made. The rest of us rode to the main track which wound its way through the forest. We were in the middle of the hunting preserve which was conveniently placed for the fortress. I imagined Romans using it. Hunting was perfect training for combat. I knew that the other three columns all had more chance of finding hunters. They would shun the road but I had the untried equites and had given myself that task. Aiden son of Miach, who was our southern sentry, brought the unexpected news that a band of warriors was marching up the road through the forest. These were not hunters!

I turned to one of the squires, "Ride to Myrddyn and bring him and the others. Tell them we have found warriors!" He galloped off. "Aiden, how many are there and where are they?"

He pointed to the south. "About a mile and half down the road and there are forty of them at least. They are leading pack horses."

"Are they wearing armour?"

He shook his head, "Helmets only and they are not fastened for war." When warriors were travelling they rarely wore armour, especially if they thought that they were safe and helmets might be pushed to the back of the head to allow air to their faces.

This was where I needed Myrddyn or Gawan. They could untangle these puzzles in an instant. I set a trap while I worked things out. "I want equal numbers on both sides of the road. Hide yourselves and do not move until I yell '*Saxon Slayer*' and my archers release." I would bring the wrath of the Saxons on me and it would allow the other men to attack unprotected backs. Why did they have pack horses? Then it came to me. They were travelling from some distance away and I remembered that Myrddyn had spoken of a wedding. It had not taken place yet and these were the guests. That made things much easier for they would not be expecting trouble. They were close to their destination and they would be relaxing.

All was silent. The birds had departed. Then I heard the sound of singing. It was the Saxons. I recognised the song as one of their story songs. It told of a great warrior who fought and killed a dragon. I smiled to myself and looked at the dragon standard carried by Llewellyn. If he rode hard then they would hear the dragon as it wailed. That would have to wait for another day. Today we needed surprise. I had five archers with me. There were four on the other side of the track. I tapped the one next to me on the shoulder and he drew back his bow. We were still and the undergrowth, which was thick with leaves, hid us. It would not impede the horses when we moved but it was a barrier between us and our prey.

I spied them. The scout had been correct. The ones at the front were nobles. They had plaited hair and their beautifully made cloaks were adorned with fine brooches. Their shields were slung over their backs and none had their weapons drawn. I waited until they were level with the archers next to me. It was an irregular column and it would have been impossible to seal off both ends. I would just have to take my chances. I wanted the nobles dead.

I nodded to the archer and, as they loosed their arrows, yelled, "Saxon Slayer!" My fifteen equites burst from the cover of the undergrowth. My archers had loosed a second flight before the first had hit and now the other four loosed theirs. Five Saxons fell. They tried to grab their weapons. I rode at the ones who had the best cloaks. They were the nobles. I swung Saxon Slayer horizontally and it sliced through the shoulder and chest of one of them. His body fell, to be trampled by Star. One of the nobles tried to grab my reins and pull me to the ground. I punched him hard with my shield and I heard the crack as the boss broke his nose. I wheeled Star to the left and swung my blade vertically to split both his helmet and his head.

I saw the warriors at the back trying to flee back down the road with the pack horses. There were five horses and their value was inestimable.

"Get those horses!"

Unfortunately all of my equites, save for Osgar, obeyed my order. I was left with just four of us and my archers. The archers had no targets for we were in the way. The surviving fifteen ran north, along the road. There were just four of us but we pursued them anyway. We would easily catch them. I realised that this would be Pelas' first combat on a horse. I hoped he was up to it. As we rode so the dragon standard held by Llewellyn wailed. It must have terrified the fleeing Saxons. Strangely as we moved forward and the dragon wailed I could have sworn I heard horns in the distance. Then they stopped and I convinced myself that I was dreaming.

Osgar caught the first laggard. He leaned forward to stab him between the shoulder blades. Pelas too managed to blood himself. His victim tried to duck under Pelas' horse's head. My young squire showed great skill in striking on the wrong side of his mount's head and killing the Saxon. I thought we might have caught them when a flurry of arrows came from our fore. One struck Llewellyn in the arm and three hit me on the helmet and shield. There were more Saxons ahead and we were being ambushed.

"Fall back! Archers, cover us."

I wheeled Star around and felt an arrow hit me in the back. I felt a tiny prick of pain. I kicked hard and Star surged forward. As we passed my line of nine archers, they loosed three flights. We kept going until we found the pack horses and the dead guards. The archers rode in behind us.

"They have given up, Warlord, but they have reclaimed the bodies."

That was disappointing for the nobles had had fine weapons. Still, we had their armour and their gold for that was on the pack horses. We had lost one equite, Dai son of Aiden. We put him on his mount. We would bury him later. Myrddyn arrived with the squires. "We had best head for the meeting with the others, Myrddyn. We have woken the wasp's nest. But we did better than I could have hoped. We killed five nobles."

"Good. Perhaps the others have had as much success."

We rode through the forest feeling elated. It had not been a total victory but it had been a surprising one. *Wyrd*!

Chapter 7

When we reached a safe place to count our treasure Myrddyn examined the wound on my back. The arrow had penetrated both the mail and the leather but it had just caused a little bleeding. Myrddyn cleaned it and applied a salve. It was not serious and the value of my armour had been demonstrated once more.

We had a day to ourselves and it allowed us to examine the armour and gold we had recovered. There were some fine jewels as well as wonderfully carved ivory and jet. I guessed they were wedding presents and gifts for King Edwin. The horses were also invaluable. What neither Myrddyn nor I could understand was the attack on us. We could not explain the presence of Saxons where they had ambushed us. All was explained when Gawan arrived. He and his equites were full of excitement but they waited for Gawan to tell the tale. His was the last column to arrive. Pol and Lann Aelle had met just a handful of Saxon hunters and they had killed them.

"We came across King Edwin himself. He had thirty warriors with him as well as ladies and some priests of the White Christ." He pointed to Daffydd. "Our Captain of Archers nearly slew him with a well aimed arrow but one of the holy men managed, I know not how, to block the missile with his staff. It split the staff but his oathsworn surrounded him with their shields. When they sounded their horn then other warriors arrived and we had to leave for we were outnumbered."

"You have done well, brother. Did you lose any warriors?"

"Aye, Warlord, two squires and an equite; Tadgh son of Tuanthal." That was a grievous loss. My father's old captain only had two sons remaining. "And we were pursued. We had to ride far to the north and then swing around in order to reach you. King Edwin has his men hunting us now. We heard hounds."

"Now I know why we were ambushed. It was an accident. They were hunting for you and found us. I have no doubt that Edwin will send even more of his warriors to scour this land for us. He will not take kindly to an attempt on his life. The woods do not suit our horses. We will cross the river and head west."

Aed spoke up. "Warlord, the waters are too high for us to ford. We will need to cross north of the fortress."

He was right. The land around the fort was swampy and the water levels were high. We had had a wet early part of the summer. "In that case we will head east and skirt the swamp. We will find a route north. Tomorrow, Aed and Dai scout to the east. Felan scout to the north."

As we headed east on a damp and wet summer's day I wondered if I had been a victim of my own arrogance. I had led us to a small victory but we could be trapped in land which did not suit my horses. The land through which we travelled was, indeed swampy. We found that, at times, we had to lead our horses rather than ride them for the weight of our horses and our armour was too much and the beasts began to sink in the swampy, muddy land. It slowed us down. Daffydd and his archers formed the rearguard and I was not worried about an attack from that direction but the further north and west we went the closer we would be to Eboracum. Edwin's hunters would be on our trails. If he was to be married then he would have many men at his wedding who could be used to augment his own forces. A human hunt was the finest sport known to man.

I walked between Gawan and Myrddyn who was light enough to ride; he wore no mail. "Can either of you see light at the end of this tunnel and a way out of our dilemma?"

Gawan shook his head but Myrddyn said, "I have not dreamed your death."

"That is reassuring."

"Of course that does not mean that you cannot be captured but I do not feel that you are in danger. King Edwin has a large area to search and we are small in number and swift. If your plan was to focus the attention of King Edwin on Northumbria and not on Mona then you have succeeded."

It was ironic but I had. We were in grave danger but Myrddyn was right. Warrior for warrior we could beat anything which Edwin could throw at us. The problem would be if we were found with nowhere to run.

We were now heading north. Felan found us. "Warlord they had men barring our route north."

We had travelled over this land when we headed to the forest. With the river to the west and the fort ahead of us then King Edwin could put a line of warriors like beaters to halt our progress. It would stop us escaping.

"How many are there?"

"He has war bands spread out." He dismounted and walked to an unmarked piece of muddy earth. "Let me show you." He took out his sword and marked the river, the fort and the marshes to the east. "The gap we came through is six miles across. He has fifty men every half mile or so. And there is a bigger warband just a mile to the north of them. We could break through one of the smaller warbands but they would be alerted and we would be surrounded." He turned and pointed. "They are just three miles away."

The land was very flat and we had no vantage point from which to spy our enemies' dispositions. The only places where one could see some distance was from the tops of Eboracum's walls. If the weather cleared then we would be visible from there too.

The others must have seen the concern upon my face. Then Pol said, "Warlord, remember when we played those games in Constantinopolis, the ones with the elephants, horsemen and so on?"

"Yes Pol. The strategos said it would make us better generals."

"There are fifty men in each warband; is that not right Felan?"

"Aye it is."

"We have thirty one archers and twenty four squires. Most of the squires now have mail and good weapons. There are three scouts. We use the archers to weaken a warband and then the squires charge them and break through."

Lann Aelle shook his head, "But Felan has said that there is a larger warband waiting for us and the others will move to surround us."

Pol smiled, "And they will do so but we will use the equites to charge the next warband when it goes to attack Daffydd and the squires. We will be hitting them from the side." He pointed to the packhorses we had brought with us. "We have twenty lances. They will break any warband. When the squires have ridden through the first warband they do not head north but they head east. That way we destroy two warbands and we have broken their first cordon."

"That still leaves the larger warband. How many are there Felan?"

"I could not get close enough to ascertain numbers but it looked to be more than a hundred."

Pol looked at me and said quietly, "And that means we would be evenly matched. Did you not tell me that one equite was worth two Saxons? We outnumber them in ability if not in actual warriors!"

I glanced at Myrddyn for confirmation. "I cannot see a flaw in the plan, Warlord, but perhaps a refinement? You should attack at dawn and use the dragon banner for both of the charges."

"But we only have one!"

"Then tonight we make another. It is not difficult and your squire, Pelas, has small neat hands."

"And where will you be, wizard?"

"I shall be with the squires for they may need my magic."

"In which case I shall lead them." Lann Aelle had made the decision for me and I was pleased. He was a good leader and the squires all looked up to him. He had been a squire more recently than the rest of us.

We only slept for a couple of hours as we needed to be moving early. Dai and Aed had reported hounds moving from the south. Edwin had sent men into the forest to flush us out. They would drive us towards their waiting warriors. The muddy ground and the wet day had both come to our aid and he had, temporarily, lost us but we were in grave danger of becoming encircled.

We had to keep Felan with us for he knew precisely where the enemy was. Lann Aelle led away his men with their new banner. They had Myrddyn and Daffydd to lead them; I was not worried. They were three sound leaders who would not panic. We moved forward and saw the lights from the fires of the warband we would attack. Kay had wondered why we did not attack at the same time as the squires. "Because we need to kill as many as possible and if we attack a moving warband then we will know that we have succeeded for they will not be able to form a shield wall.

We waited in the dark and waited for the noise of the attack. We were just six hundred paces away in the dark. It was nerve wracking. I knew, in my head what would happen. The archers would move closer, on foot, and loose from the shortest range possible. After five flights they would mount their horses and Lann

Aelle would lead the attack. The wailing of the dragon banner would be our signal but we also knew that the screams and cries of the wounded and dying would carry great distances at night. We would attack as soon as we heard the wail of the dragon banner. None of us were mounted yet. We were saving our horses and keeping a low profile. There was no moon but it paid to be careful.

As soon as we heard the cries in the night I said, "Mount!"

The camp ahead of us soon filled with noise as men grabbed the weapons which were already to hand. They would race to the sound of their comrades being attacked. I knew that all would be dressed for war. Men would sleep and rest in their armour. The wailing of the dragon was the signal. I was not carrying a lance but those around me were. I raised my sword, kicked Star in the flanks and we leapt forward. There were two lines of thirty one warriors and we were bearing down on fifty Northumbrians who were expecting an enemy to their fore. This was open farmland and we had few obstructions before us.

The night aided us for they heard the hooves but were unable to judge the direction from whence we came. As soon as our dragon banner wailed some of them looked around. By then we were less than a hundred and fifty paces from them. They panicked. Some continued running east and some stopped and tried to face us. Both were the wrong decisions. The warband just spread itself out and became thinner. The lances to my left and right punched holes in the Saxon shields. I saw the warrior who had been spared a spear looking relieved until my sword smashed down and caved in his skull. We just appeared out of the dark night. And then we were through. I wheeled, as did the rest, to the sound of the hooves and I saw, to my great relief, Lann Aelle and Myrddyn leading the squires. I turned north.

Some of the lances had been shattered but it mattered not. We still had more than twenty amongst my men. We kept a steady pace as the three scouts took us towards the large warband. I could imagine their anxiety as they had heard the twin wailing dragons and the thundering hooves coming from the night. I was thankful that the night was as black as Wyddfa's cave. It added to the eerie feel.

Ahead of me I heard the Saxon horns blowing. Whoever was in command was attempting to gather their forces together. They were too late! We had the advantage that we could just head north. If we met the Saxons then we would fight them and destroy them. The Saxons were racing to the aid of their comrades but the noise in the night made it harder for them to work out where the danger was. The Allfather had helped us by giving a cloudy, moonless night. Dawn was still an hour away. By that time we would either lie dead or be running free.

Although we were moving swiftly we still maintained our lines. All rested on my equites. The squires and the archers would follow us through the hole we punched in the Saxon line. Suddenly I saw movement ahead. It was the Saxons and they were moving obliquely across our front to reach the stricken warbands. They saw us as we saw them. The fact that they were running and we were galloping meant that they had little time to lock shields. The long spears and lances punched through their flimsy wooden wall. Those of us with swords and maces used them to batter through the shields. Our horses' hooves were deadly weapons. Men fell to the floor, struck by the horses and the hooves of those following crushed skulls and shattered their limbs as they lay prone on the ground. We cut a bloody hole through the heart of the warband. My archers did not use their bows but their swords were as effective in such a confused field. We kept going until I felt the stones of the Roman Road beneath Star's hooves. I halted. "Felan ride to the south and see if we are pursued. Aed, find us somewhere to camp to the north and west."

As I turned to view the lathered horses and weary warriors I saw the thin light of early dawn in the east. "Pelas, see how many men we have lost."

I dismounted, as did all of my equites and squires. The horses had ridden further and faster than was wise. They needed to be cared for. We would walk north for a few hours unless we were pursued. I saw men gulping water from their skins and then pouring some in their hands for their horses. Man and rider were as one. We suffered or succeeded together.

Pelas returned with the count of our losses. "Two archers, three squires and one equite, Aneurin, Warlord."

It could have been worse but the equites were hard to replace. We had lost three and there were four less squires to replace them. It was unlikely that we would know how many men we had slain. I suspected it was many times the number we had lost. I also knew that many of those who had not been killed would have been crippled and unable to fight in a shield wall again. King Edwin would hunt for us and that meant that he was less likely to attack Mona. If Fergus and Aengus could succeed then we would have bought Aelle the time to build up Mona's defences.

Dawn had broken when Felan returned leading two of our horses. "I found these wandering after us. Their riders were dead. I found their bodies. The Saxons are not pursuing. I saw them looking to their wounded." He smiled. "There were many of them."

When Aed returned he led us to the Nidd. It was a three hour ride but we could defend the narrow gorge if attacked. We had visited there once with my father and Myrddyn. We had found a cave with a Roman sword and witches made of stone. It was a good place to hide as the Saxons shunned it, fearing the dead and the spirits. We would use it to help recover the horses and to plan our strategy. It was now long past midsummer and soon it would be harvest time. This would be the opportunity to hurt the Northumbrians.

"Kay and Daffydd, I want sentries a mile out from the camp. Use pairs of men; one sleeps while one watches."

"Aye, Warlord."

Myrddyn pointed to the cave, "Gawan that is a cave of the dead. I will sleep there. The spirits may talk to us."

"And I will join you."

Pol, Lann Aelle and I watched as the two men walked happily into the cave of death. It frightened me but not my young brother. It was just the way we were. Pelas took Star off to feed and water him. Both had served me well.

Although I was tired I needed to talk. I went with Pol and Lann Aelle to the river. The soothing sound of the water rushing over the stones was reassuring. It reminded me that Icaunus was close by. He had oft times protected us. We had yet to lose a warrior during a river crossing.

"Lann Aelle, where do you think that we should raid?"

"I think south and east will be too dangerous at the moment. We know where Edwin and his men are. They will be searching for us.

Oswald and Oswiu will have discovered that we have killed their men and he will be scouting the east."

"You are saying that we should work north and west?"

"We know the land and we have a shorter journey to our cache of weapons should we need it."

"You counsel well."

Pol threw a stone into the bubbling waters. "What do you make of the brothers, Warlord? It seems they are not part of Edwin's army."

"I think they are allies but it may well be that they have ambition. Perhaps we could ferment discord."

"How?"

"I am not sure. When my brother and the wizard have dreamed, they may have thoughts on it." I stretched as I yawned. "We will leave tomorrow afternoon. We can strike at Stanwyck. It is not far from here and we can rest there once we have captured it."

"You are sure that you can capture it?"

"It is the one place I am certain of. Our fathers were born there, Lann Aelle. It was from thence that the Saxons first drove our people west. We will capture it and this time we destroy its defences. They will not use it again."

I thought I would sleep well but it came in fits and starts punctuated by pictures in my minds. They made no sense. I saw Irishmen fighting Irishmen. I saw Caer Gybi burning. I saw dragons fleeing west. When I woke I did not feel rested. It was late afternoon and my warriors were all asleep save for the sentries. I wandered to see Star. Pelas was sound asleep and close by. I stroked Star and examined him for injuries. I knew that Pelas would have done so already but he was my horse still and I knew him better than any. He appeared unharmed although I noticed he looked a little gaunter than usual. I spied a wild apple tree by the river. I wandered over and picked three of the riper fruits. I took a bite and they seemed a little sour to me but they were Star's favourite treat and I took them back to him. He savoured each one as he ate it. The sour taste did not seem to bother him. After letting him drink from the river I tethered him again.

I strapped on my sword. I needed no mail yet. I walked the camp until I came to the first of the sentries. I spoke quietly for one was sleeping. "Have you seen aught?"

"No Warlord." The squire looked up at the cliff and the cave. "This place frightens me. I was told that there is a cave yonder and within it lays a stone witch." I nodded. "And yet your brother and the wizard sleep there."

"The dead do not frighten them. They walk in the world of the dead but I am like you, Dai son of Daffydd, I prefer the living to the dead." I noticed that he was wearing a short byrnie. "Is that Saxon?"

"Aye Warlord, Pol gave it to me after we had routed the warriors in the forest."

"Good, then soon you will be an equite."

"It is my dearest wish, Warlord."

Dai was not from Rheged. His father, Dai, had been King Cadwallon's squire and then leader of the oathsworn. When he had died fighting the Northumbrians he had been orphaned and the king had asked me to train him as my father had trained him and Dai. It seemed his allegiance was now to me.

My brother and Myrddyn came down after dark. We had all woken and were busy cooking hot food. We felt safe here for we were far enough to the west of the road to be safe from Edwin, at least for a while. Pol and I were sat with Lann Aelle when they came. Both had a worried look upon their faces. "Did the dreams not go well?"

"They were dreams," sighed Myrddyn, "but their content was somewhat disquieting." He nodded to Gawan, "Your brother can tell you. I need to make water." He shrugged, "It is my age."

Chapter 8

"Did you dream the same?"

"I do not know but Myrddyn seemed to know what I had dreamed."

"And there is trouble?"

"Dreams do not tell you what is; they just give you glimpses into what may be. I saw Fiachnae mac Báetáin falling and then there were waves of Saxons flooding over the Roman Wall and they fell upon Deva. There were Hibernian ships stretching across the horizon and they hid Mona from my sight. I saw King Cadwallon and he lay slain with King Edwin and Oswald standing over him."

The dreams sounded catastrophic. Usually there appeared to be some ray of hope or a solution to the problems they suggested but the spirits seemed to offer only despair. I wondered if Gawan's state of mind had affected his dreams. Myrddyn only had himself to think on. "You were worried about your family. Perhaps that affected your dreams. "

"Perhaps but Myrddyn had seen the same too. And then I saw many ships leaving Manau and sailing to Mona." He hesitated. "Mona was burning behind the wall of Hibernian ships."

Lann Aelle said, "It is a sign that we should return home!"

I shook my head, "That would be a mistake. We have been here just a short time and yet we have already achieved much. Another two or three moons might be all that we need." I turned to Gawan, "You said yourself that you do not know when these events will take place, if they take place at all."

"You are right brother but I cannot help worrying."

Myrddyn's voice came from behind me, "Worrying does not solve problems; it creates them. The Warlord is right. The dreams we both had may tell us what will happen at some time in the future."

We stared into the fire. My pictures suddenly made a little more sense. Pol threw another branch onto the fire. "Even if the dreams are true the Saxons on Manau do not have enough ships yet to attack Mona and King Cadwallon is still at the Narrows. We know King Edwin is here, we saw him! I agree with the Warlord."

"However, we will not stay beyond Yule. I do not want my brother worrying about his family in the short days of winter but we will leave our mark on Northumbria. King Edwin will know that we have visited our vengeance upon him." I looked at my leaders one by one. "We will take as much of the harvest as we can and feed our people."

"That means wagons or carts."

"It does. We begin at Stanwyck and work our way along the Dunum Valley. We will send whatever we gather to the Belisama. Daffydd can carry it home."

Myrddyn nodded his agreement. "Then you will be sending riders back?"

"I will. We will send two squires to Deva. I will ask Daffydd to be at the estuary by the night of the bone fires."

We reached Stanwyck before dark. We knew the hill fort well. Leaving our horses in the woods to the north I led half of the men towards the northern gate. Lann Aelle and Gawan led the other half to the southern gate. As I had expected word had spread about the Warlord rampaging through Northumbria. We had watched as many of those in the outlying farms trudged towards the security of Stanwyck's walls. This suited me for it gathered them in one place and meant we could take their crops and animals more easily after the fall of the fort.

The ditches at Stanwyck are ancient. They were there before the Romans had reached Britannia. My grandfather, after whom I was named, had ordered the erection of the two gates which we would now use. The wooden walls had been put up at the same time. They were older than I was. I doubted that the gates had been well maintained and I knew that they would not have laid traps in the ditches. With our archers covering us I led my forty odd warriors towards the walls. There were sentries but it did not matter if they saw us. Daffydd and his archers would silence them and we knew how to scale walls.

I had left Llewellyn with Myrddyn and the two wounded squires to watch the horses and it was Pelas who watched my back. He had grown much since he had killed his first man. He was not yet experienced enough to stand in a shield wall or to ride as an equite but another summer would see him being considered.

We reached the ditch and waited out of sight behind the mound. We watched the sentries and as soon as they moved we flooded over into the banks of the ditch and lay waiting in the bottom.

When they moved again we ran to the wooden walls. It would be the squires who would be hoisted over the walls. They were lighter and quicker. They would not have to deal with armoured warriors and their knives and swords would make short work of them. Bors and I held my shield. Pelas put his foot upon it and rested his arms on our shoulders. When he was set he nodded and Bors and I thrust him upwards. He had just reached the top when we heard the cry of alarm from the other side of the fort. I heard the arrows as they flew towards the sentries and heard their cries as they tumbled from the walls. I looked up and saw that Pelas had disappeared. The other squires soon joined the first ones and we ran to the gates.

Inside I could hear the clash of metal on metal and the shouts of combat. I had two men ready with axes in case we could not gain entry but, as we reached the gate I saw it creak open and Pelas was there with two of the other squires. I saw that he was bleeding. The concern must have shown for he shook his head and said, "It is nothing."

He was a warrior and we had to bear such things. We burst into the hill fort. This was the biggest fort we had seen. It was even bigger than the Roman ones we frequently used. Only Eboracum and Civitas were bigger. I said to Pelas, "You and the squires wait here. No man leaves alive but do not hinder the women and children."

"Aye Warlord."

This was less a battle and more of a hunt. The women and children soon discovered that we were not interested in them. It must have surprised them for when Saxons raided they violated and then enslaved the women and the children. We just let them go. They ran. The men fell as they fought to hold us back. Eventually we had the last four cornered near the hall of the chief. While the squires went from hut to hut gathering anything which might be of value I questioned the four prisoners. Two were wounded and were likely to lose limbs. They would be either sold as slaves or used as slaves on Mona. We could not afford to let men go free. They would breed more Saxons. Had I been a cruel man I would have applied that logic to the women but I could not.

"Who is your master?"

The four remained obstinately silent. "This place you have taken is where my grandfather and grandmother died and where my father was brought up. I have no reason to be kind to you. You, or your fathers, killed my grandparents. If I chose I could have you blinded, castrated or merely maimed. I have allowed you to live and to live whole. My healer will be here soon to see to your injuries so do not try my patience!" I roared out the last word and they all recoiled.

"Prince Oswiu is our lord and master. We serve him and he serves King Edwin."

"That was not so hard. I see you have gathered in many of your crops and your young animals. It has been a good year?"

My voice was calmer and almost conversational. "Yes we have done well."

"And when do you extract tribute from Rheged?"

"As soon as..."

He got no further as the man next to him hit him in the ribs with his elbow. "Finish what you were going to say." Once again there was silence. I nodded, "I think that you were going to say as soon as Prince Oswiu arrives which means he is due." I nodded. "Bind them and mark them."

Kay went to the fire and thrust two daggers in it. The men began to plead for mercy. They knew what was coming. They were to be branded. If they escaped then my people would know that they had been enslaved.

By the time dawn had broken we had collected the bounty of Stanwyck. We had done well. There were many sheep; my father and Lann Aelle's had herded them on these very fells. There were three cows and the villagers had gathered in much grain as well. It was mainly oats and barley but they had some wheat. We also found two carts. Most of the grain went in the carts.

"Kay. Take four equites, four squires and four archers. Use two of the horses for one of the carts and the four slaves can pull the other. Head for Belisama and await Daffydd. Take most of the sheep and the cows too."

"Aye Warlord. When should we leave?"

"Now. With the animals it will take some time. Go back through the valley we used. Give four of the sheep and one of the cows to the villagers. It will help them to remain loyal."

Pol asked, "And what do we do, Warlord?"

"Today we rest but I want this place burning in the early hours of tomorrow. By the time the sun breaks I want a cloud of black smoke to tell Oswiu that we have burned Stanwyck."

Pol grinned as he nodded his approval, "And he will race here with his warband ready to pursue us."

"Except that we will not have gone we will be waiting for him."

The men tore down whole sections of the palisade and piled the wood onto the huts. We found pig fat and oils and we doused the rest of the walls with that. We needed flames at night. When dawn came we would add material which would make it smoke; the bodies of the dead Saxons.

My three scouts and six of the squires were spread out five miles away from Stanwyck. There were many woods and copses in which they could hide. The warband would be on foot and I knew that if they came we would know of it. Bors was not certain that they would come.

"Why should they care if this fort burns?"

"Because there is nothing else which compares with this one." I pointed to the north, "There is the fort at Morbium and Eboracum. They are the only forts which defend from the west. You saw the riches of this fort. He will have lost much food for the winter if he loses this. We have hurt Edwin, we have hurt Oswald and now we hit Oswiu. When we have finished here we go to Morbium and the Dunum Valley. From now on we pull further west and draw the Saxons away from safety."

"But why?"

"Because, Bors, I want them to think we are pulling them into a trap. They will not believe we are so few. By the time they catch up with us we will have less than fifty warriors. Next year, when we repeat this they will come on recklessly but by then we shall have King Cadwallon and his army to help us."

"You think that far ahead, Warlord?"

Pol laughed, "You must visit Constantinopolis. There they plan even further ahead than that."

The fire burned so brightly that it made it seem like daylight. By the time dawn broke it had taken hold and the bodies were hurled in to the hall. Myrddyn ordered that leaves and fresh branches be put on the burning ramparts and soon there was a black cloud rising high into the sky.

We moved out of the burning hill fort and headed east. Oswiu would expect us to have fled further west once we had destroyed his fortress. He would neither be wary nor worried about ambush until he reached it. We would strike before he did so. We knew that he would be on his way west from what his villagers had told us but we had no idea how close he might be.

Dai was the scout who found them. "Warlord, they are four miles away coming from the east. There are a hundred of them, at least, and they have five nobles on horses."

There were less than seventy of us remaining with deaths and the messengers we had sent. We were made up largely with archers and equites. The Northumbrians would be using the sunken lane which meandered its way towards the hill fort. It was an ancient track way. The Romans had never built a road here. There were trees and bushes which lined it.

"Daffydd, Take your archers and line the track way."

"Aye Warlord," he hesitated, "we are getting low on arrows; should we conserve them?"

"No, if you use all of them then you and the archers can ride to the Belisama and replenish. It is why we brought them with us."

After they headed down the track way to their ambush site I spread the equites out. "Osgar, take charge of the equites. Myrddyn will be close by. Your task will be to fill in any gaps which appear in our lines and to stop them outflanking us." I saw the disappointment on his face. He would have preferred to be with the other equites fighting by my side. "This is important Osgar. The men you lead will be equites soon. This is your chance to be a captain."

"Aye, Warlord. I shall not let you down."

As we waited I realised that Oswiu had not been far away. I had stopped his tribute raid. The lands of Rheged would keep their harvests and their children for this year at least. They would be stronger. I knew that if I had had more men I could have stayed over here and denied the Northumbrians the freedom of movement they enjoyed. Our mobility was our secret weapon. Even though we had been outnumbered by Edwin there was no way he could have caught us. This was the land of the horse. Back in Cymru he could have blocked passes and we would now be dead. It was a lesson I needed to learn from.

We had chosen a place where we had the high ground. The sunken lane turned between some oak, birch and yew trees and then climbed to begin the ascent to the hill fort. We waited there so that when they turned the bend they would see us. As soon as we charged them then my archers would rain death upon them. I was with the last ten lancers. All the other longer weapons had broken. The rest used spears but they were no longer than the spears the Saxons would use. Our advantage was our horses.

Oswiu's banner was a white one with a red boar upon it. I saw it above the hedges as they made their way towards us. I raised my sword; it was the signal to be ready. When I lowered it then we would charge. As soon as I saw the horsemen appear I lowered my sword and we galloped towards them. A sudden gust of wind sent the pall of smoke from behind us so that, when the dragon standard began to wail, the smoke from the fire joined us and wreathed us in black and grey clouds. It masked our numbers and made us even more terrifying. I roared, "Saxon Slayer, and Rheged!"

We thundered down the slope towards them. The horsemen had turned and fled. Saxons rarely used horses and they certainly never fought from their backs. The narrow track way made it almost impossible for the warriors to prepare lines to meet us and avoid their fleeing leaders. When the arrows fell we hit them. The track was wide enough for four horses and I rode with three lances next to me. We scythed through them. I raised my sword and brought it down on the helmet of a Northumbrian who was trying to spear the equite next to me. It was pandemonium as the Northumbrians turned to flee. That was our undoing. We could not get beyond the bodies of the dead and the dying. Although forty Northumbrians perished, their leaders and fifty odd others fled. We simply could not reach them for the wall of dead and dying. It would have tired the horses to no good purpose.

I sent my archers back to the Belisama. They needed to replenish their supplies of arrows. If they passed the captured animals and slaves they could escort them. "Wait on the Belisama. I will send word to you if I need you." The archers rode off and we headed north. It had been another victory but it tasted bitter. I had had Oswiu within my grasp and the slippery eel had escaped. His death would have to wait for another day.

Chapter 9

We managed to capture one wounded prisoner who could talk. He boasted that the two brothers were coming for me and that they had plans to burn my halls on Mona. After we gave him a warrior's death I spoke of this with the others. "This sounds to me like the two brothers boasting to their men. I cannot see them risking their own warriors to best me."

"The Warlord is right. Their aim is to gain the throne of Northumbria and then defeat the alliance of the west." Myrddyn's words confirmed my own thoughts.

We had bought ourselves valuable time. We had bested both Edwin and Oswiu. Oswald had been hurt. I sent Daffydd to Belisama to collect more arrows and led my small, but highly mobile force of equites north to Morbium.

We passed no inhabited farms on the way north but we burned every building and hut we found. We could not take the animals with us and so we ate well and scattered what we could not eat. The land between Eboracum and the Dunum would be laid waste. As I watched the halls and fields burning I had to keep reminding myself that I was doing this for Rheged. We needed to starve the beast that was Northumbria.

When we reached Morbium we found it empty. There was nothing to destroy. We had a roof over us as we slept beneath the first autumn storm. Myrddyn explored the fort. This was where my father had discovered the nails for the caligae. Such a small find and yet one which had such a profound effect on his life and the way that we fought. Myrddyn made an equally dramatic discovery. He found an empty ship moored by the bridge. When he examined it he found, within it, a few remnants of a cargo of iron ore.

"We have taken their food, Warlord, why not take their iron?" I must have looked puzzled for he continued, "East of here there are iron mines and they smelt and forge their weapons. If we could destroy their forges and steal their iron then they would have fewer weapons."

"How far away are they from here?"

"Less than half a day. We could go on the morrow and sleep here tomorrow night." He stroked his beard. "And as the forges are on the northern shore we could do so with impunity. He pointed to the empty boat. "They must use this as a distribution point for the north and the south."

"Then tomorrow we will ride east!"

I was not expecting much opposition at the small port on the northern bank of the Dunum but the workers there proved to be made of as strong a metal as the one they worked. We galloped through the open gates and the Saxons within grabbed hammers, axes, shovels, indeed anything which might be used. It was brave but it was futile. They were not warriors, they were craftsmen and they died. Their deaths were as important as any warrior we had killed for they were harder to replace. We burned the settlement and threw the pig iron into the river. There were some sword blanks which we took and carried them back on the horses which we found. We had not planned the raid and yet, in the long run, it proved to be crucial. The Saxons took a year to begin to produce weapons again. Of course, at the time, we did not know that. We just returned in high spirits to Morbium to enjoy the food we had taken and the barrel of beer which had been discovered. And the following day we began our journey west and to the River Belisama.

We crossed the bridge and used the southern side of the Dunum. We would pick up the Roman Road which led from Cataractonium just a few miles down the river. We did not look like the glorious mailed warriors who had landed just a few weeks earlier. Our horses looked thinner and our mail was flecked with rust. There had been flaws in my plans; I saw that now. We needed a base from which we could launch our attacks on Edwin. We needed spare horses. I remembered that my father had kept three horses. I now saw why. There had been a time when I had kept two and now I was down to one. We needed more horses. I knew that there were fine animals in Frankia. Time was we would have sailed there and bought them. Now we could not afford to be away from our island home for the eight weeks the voyage would take.

We only burned four farms on the first day of the ride west. The farmers fled when they saw us coming. Once we reached the crest of the hills which divided Rheged from Northumbria we turned south west and left the road to follow the ancient tracks. Autumn had arrived with a vengeance. The winds, thankfully, were from the east and pushed us along but the wind and the rain permeated our clothes. We were grateful to find abandoned houses in which to sleep. The next day we pushed on. We reached the Roman Road which ran down the western side of the country. If we pushed the horses hard we could reach the Belisama in two days. I would take three. There was no hurry. There were no Northumbrians on the west of the divide. My men I had sent west earlier would be at the Belisama now. Daffydd would have fortified the old fort on the river. We were not being pursued and there were no enemies to worry about.

It was mid afternoon when Aed and Felan galloped in. "Warlord! We have seen Hibernian ships off the Lune. They are slavers!"

"How many boats did you see?"

"There are ten of them in the estuary. I estimate more than a hundred warriors although there were not those numbers by the side of the river. There looked to be just sixty or so warriors."

I turned in my saddle, "Arm yourselves. Myrddyn and the squires watch the horses."

My wizard mused, "I wonder if this is the dream we had?" He looked at Gawan.

My brother looked concerned, "In which case the rest might be just around the corner. I fear the worst."

"Then do not!" Myrddyn barked his words at my brother. "You are privileged to see the future. Your duty is to tell your brother what you dream. Think of the people of Rheged first and not just your family."

Gawan recoiled at the words. "That is because you have no family!"

I saw Pol and Lann Aelle start at Gawan's reaction. No one spoke like that to Myrddyn. Miraculously he did not look angry, he looked sad. "I wish that were true for then there would be no sadness in my heart at the loss of Brother Oswald, Myfanwy and my dearest friend, your father Lann. I have to make my heart cold. If I did not then I would go mad. This gift you have Gawan, son of Lann, is also a curse. Remember that. I will wait here Warlord."

He seemed smaller and sadder as we rode south towards the estuary where the Hibernians sheltered with their boats. Aed had told me that they had slaves already. "I think there must be warriors out hunting more of our people for there were not enough men to crew the boats."

"When we reach the estuary you and Dai find the others and shadow them. We will deal with the ones at the river first." We halted in the woods just half a mile above the river. The estuary was wide at this point but it was also shallow. They had the boats well out in the river. We saw the tethered slaves. There looked to be twenty of them and there were animals too. It looked to me as though they were waiting for other warriors to join them. The tide was out and they would need to wait for the high tide to load their ships. I could see no more than fifty warriors. Aed was right. From the banners they were the Uí Néill.

I turned to my warriors. "We charge them and drive them into the water. Pelas and Llewellyn, you secure the slaves and protect them."

It was a crude plan but the absence of half of the warriors meant we had to strike quickly. In a perfect world we would have approached silently and taken our time. We would inspire fear instead. I drew Saxon Slayer. The edge needed sharpening and it required a good clean but it would still bring death to these slavers.

I raised my sword and, leaving the trees, we galloped down the gentle slope towards the beach. It was the dragon standard's wail which alerted the Hibernians. They are brave warriors but they do not fight as one warband. They crave the glory of individual combat and they raced towards us and their own death.

We were not riding boot to boot. There were fifty of us and we were spread out. I saw Pol's lance as it speared a warrior with spiked and limed hair. The force of the blow shattered the wooden lance but the warrior hung like a piece of meat as the tip dug into the ground. The screams of the slaves married with the war cries of the Hibernians and above it all was the eerie wail of the dragon.

A heavily tattooed chief who was bare-chested and swinging a two handed sword advanced towards me whirling the blade above his head. If I approached him then Star would lose his head. I feinted to the right with Star and as the warrior adjusted his feet I wheeled to the left. He would expect me to keep my shield between me and him. I was risking a mortal blow by exposing my right side. The tip of the sword whirled desperately close to my leg but it missed and I swung my sword at his unprotected neck. Had my blade been sharp then he would have lost his head. As it was it bit down and ground into his collarbone. He screamed his pain and tried to swing his sword at me again. Star had kept on moving and the wound had slowed the warrior down. I made a back handed slash and this time my blade bit into his neck and he fell to the floor in a puddle of his own blood.

My equites were driving them into the shallows and the waters turned red with their blood. The unarmoured warriors flung themselves into the sea and began to swim out to their ships. I had just turned when Dai galloped in waving his arms. "Warlord the rest of the warband is just behind us!" I saw Aed turning in his saddle and releasing arrows.

"Reform! Leave the wounded!" The well trained warriors wheeled and followed me as I left the sea. We were now at a disadvantage for we had to charge uphill. As we trotted towards Aed the warband appeared. There were as many as we had already fought and we were tired.

As soon as the leader of the warband saw us he tried to form his men into lines. I did not think it would work for they were Hibernians. We now had a mere five lances and spears but we were fighting men without armour. I sheathed Saxon Slayer and took out my mace. I had been given the weapon by the Emperor of Byzantium. It was a beautifully made and well balanced weapon. I slipped the leather thong around my wrist and yelled, "Charge!"

It was hardly a gallop but we had momentum. I held the mace behind me and as I charged I began to swing it. A warrior in the front rank tried to spear me and I lifted the shield to the right side of Star. The head slid harmlessly along the leather wolf and my mace connected with his face. His face disappeared in a red mush. Pieces of skull and brain showered those behind. Star crashed into the side of a warrior who was trying to stab Lann Aelle. I brought the mace down on to the skull of the Hibernian next to him. The metal flanges smashed through the metal helmet and broke his head. He slumped to the ground, dead. I found myself through the warband. There were tethered slaves ahead and two warriors guarding them. I galloped towards them. Both men dropped their ropes and ran towards the river. They had had enough.

Star was winded and I reined him in. I dismounted and cut the rope of the first few slaves. "Release the rest and wait here until they are all accounted for!"

I left the slaves to free themselves, remounted and returned to the fray. The Hibernians who had survived were already in the water, swimming to their waiting ships. I saw that over forty of their fellows lay dead on the beach or bobbing up and down in the water. This had been *wyrd*. We had been directed here so that we could save the villagers. I counted thirty eight of them. They were mainly women and children but there were some men amongst them.

We watched the Hibernians sail away. They barely had enough crew to man their ships. I could not see the Uí Néill raiding again this year. I had met them twice and bested them both times. They would curse my name in the long nights of winter. When I reached the beach I saw Myrddyn attending to the wounded. Pol put his arm on my shoulder. "We lost two more equites, Daffydd son of Aiden and Scanlan the Bold."

I nodded. It might be a small price to pay but it was one we could ill afford. The villagers had been saved but the cost had been high. We discovered that the villagers had all come from two settlements just up the river. Men had escaped and warned a third village. The raid could have had far worse consequences.

My squires escorted the villagers back to their homes and we camped by the estuary to bury our comrades and reflect on the day. Pelas tried to put an edge on my sword using some of the stones lying on the beach. It was better than it had been but it would need our smith to repair it properly.

Rather than heading back, east to the road, we crossed the estuary at low tide the next morning. It took just a few hours to reach the fort where we found Daffydd and the booty. We told him of the Hibernians.

"We did not see them" He pointed to the north. "Of course they would have been sheltered by the headland."

"Any sign of our ship?"

"Not yet but the squires have returned from Deva; the message got through. We just need to wait for them, Warlord."

"It will do the horses good to rest for a few days and eat this fine sea washed grass. We will make the fort habitable while we wait. Did you see the villagers at Aedh's village?"

"Aye Warlord. It looks much more defensible. They have improved since we were last there."

"Take them some of our arrows and some of the weapons we took from the Hibernians. They are not the best but they are better than what they have." He nodded, "Scout the land to the east in case the Saxons have pursued us."

As we waited by the coast we were rewarded by balmy blue skies. The storms we had suffered crossing the land had been replaced by pleasant weather. Sometimes this happened. Perhaps the gods were smiling upon us once more. Star and the other horses began to put on weight again. The hunters found much game and we ate well. If we did not have the animals and the grain then I would have been tempted to return to my home on my ship when it arrived. The thought was fleeting. I would not leave my men to make the last fifty miles on their own.

I walked the shore with Gawan and Lann Aelle. "Your son has done well, cousin."

"I am pleased. He admires you greatly, you know?"

"I am sorry."

"No, do not be. It was the same when I was squire to your father. When I grew I felt guilty that I had shown him more love than my own father. It is something in the relationship between equite and squire." He looked at Gawan, "And what of Arturus? Will he become a squire?"

"He wishes to be but my wife…"

"It is the same with all women. They carry them and bring them into the world. They know that there is a likelihood that they will die in war and do all that they can to keep them safe."

It was pleasant for the three of us to talk of such ordinary things. The schemes and strategies, the quest for power, all were briefly forgotten as we spoke of children and our hopes and fears.

Daffydd ap Gwynfor arrived three days later, two days after my Captain of archers returned from the village. He waded ashore and I could see from his face that he had bad news to impart. He came directly to me and spoke, "Disaster assails us on all sides, Warlord. Fiachnae mac Báetáin has been slain in battle by Fiachnae mac

Demmáin, king of the Dál Fiatach. There is now peace between Edwin and the men of Strathclyde." I looked at Gawan. That had been part of his dream. "And Fergus and Aengus have been defeated. The survivors await you on Mona."

"What happened?"

"They landed and had initial success, taking the village to the west of the island but then Aella, the chief of Manau gathered his men together and drove them back to their ships. They came back in one ship. Fergus died and Aengus suffered grievous wounds. He is being cared for by your brother."

I looked at Myrddyn but it was hard to gauge his feelings. Gawan, Lann Aelle and Pol looked as though we had lost a war. I knew what they felt. We had done all that we could but it might not be enough to save us.

"Thank you, Daffydd. Take the animals and slaves back to Mona. I will bring my men back by road." I nodded towards Myrddyn, "Take Myrddyn with you and any of the wounded."

"I require no charity, Warlord. I can ride with the best of them."

"I know, wizard, but you are the finest healer on the island and those skills will be needed on Mona, will they not?"

"You are correct. You are becoming wiser, Warlord, it must be my influence."

The boat was quickly loaded and headed west. We mounted our horses and began the long ride back to our land. It was a land from which we had not removed the threat of the Saxon and I would need to discover a new strategy to save Rheged.

Chapter 10

We were weary when we trudged across the ditch of Deva into the safety and warmth of the fortress. The autumn rains had come in earnest and we looked like ragged refugees rather than successful warriors. Gawan was pleased to be back in the bosom of his family and I left him with his equites. Daffydd and his archers also remained there for the fortress had more room for them. I headed home with Lann Aelle and Pol. We had three days to discuss the catastrophic events which had destroyed my plans,

"I did not think that the Hibernians would capture Manau but I did not think they would suffer such losses."

"We do not know, Warlord, how many warriors they lost."

"We know that they came back in one ship. That suggests great losses; besides the greater loss is Fiachnae mac Báetáin. He had forced Edwin to protect the northern boundaries with many men. They are now free to come south and make war upon us. We will need to rethink our strategy."

Pol, who was always positive, said brightly, "We have proved that the long spear and the lance are more than effective. I think that we issue them to all of our equites." I nodded and smiled. He was right. "And I think that the squires have proved themselves. We have mail for most of them and we can use the weapons we captured to have the smiths make it for the others. Our speed and our tactics worked."

Lann Aelle injected the word of caution. "We still need more horses and we need more equites training. Our two most successful assets are the archer and the equite. Both are expensive. You cannot just give a man a horse or a bow and say fight. It takes years to train them."

"Then we use Tuanthal for that. We ask him to train as many equites as he can. We will pay a bounty to families to give a son to be trained as an equite."

Although it was my idea I was pleased with it. I remembered the rich farmers who had not wanted to be responsible for their own defence. This would be a way of making them care. If each had a son who was an equite then they were part of the fight.

We reached King Cadwallon's stronghold during a torrential downpour. It took away all the good feelings we had had. The King was equally concerned over the setbacks. "Penda is urging King Ceorl to fight against Edwin but the Northumbrians have grown strong. They are building forts, called burghs, all along the border. We think it is not to keep us in but to provide refuge for the warriors who will raid our lands for slaves and cattle."

I looked up. "Has he started yet?"

"Not yet but the forts are in the early stages of construction."

"Then we attack now! The more we can delay the building of them then the more we delay the raids."

The king smiled sadly, "Warlord your heart may be willing but your flesh is not. I watched you and your men as they rode in. They are exhausted and you cannot fight until you have rested. I will lead my equites and we will delay them."

I knew that he meant well but compared with my men his were half trained. They had neither the discipline nor the aptitude. His warriors were the finest archers and the doughtiest of spearmen but horsemen they were not. He was, however, a king and I could not gainsay him. "I urge you to use archers too. The Northumbrians have yet to learn their value."

"As you know, Warlord, our archers are second to none."

As we headed, the next day, across the island, I spoke of my fears to my two closest friends. "I am not certain that the Cymri will be able to do what their king has in mind."

"Even if they do not succeed they may well slow down the building process. He was right, Warlord, we are in no condition to fight. We need until the New Year to recover and rebuild."

I stared south. If I was to be inactive then I could do something useful. I had no family to tie me to the land. "Pol, we will travel to Frankia and buy horses. I had thought we could not afford the time away from Mona but if the king can buy us some time then Tuanthal can train the equites while Lann Aelle here can help his father improve the defences."

Pol brightened, "I have heard that the Barb horses from North Africa are the best."

"That would mean visiting the Muslim world and even the Byzantines fear them. We will try to trade for them but from a safe distance." I had no wish to suffer at the hands of that cruel people.

The last ten miles to my home were spent in working out the finances needed for such an expedition. The simple fact of bringing them back would cause us problems but it would exercise my mind. Since I had heard the news of the demise of my allies I had found my thoughts becoming darker and darker. It was as though I was falling into a tunnel and there was no escape. Planning gave me hope.

My sentries cheered me as we rode through the gate. I did not know why for we looked like bandits rather than equites. We all took our mounts to the stables. There we were able to give them grain and rub them down. After we left them I noticed that my men had smiles upon their faces. Our animals were like our family. Caring for them gave them good feelings. Pelas helped me to change from my mail. I put on a tunic and headed for the bath house. It would clean my body and purify my heart. "Pelas, do not bother with the armour and the sword today. Tomorrow is soon enough. You have done well on this, your first campaign, go to your family and enjoy yourself."

He looked at me seriously, "I am your squire, Warlord. I will take the sword and your mail to the smith. When they are repaired I will clean them and sharpen Saxon Slayer. Then will I be able to enjoy myself without the burden of my work hanging over me."

"You are a good squire and I bow to your dedication."

The bath house was empty. My warriors were cleaning their own weapons and armour. It allowed me the luxury of solitude and I could think. I was in the tepidarium when I heard them enter, led by Pol. Osgar saw me and began to back out, "I am sorry Warlord; we will come back later."

"No, come in now. We are all warriors together. We share the same hardships, we should share the same pleasures. Besides, I have almost done and then you younger warriors can talk without worrying about me."

I lay in the lukewarm water and listened to the good natured banter between the equites in the caldarium. It would do them good to let off a little steam in the bath house. I slipped away without saying farewell. I could have sent for a servant to dress me but I was enjoying the solitude. I slipped out of my room and went to my solar. Times past I would have shared a goblet of rich red wine with my father and perhaps Myrddyn and Brother Oswald. I poured a goblet and stood looking out of the window to the south. Was Pol right? Should we try to get the best horses possible? The problem was we would have to negotiate the Barbary pirates and some Muslims were fanatics. They hated Christians; who knew what they felt about those of us who worshipped the old ways? I would ask Myrddyn and Gawan.

There was a knock on the door and a slave stood there. "Warlord, Myrddyn asks if you would join him in the infirmary."

I sighed and swallowed my wine. My solitude was ending. "I will be there momentarily."

I contemplated tying my hair back or even plaiting it but it was clean and it was lustrous, I would leave it about my shoulders. I had no wife now to tell me it did not suit me.

The infirmary had been Brother Oswald's idea. It was a building separated from the others. Ironically it had been completed too late to save him. He had said we could use it for those with the plague or other infections. They could be cared for without infecting others. Had it been finished on time he might have been spared, along with my family. Myrddyn was waiting at the door. "Come Warlord, Aengus is between life and death and I do not know if I can save him. He must speak with you before he goes to the Otherworld."

"You can save him!"

"I can try but his wounds are serious; they could be mortal."

The bed in which the Hibernian lay was away from the rest of the sick. He had heavy bandages covering half of his face. He had lost his right eye. His right arm had been removed and his right leg was heavily bandaged too.

He gave me a weak smile as I approached. "Warlord, I am glad that I saw you before I went to the Otherworld."

"You must fight, Aengus. I would have you stay here with us."

He gave a hollow laugh, "A one eyed, one armed warrior is no use to anyone."

"That is for me to decide. I want you to cling to life. Myrddyn is here now and he is the greatest healer that ever lived."

"I will try but if this is my time I need to speak with you before I cross over."

"Go ahead then."

Myrddyn said, "I have other charges. I will see to them while you talk." He touched Aengus' hand. "I will do all that I can to save you."

"Your wizard is a good man, Warlord. I used to fear him but now I do not." He winced as pain struck him. Opening his eye he said, "My men and those of Fergus fought well. I would have you know that."

"I believe you."

"I know that we came to you with a poor reputation but you gave us honour and we tried all that we could." He closed his eyes as another spasm of pain coursed through his body. "We did not have enough discipline. I have spoken with the men who survived, and the women. They all wish to serve you still. I beg you to let them and to care for them. Like your wizard you are a good man and one we would follow."

"Of course but you said women?"

"Aye they would not be left behind and they came with us. They fought alongside us and some died but they died happy for they were with their men."

"If that was your only worry then I can put your mind at rest. I will watch over your people and they can fight for me still. Now you get well. That is a command."

Myrddyn waved me over. I saw a woman. I thought that she was dead for she was so still. It was Aileen, Fergus' sister. "It is the woman who thought little of you, Warlord. Apparently she thought enough of you to accompany her brother to Manau and to fight the Saxons there."

"What is wrong with her?"

Myrddyn pointed to her middle which was heavily bandaged. "She received a sword thrust to her vital regions." He shook his head, "I had to work hard for there were serious wounds there. But it is her head which poses the greatest risk. She has received a blow to the side of the skull. I believe that there is a fluid just inside the bone and it needs draining."

"You are jesting!"

"No. When I visited Constantinopolis with your father I read of Greek surgeons who had relieved such pressure. I also spoke with the Greek healers. They wished to learn of my skills and I shared theirs. They drill a small hole where the pressure is and relieve it. I am confident that I can do it."

"But if you fail!"

"Then she will die but will she be any worse off than this life of the living dead?"

"You will do this? You will drill a hole in her skull?"

He looked at me with his old sad eyes. "Yes Warlord, but you must assist me. I need another pair of hands to hold her still and I believe there is a connection between the two of you."

"She hates me!"

He nodded, "And that is the connection; love and hate are closer than many think."

I would have to do it. To refuse would be dishonourable. "When do we do it, tomorrow?"

"Now! Every moment we waste makes it less likely that we can call her back from the other side. Even now she is speaking with her brother, Fergus." I was stunned. "Wash your hands and use vinegar to do so."

"Vinegar?"

"Warlord, just do it."

When returned he had a small hand drill ready; it looked like an auger used in shipbuilding but was much smaller. "You must hold her head as still as you can. One slip from you and she could die." He smiled as he said it. I placed my hands upon her head. I noticed how beautiful she was. Her hair shone and her skin was as clear as Roman marble. She was a brave young woman and needed to live. I held her head tightly.

"Move your left hand a little. I must drill there." He looked at me and he gave a sad smile, "I pray you Warlord, hold her as tightly as you hold Saxon Slayer in battle for we battle death. I have never done this. One mistake from either of us and this brave young girl will die."

"Do it wizard. I will keep her still."

I concentrated harder than at any time in my life before. I noticed that he had cut away some of her long, red hair so that the bruised skin was visible. It looked harmless enough; it looked like my body after a battle. The bruises normally went away after a couple of days. Perhaps the head was a more dangerous place for such a bruise. Myrddyn took out a sharp knife and made a slit in the flesh at the side of her skull. He carefully parted the skin and, after examining the flesh, began to turn the drill. It made a strange whirring noise but I could not see it working. How could it get through bone? I glanced at him. "I am drilling through the skull. It takes time and I have to be careful. I can only hope that it is not as thick as yours Warlord."

I focussed on the girl's face. She could be no more than eighteen summers. From what I had been told she had fought against the Saxons. I knew young warriors who would not have survived such an encounter. There was something about this young woman which intrigued me.

Suddenly Myrddyn stopped and withdrew the drill. He placed it on the floor and held a candle to the side of her skull. He nodded, seemingly satisfied and then he took a long thin scoop and inserted it into the hole. A blob of reddish purple material dropped out into the pot he held. He shone the candle there for a few moments longer and then nodded. "Just a couple more moments and I think that we will be done." I saw him take some catgut and a needle. He placed them ready to hand. He took a small metal disk and gently pressed it over the hole. It was an exact fit and slipped into the bone well. Myrddyn had been busy.

"Put your finger on this piece of metal whilst I sew." The piece of metal was so small that when I put the tip of my finger over it the metal could not be seen. Myrddyn joined the two flaps of skin, lifting my finger as he did so and then he stitched, neatly, the flap of skin, back in place. He sat back and smiled, "And now we wait. Well done Warlord. You can assist me again!"

I found that my hand was shaking. "I hope not, wizard!"

He laughed, "Go and have a drink, Warlord." He chuckled. "I can see this becoming another legend if it succeeds." He nodded to the other end of the infirmary where a small crowd had gathered. We had had an audience.

I went to the main hall and found that I was now ravenous. I sat at the table and quaffed a whole goblet of wine. Pol and Kay joined me. As the food was brought we talked.

"I have spoken with the Hibernians. They did well, Warlord. From what they said they became over confident after their initial success and when Aella brought his whole force they were tricked into an attack when he pulled his centre back."

"He outflanked them."

"Aye, had either of us been leading the men then it would not have happened. They feel they have let you down."

"I know, I spoke with Aengus and he has asked me to lead them. They can be trained here and protect my home."

"That will make Aelle happy then."

"Where is my uncle?"

"He went with Lann Aelle to show the improvements he had made and to ask his advice."

It was good that the two were coming closer. My father had taken Aelle's son away from him. He had sent me to fight far away. I knew now that he had done so to protect the land but I missed him now. I thought of all the times we might have spoken and the questions I would have asked of him. I had not thought he would be taken away as he had been. I wondered if the wizard had some way of going back in time. I was jealous of Gawan. He could still speak with my father. He and Myrddyn would visit Wyddfa at Yule to the dream cave. I could not. Lann Aelle and his father should have more time together. When I campaigned, the next year, I would leave Lann Aelle with his father. Outside of Pol and myself, he was the best stratagos we had.

"You appear lost in your thoughts, Warlord."

"I am Pol. I am thinking of my father and how I wish I could walk these walls with him and talk. I did not talk enough when he was alive."

"You and he were not meant to talk, Warlord. It is a sad fact of life that the two of you were born to fight for Rheged. There are many people who are free today only because you and your father fought for them."

I pushed away the empty platter. "It seems Pol, that we take one step forward and two back. Just when we bloody Edwin and the brothers we lose two valuable allies."

"And yet our greatest ally, King Cadwallon, was not used. His strength is undiminished. It is sad that we lost our other allies but they served their purpose. They bought us time. They have given us a winter to get the horses and to train new men. Our crops were harvested; the Northumbrians were not. There will be a hard cruel winter for many. We hurt them." He held up his beaker, "This is half full, Warlord. Do not be fooled into thinking that it is half empty."

"You are right Pol. I am wallowing in self pity. Our old teachers from Constantinopolis would be less than happy with us. Come and we will go and speak with the Hibernians."

We took the jug of wine and went to the table where the survivors were seated. They looked miserable and downhearted. I saw that there were but fifteen of them remaining. There were four others, along with Aileen, in the infirmary. They made to stand. "No, do not stand. I am here to drink with brave warriors who fought well for me."

One of the older warriors shook his head, "But we failed! We had to flee with our tails between our legs."

"What is your name?"

"Fiachnae."

I poured some wine into his beaker, "Well, Fiachnae drink with me for there is not a warrior in my army who has not had to flee a field at some time. It does not make you less of a warrior. It gives you something invaluable; experience. You learn from what you did wrong. All of you will have learned from your defeat." I pointed with the jug towards the infirmary. "I have just left Aengus and Aileen fighting for their lives. With the Allfather's help they will survive. I promised Aengus that all of you can serve with my men if you have a mind. Will you?"

I saw hope light their eyes as they all chorused an, '*Aye Warlord*!'

"Then tomorrow you can swear an oath on Saxon Slayer. We will teach you how to become warriors like us. You will learn to fight as one behind a shield and wearing armour. You will not flee the field again but your enemies will."

Chapter 11

The talk with Pol and then the Hibernians helped me to sleep much better than I had for some time. I awoke with a positive attitude. I went, even before I had eaten, to the infirmary. I saw Myrddyn there, looking tired. "Have you slept?"

He shook his head, "When they are both out of danger then I will sleep. Aengus appears to be through the worst of it. This is one of the many times I miss Brother Oswald. He too was a healer and he could have aided me. Needs must I should train someone to do this when I am in the Otherworld."

"Do not even jest about such things! It is hard enough to live without my father. I could not manage without his wizard too."

"Even the tallest tree in the forest must fall some time but it will not be for some time yet." He nodded towards Aengus. "I have found the last of the poison and he will live. He sleeps peacefully now. Let us go and see the one with the strong heart. She fought all night against death. She clings to life and that heartens me." She looked very pale in the thin morning light but her breathing appeared steady. Myrddyn put his hand to her neck. "There is a steady beat."

We had been there for a few moments when she opened her eyes and stared up. "Am I in the Otherworld?"

I smiled and took her hand. "No Aileen, sister of Fergus, you are in Caer Gybi and you are safe thanks to the hands of Myrddyn the healer. He brought you back from the other side."

"With a little help from the Warlord." Myrddyn added.

"I am sorry for the harsh words I uttered, Warlord. I was angry and I regret my outburst."

I noticed that she held my hand still. "I understand and had I been in the same position then I, too, might have said such things but you are safe now and I have promised Aengus that I will look after all of the Hibernian people who fought for me."

She suddenly started, "My brother?"

"He is in the Otherworld but he died with a sword in his hand and he will be telling them all of the courage of his sister, Aileen."

She blushed and put her hand to brush her hair away. She found flesh and he eyes widened. Myrddyn took her hand and put it beneath the covers. "We had to cut your hair for there was a problem inside your head. We removed it but you have a small piece of metal just here." He gently touched the stitches. "Do not worry it will do no harm and your hair will grow."

I smiled, "You will be as pretty as you ever were."

She smiled, for the first time, back at me. "Thank you, Warlord, that is kind. It is an untruth but it is a kind one for a girl who is now alone in the world."

"No Aileen for when the Warlord swears to care for someone then they are never alone for they are in his family. You get well and when the wizard is happy we will talk of your future. You just need to get better."

Pelas brought Saxon Slayer to me as soon as I had eaten. He must have badgered the smith for it shone and looked like new. "Well done, squire, for we need it this morning." I took it to the Hibernians. All of them knelt and swore an oath. Aelle and Lann Aelle were present along with my equites.

"Until you are all trained I would have you here in Caer Gybi as part of the garrison. My cousin Lann Aelle and my uncle, Lord Aelle will be responsible for your training."

As we went back to the hall Lann Aelle said, "That sounded ominously like goodbye. What have you planned, cousin?"

"Pol and I will travel to Frankia. I intend to buy some horses. We need to breed our own herds. I am sure that had my father been granted more time he would have realised the potential of this island which is perfect for raising horses. We will buy a good stallion and some mares. Within three years we should have enough horses to campaign in Northumbria for a year."

Aelle nodded but looked sad, "I hope that I will still be here when you return, nephew."

"Of course you will. What ails you, uncle?"

"Old age. There is only Myrddyn left now of those I fought alongside as a young man. The Otherworld is calling."

"Then tell it to wait for I am not ready to let you go yet. We all need your sage advice and memories." I looked pointedly at Lann Aelle who nodded his understanding.

It took a few days to prepare the ship and gather the gold coin. We had traded well over the years and we also had collected much gold and blue stones from the mines in the heart of Cymri. We would use that now to buy us hope for the future. All of my equites wished to accompany Pol and me but I needed the experience of Kay and Bors to aid Lann Aelle with training of the warriors. I still worried about another Saxon attack. The ease with which Aella had defeated the Hibernians made me wonder about the strength of the forces on Manau. I left the strongest force I could. I took just Osgar and six of the younger equites. With Pelas and Llewellyn I was happy that we would be protected. We were not invading Frankia; we were trading.

Aileen was up and about and Aengus was awake and recovering before I left. Myrddyn was pleased with the recovery of both of them and Aileen had shown some skill in caring for the sick. I left them happily knowing that they all had purpose in their lives once more.

The journey south was familiar to us all. We traded with Dyfed and Gwent on a regular basis. Daffydd had also made many voyages to Constantinopolis although not in recent years. We seemed to have receded in the last few years and stopped looking out. That was not good. Perhaps this voyage was meant to be.

We had just passed through the tricky waters of Scillonia Insula when Daffydd asked me of our destination. "Frankia is a large place, Warlord. Where specifically would you have us land?"

This was where we missed Brother Oswald. He was well read and he knew how to decode the books and writings of Osric. He would have known precisely where we should land. "I am not sure; where would you suggest, Captain?"

Daffydd rubbed his beard. "The land of Austrasia is the most civilised place to land. I believe they have a king called Dagobert. "

"Brother Oswald told me of kings who were called Merovingian. They lived in Frankia."

"Aye, Warlord, we read of them in Constantinopolis. They were great horsemen." Pol had enjoyed his time studying in the capital of the Eastern Empire.

"Then that is where we will go. Have we still the maps which Brother Oswald made?"

"I will fetch them."

When we looked at the maps we saw that they showed the old Roman provinces but, fortunately, they gave the place names. They were all marked in red. The names might have changed but the places themselves would still remain. We saw one on a river; it was called Abbatis Villa. "That looks as good a place to start as any." And so we headed east towards the north western coast of Frankia.

Wyrd does not always allow us to make our own decisions. Even as Daffydd put the steering board to head north and east a storm came from the north east and drove us ever south. Daffydd and his crew desperately fought to keep us heading east rather than west for the edge of the world lay there. It seemed the Gods did not want us to visit Abbatis Villa. We fought the storm for three days. The sails were in shreds when it abated. We saw no land but just rain, storm clouds and seas which threatened to engulf us and send us to the bottom of the ocean. When dawn arrived and the clouds lifted we found that that we were off the mainland of Frankia but we had no idea where. The maps did not help us. We knew, from the position of the sun, that land was to the north of us and there was a distant island to the south east of us. That led Daffydd to deduce that we were close to the land of the Bro Waroc'h. He had never landed there but he had heard that they were the descendants of the last Romans to live in our land and the ones who had fled the Saxons when they came.

"You mean they are our people?"

"They were but I have never landed here before. It is a savage coast and dangerous." He pointed to the island. "It is protected by sharp teeth such as that. It is *wyrd* that we are here now." He pointed to the north. "There is, I believe, a port there. I have heard it named Gwened."

"That sounds like our language. We will need to repair will we not, Captain Daffydd?"

"Aye, we will."

"Then we sail to Gwened and see what *wyrd* has in store for us."

Daffydd was correct, it was a wild and savage coast. It made ours look positively welcoming. There were steep cliffs and savage looking rocks guarding the entrance to the port. There was an oppidum but my heart sank when I saw the cross of the White Christ atop a stone church. These may have been our people once but now they worshipped the White Christ and I feared for our welcome. We had little choice. Our ship needed repairs to the hull and to the sails. We would have to venture into the port. The two arms of the harbour meant that we would only be able to leave if the inhabitants allowed us to. Once in we might become trapped.

As we tied up an armed delegation came towards us. There was a holy man and ten armed and armoured warriors. Bows were aimed at our ship and I noticed that two smaller boats had been rowed to the entrance of the harbour to block us in. Although we had no mail on I had Saxon Slayer and Llewellyn carried my dragon banner. I stepped off the ship once the gangplank was in place and my equites formed a guard of honour.

I decided to take the bull by the horns and speak first. "I am the Warlord of Rheged." I pointed to the *'Gwynfor'*. "Our ship has been damaged by the storms and we beg your indulgence to repair our ship."

I saw a reaction from both the priest and the leader of the warriors. "I am Caradog son of Conmar. We had heard that Rheged lived still. Does the king survive yet?"

I shook my head. "The last king was Pasgen and he died. The line of Coel and Urien has disappeared. We are all that remain."

Caradog nodded to the archers who lowered their weapons. "You are welcome." He hesitated. "You say your ship needs repairs?"

I smiled, "We have gold and silver to pay for the materials. We are no beggars to ask for charity."

I saw the relief on his face. "This is Bishop Judicael."

I nodded and saw a frown cross the priest's face. We had not shown due deference. "You are not Christian?"

"No, we follow the old ways."

Had I burned him with a brand I could not have had a more extreme reaction. He almost recoiled. I suspect that if we had not spoken his language then he might have ordered Caradog to attack us there and then. As it was a look passed across his face of pure hate. I thought that was ironical. Brother Oswald had told us that the White Christ was both all forgiving and moderate. His followers seemed to be the opposite. He stormed off with his two tonsured priests scurrying behind him. We must have offended him just by our presence.

Caradog smiled, "It seems you have upset the Bishop. He does not like pagans. You are our distant kinsmen and welcome. Come to my hall and we will sup while your captain sees to his ship."

We followed him up a path leading to a twisting stone lined track which led to the gate. The walls were stone topped by wood and I saw many stone buildings within the walls. The hand of Rome was visible everywhere.

"Where were you headed, Warlord?"

"We were going to Austrasia to buy horses."

He laughed. "I am afraid that the moment you opened your mouth you would have been attacked."

"Why? We have done them no harm. Indeed until a few days ago I had never heard of the place."

"That is our fault. We war against them. Their regent, Pepin of Landen, has tried to take our land and expand the empire of the Merovingian kings." He smiled, "We are too big a morsel for him to digest."

"Your land looks to be rocky and hard to assail." We had entered his fort and I saw the machines of war such as we had and the well armed sentries. "And your men look like they know what they are doing."

"When our people first came here almost two hundred years ago they were the last Roman soldiers to leave Britannia. We are all descended from them and we do them honour by maintaining their high standards."

When we entered his hall, I could see that it was built in the Roman style. There were fine pots and jugs of wine on the table. It felt like being at home. The floors had mosaics upon them and there appeared to be the heating we had in our fort.

We sat around his table and some of his men joined us. I could see both sets of warriors examining, surreptitiously, each other's armour and weapons.

"I have heard of the Warlord but you seem somewhat younger than I expected."

"That would have been my father, Lord Lann."

"The warrior who flew with Myrddyn into Morcant Bulc's castle and slew him."

I did not correct him. The legend had spread far and wide. "Aye and Myrddyn lives still."

That interested all of them. "We have heard of him. He is the most powerful wizard in the world; although our Bishop would dispute that. He thinks all wizards and witches should be burned."

"But not you?"

"I am a Christian but I have heard of too many strange events to dismiss wizards as something evil."

I was happy talking to this man. He reminded me of my father. He had a similar look to him. The grey flecks in his beard told me that he was no longer a young man. Myrddyn always said that wisdom came with age. "If we are not welcome in Austrasia where would you suggest we buy our horses from?"

He suddenly looked interested. "You wish to buy horses?" I nodded, "There are none left in Britannia?"

"The horse breeding lands are in Saxon hands and they do not ride horses. Our stock needs rejuvenating."

"In that case we can help you. We trade for our horses with the lands of the Al-Andalus." I frowned. I had not heard of it. "They are the Arabs who have conquered the land to the south. We fight the same enemies, the Franks. I think they believe that the enemy of my enemy is my friend." He shrugged. "It suits us for we have the fine Berber horses. It helps us to defeat the Franks."

"And would you sell us some?"

"We might but I would get to know you first. Will you and your bodyguards stay here for a couple of days? It will take that long to repair your ship. I was amazed that it made it into port."

"So are we, it was *wyrd*."

He laughed, "And that is something else which we have lost. The church says that there is no *wyrd*, it is all the will of God."

"And is that not *wyrd*?"

He clapped me about the shoulders. "I like you, Warlord, the next few days should be interesting."

We were given the freedom to wander around town but I noticed there was always one of Caradog's guards on hand to explain what we were looking at. I did not blame him. He was a careful ruler. I made sure that we visited the ship to make sure that we were being treated fairly. Daffydd had a wry smile on his face when I asked him. "Let us say the canvas and the wood we have purchased must be of the highest quality for we paid a pretty price for it."

"Needs must, Daffydd. We have the gold and silver to pay for it. I think we might have raised our prices in the same situation."

"Perhaps, although I like to think not." I left my captain knowing that he would do all that he could to ensure the ship was seaworthy before we left.

Many of the nobles came to visit with us although the priests assiduously avoided us. It was as though they would be contaminated through conversation and contact. We discovered many links in our histories. The stories we told of our pasts were the same. That evening they threw a feast for us. I suspected we had either paid for it by our repairs or we would be paying for it when we bought horses. However, Caradog had us over a barrel. Where else could we go? We each took it in turns that day to tell the tales of our battles and our losses. They became quite fascinated by the sword and its origins. The idea of a sword being dug up and then cast into the water hearkened back to a shared past. Had the priests been there they might have cast doubts on the stories but the warriors knew the bond between a warrior and his sword was a strong one. We heard their stories too. It seems that they had two revered fathers. One had been the Warlord, Flavius Atius, who brought them from Britannia when the Romans left and the other was Caradog Strong-arm who seemed to have brought others over not long before my father was born. It seemed we were closely related.

Caradog drew me to one side. "Tomorrow we will travel inland and visit our horse farms. I should tell you, Warlord, that our horses will not be cheap."

I nodded, "If I had wanted cheap then I would have stolen them from the Saxons. I want good horses. I want horses that can wear some armour."

"I have heard of armoured horses but they are in the east at Byzantium and Persia."

"I have visited there and seen them. That is what gave me the idea. Our horses are good but they cannot bear the weight of an armoured rider and their own mail."

"You have brought your mail with you?"

"We have."

"Then wear it tomorrow. It will give you a truer picture of what our horses can do."

We returned early in the morning to retrieve and don our armour and helmets. Caradog was impressed with the quality. "We have nought as fine as this."

"We modelled it on the armour of the east. Our smiths are now skilled at making it. We also have fine maces and long spears too."

"You did not bring them?"

I shook my head, "They are only of use when mounted."

"We would be interested in trading for them from you. The Kings of Frankia do not like to trade with us. They prefer to war with us. We have their captured weapons but yours are better."

We were taken to the stables. They only had spare horses there for three of us. I took Pelas and Pol. Caradog apologised, "We do not keep many horses here in our stronghold for we like our horses to have the freedom to exercise."

We travelled north for half a day. Caradog had provided an escort of his own men. "We do not fear the men of Austrasia but sometimes they raid deep inland. It is as well to be prepared."

"Do you not have forts along your borders?"

"Aye we do but they are cunning and sometimes trick the border commanders. They only manage that once for we are quick learners."

In many ways they were in a similar situation to us. We could block an enemy in the passes along the Clwyd but we were vulnerable to an attack from the sea. I envied Caradog. If Aella had not made the mistake of landing so close to our fort then he might have succeeded in hurting us. I would have to spend some time with Pol and Lann Aelle. We needed better defences.

The land through which we passed reminded me of the land around Stanwyck. If we could only recapture that land then we would have the right conditions to raise fine horses. We rode up a gentle slope and when we reached the top, we saw a huge field filled with a huge herd of horses. There were fences around to keep them penned. Caradog swept his arm around them. "These are the young horses. We break them in as we need them."

They were muscular and powerful looking animals. They appeared to stand about fifteen hands high although some were a little bigger. "They are just what we require."

"We will visit with the horse master. He lives in a hall just along the valley."

We found stables and a small hall. The horse master was a sour looking individual who proved that looks sometime belie what lies within. He was the friendliest of men. He saw my look of surprise when he laughed at something Caradog said, "I am sorry for my looks, Warlord. They are the result of a kick in the face when I was young. I have learned to avoid hooves since then." He led me to the stable block. "We have the best horses here. I have my stallions. These are the best five that we possess."

There were three chestnut horses, one jet black and one grey stallion. They were all kept separate. Macliau, for that was his name, spoke to them as though they were humans and he seemed inordinately fond of them. When he had shown them to us he asked, "Well, Warlord, what do you think to my beauties?"

"I think they are magnificent."

He nodded proudly, "I always like it when the master brings visitors to see them."

Caradog said, "The difference this time, Macliau, is that the Warlord wishes to buy one and some of your mares."

He looked shocked, "I don't mind trading the mares but I cannot lose one of my stallions."

"Macliau, you are the guardian of these beasts. They belong to me."

I actually thought that he would weep but he merely hung his head. "Yes, master. Which one would you like, Warlord?"

To me they all looked superb beasts. I could understand the horse master's dilemma. "Macliau, you choose one for me." He and Caradog showed equal surprise. "You are obviously closer to them than any man and you will know which the best is for me. I would like you to choose."

"You are being cruel now, Warlord. I cannot choose."

"Imagine then that you are buying one. Which one would you choose to buy if you could have but one?"

"That is easy." He went to the white one, "Snowflake here is the best."

"So I should have him?"

He did not answer at first but he stroked its mane and its nose. "What do you want them bred for?"

"War horses."

"Then Snowflake is not the stallion for you."

He went to a chestnut. "Wolf here has broad shoulders. He is powerful. He is not as fast as Snowflake but he can keep going with heavier loads. Wolf would be my choice."

I smiled, "Had you just told me his name I would have chosen him."

The two men looked at each other and then at me. "Why, Warlord?"

"Had you seen my shield you would have seen the symbol of the wolf. My father was called the wolf warrior. I bear the wolf shield and lead the wolf brethren. It is *wyrd*. We do not need speed we need endurance. We will buy him."

"But I have not yet told you my price."

"Caradog, I will pay the price you ask."

"You are a poor trader then. Why do you not haggle?"

"Because I believe in the gods. If you cheat me then I believe that *wyrd* will ensure that you pay in the future." I shrugged, "Of course you do not believe in such things so name your price."

"You are most interesting, Warlord. I will not cheat you. Come we will let Macliau pick out your six breeding mares and we will speak of gold."

When we returned to the fort we were all satisfied. I had seven fine horses. It had cost me a small chest of gold but it had been worth it. I also gave both Caradog and Macliau a pendant each to hang around their necks. I had had them made before we left. They were a wolf with a blue stone for the eye. "But you have paid us Warlord, why give us the gift?"

"The gift is to seal our friendship. We are one people separated by a stormy sea of Saxons and Franks. This will remind you that there are others such as you. We believe that such a gift binds us closer than gold." I shrugged, "You do not need to believe so long as we do."

They nodded and I saw that they valued the gift. Perhaps they stirred distant memories. I was pleased that Myrddyn had asked me to take some of my pendants with me. *Wyrd*.

That night the feast was even finer. A young warrior approached Caradog and spoke quietly. Caradog nodded and said, "Warlord, this is my nephew, Llenlleog. He has just finished his training to be a warrior. He begs leave to visit with you and to learn of Myrddyn and the dragon beneath the mountain."

"Is he not Christian?"

"Let us just say that my nephew has an open mind and has butted heads with our bishop before now. I would consider it a favour and if you would grant it I will send another four mares next year."

"You need not for I am happy to do the favour. We always need equites who can fight."

"Then consider them a gift from me to you to remind you of our kinship."

The bond was made and, when we sailed three days later, there was sadness all around. All that is save for the Bishop who was more than happy to see the pagans depart. I watched as he cursed us from the harbour wall as we left.

Chapter 12

It had taken us two days to construct the stalls in the hold to ensure the safety of the valuable horses. We had prepared two but had not known how many we would be able to buy. Llenlleog was young but he knew his horses and he made sure that the animals would not be distressed on the journey north. His own horse, Eliane, had been brought too. Llenlleog chose to sleep in the hold with the horses. He had shaken his head and smiled when we suggested he might share the cabin with the other equites. "I will rest easier if I am close. If they become upset I shall sing to them."

That was how we knew when the animals were fretting; we heard the voice of Llenlleog drifting up from the hold. He had a fine voice but more than that it was soothing. It proved effective each time it was heard.

Pol was happier about the new alliance rather than the horses. "It is good to know that we are not alone."

"They cannot come to aid us Pol. They, too, have their own war to fight."

"It does not matter, Warlord. Before we met them we thought that the world was Saxon and was closing in like the walls of a tomb. We now know it is not. Gawan and Myrddyn will make much of this."

He was right, of course. However, the negative side of me, the side which sometimes saw things half empty, also saw that both peoples had somewhere to flee to if they were overrun. I suspected it would be we who would be flying to the land the Romans had called Armorica.

The autumn weather proved to be precocious and unpredictable. Sometimes the wind was on our beam and we almost flew across the waves. The next day would see it constantly in our face and we would have to tack, endlessly, back and forth. When we reached the Scillonia Insula the winds were so bad that Daffydd was forced to take shelter between two of the larger islands. We anchored with two strong sea anchors. He turned to his first mate, "Go ashore and see if there is any water."

I shook my head, "The equites and I will do that. You and your crew have slaved for days. Let them rest and we will do something useful for a change." In truth we were all grateful to be off the pitching and tossing ship.

Llenlleog came with us. "I will see if I can get some grass for them to eat. Even a handful each would be better than nothing."

We jumped into the sea. The sheltered anchorage and the ship itself afforded some protection from the waves but we were all well soaked before we reached the beach. There was a hill in the middle of the island and a few scrubby and stunted trees struggled to rise above the skyline. I pointed, "If there is fresh water then it will be there."

As we headed up the hill I noticed that there were tracks on the beach. The wind and the rain had made it hard to see if they were animal or human but both required caution. I drew my sword. When we reached the top Llenlleog found the grass he wanted. He took off his cloak and used it as a container for the grass. The rest of us searched for water.

"Here, Warlord," Pelas voice drifted over from a cairn of rocks.

We joined him and saw a small spring bubbling up. Pol put his hand down to taste it. "It is good."

"The problem we have is how to fill the barrel."

Osgar smiled, "I would think, Warlord, that we use our hands." He took the bung from the barrel and, after picking up a handful of water from the spring he poured it into the hole.

One of the other equites, Belas, said, "But that will take hours!"

Pol laughed, "And you have somewhere important to go have you, Belas?"

We took it in turns to collect the water. The wild wind whipped the occasional flurries of rain into our faces. Occasionally it would stop and on one of those occasions I caught a whiff of smoke. I looked to the ship to see if it came from there but that was in the wrong direction. "I smelled smoke."

"Are you certain, Warlord? There is nothing on this bleak little rock."

"Yes Osgar. My nose does not deceive me." The barrel was almost full. "Pelas and Pol come with me. The rest of you continue to fill the barrel." Llenlleog had collected his grass and we saw him in the rocks collecting shellfish. He was a resourceful youth.

The island was about one mile in length and half a mile wide. It was hard to see where any fire would be. We searched the island from one end to the other. Even my old friend Pol was beginning to doubt my sanity. "Perhaps you wished for a fire to dry out your clothes."

I heard the trace of mockery in his voice, "Perhaps. The next time this rain stops we will stop and sniff the air." Almost as though I had commanded it the rain stopped and my two companions dutifully sniffed like a pair of hunting dogs.

Suddenly Pelas shouted, "The Warlord is right! I can smell smoke too."

"Spread out and look down rather than up."

We made our way down the slope. The equites filling the barrel were just thirty paces from us. I could see their curious looks. It was Pol who found it. He waved his arm to attract my attention. When we reached him he pointed to a jumble of rocks. There looked to be a hole there. I nodded and, with Saxon Slayer held before me I walked towards it. The closer I came the more I could see that it was a cave. That was where the smoke was coming from. It appeared to be pitch black inside; I had expected the glow from a fire. I held my left hand out to find the walls. As the cave became lower, so that I had to crouch, so it also turned right and I saw a glow. There was a fire and the smell of smoke was stronger.

A thin voice crackled in the dark, "You can sheath your sword, Warlord, unless you are afraid of one woman."

I felt the hairs on the back of my neck stand on end. Who was here and speaking my name? I edged forward and I heard the voice cackle, "Still afraid? If I were Edwin or another Saxon then you would be attacked already. Your brother would not be afraid of the dark or the cave. Come we will not harm you."

I felt Pol's hand on my back. I must have stopped. This was ridiculous. I was the Warlord. Was I truly afraid of a hole in the ground and a woman's voice? I stepped forward ready to skewer anyone who tried to strike me.

As I stepped into the open space I saw the fire and the back of a woman. I remembered the cave we had found with the stone witches. Was this place the same? Then I remembered that Gawan and Myrddyn had survived a night there. The thought of my two mystics gave me the courage to step into the light. The woman turned around and smiled. It could have been Aileen's sister!

She smiled. "Sheathe your sword. You are safe. Tell your companions that I will not eat them either… yet." She laughed and her laughter seemed to fill the cave.

I did as she had said. "You said we; where are your companions?"

"They are all around. This is the world of the spirits." She smiled at me, "Your father's spirit and your grandmother's are both here. If you were Myrddyn or your brother then you would hear them." She shook her head, sadly, "I am sorry you have not the gift. If you had then it would give you comfort. Now sit. Your clothes are wet and the barrel is not yet full."

Pol and Pelas both had weapons drawn. "Put away your weapons my friends. It seems we are expected."

There was a pot on the fire and the woman took a ladle and filled three bowls. She handed one to me and a wooden spoon. "Eat." She hand Pol and Pelas the other two. I hesitated and she laughed. "You wonder if it is poisoned?" She reached over and took the spoon from me. She sipped some. "A little hot but you can always blow upon it. Now eat."

I took the spoon and ate some of the shellfish stew. It was good. While we ate I studied her. I had said woman but she was barely that. I took her to be seventeen or eighteen summers. Had I not known that Aileen lay in the infirmary with a partly shaven head I would have sworn that she sat before me. She smiled at me as I ate. I put down the empty bowl.

"Thank you….?"

"You need not know my name. You were sent here to speak with me."

"Who sent me here? The storm drove us to shelter here."

She nodded enigmatically, "Just as the other storm drove you to find your kinsmen and the horses. Do not be so arrogant Warlord. You do not decide your actions. The spirits work in their own mysterious way and you are tools only."

"Then why am I here?"

"So that I can speak with you and guide you. Your world is about to change." She looked sad. "You are going to lose. The Saxon sea will engulf you. You have held them back long enough but there will come a time when you will be defeated. It will not be for some time but defeat is coming."

My head slumped forward and Pol shouted, "Do not listen to her, Warlord, she is a witch and she is sent to trap you with her words."

The woman stood and she seemed to fill the cave. Her voice echoed around its walls, "Of course I am a witch! Just as Myrddyn is a wizard and I am on the side of the Warlord and our people!"

She subsided and smiled at me. It encouraged speech. "If we are to lose then why fight on? Should we flee to our kinsmen?"

"No, for they will lose too, but there is hope and the hope is within you; it is in your blood. Your father's sacrifice was to buy time. You must use that time well. There will come another warlord long after you are dead and gone and he will recover your homeland. Your blood will save Britannia."

"But you say my blood; you mean Gawan and his children?"

"No, I mean your children. The spirits do not talk to you but they will to your children if you choose well."

I was confused, "Choose? Who?"

She did not answer me but, instead, closed her eyes. She began to speak, almost to chant and the words were not directed at me. "You are right. His heart is pure but his mind and his eyes are closed." A silence filled the cave and I felt a chill creep up my spine. A voice from inside me said, '*Close your eyes.*' I did not recognise the voice but it seemed familiar. I did as I was told. I saw, when I closed my eyes, a woman and she played with a child. I saw the child leave her and grow until he became my father. He disappeared and then I saw Aileen. I suddenly felt a hand on my shoulder. I opened my eyes and saw Pol and Pelas looking terrified.

"We thought you had gone! You went still and began to murmur." Pol suddenly whirled around. "Where is the witch? Pelas take a brand and search for her!"

"No, Pol. I can see now. I understand. Let us go, our men will be worried."

"But where is the witch?"

I shrugged, "I know not. But I have had a glimpse into the world of Gawan and Myrddyn. We have much to do."

As we made our way back to the ship I thought of all the questions I should have asked. She had said we would lose. When? She had said my blood would save Britannia. How? I would have to ask Myrddyn to dream again under Wyddfa. I now knew who the voice was. That was my grandmother. I also knew who would be the mother of my children: Aileen. I just had to turn the hate into something else.

Miraculously, as soon as we boarded the '***Gwynfor***' with the water, grass and the shellfish the storm abated and we were able to sail north. Pelas could not remain silent and he told the others of what he had seen. Fortunately, he did not speak her prophesy. I would swear the two of them to secrecy. If my men thought there was no hope then they would not fight.

"We saw no one leave the cave, Warlord."

I shrugged, "Perhaps she was a messenger from the spirit world. We will ask Myrddyn when we return. Osgar see to the water with the other men. Llenlleog, see to the horses." When they had gone I drew Pol and Pelas with me to the bows of the ship. "You must swear never to reveal what was spoken in the cave. It remains with us." They both nodded. I took out Saxon Slayer and held the hilt towards them.

They both grasped it and said, "I swear."

I sheathed it and Pelas asked, "But are we to lose?"

"Remember what Myrddyn said, the spirits do not speak of now but the future. We keep fighting and you two must watch over my children for they are the future too."

"What children, Warlord?"

"The children I shall have, Pelas. And that is how I know that the end is not imminent for there are, as yet, no children. But there will be."

We tacked our way up towards Mona and we wore our armour. There were Hibernian pirates in these waters and we would not take any chances. I was relieved when the island of Mona loomed up in the early hours of one of the late autumn mornings. I would not have liked to take that voyage later in the year for the seas were, even now, becoming more violent.

Llenlleog took a great deal of time to ensure the safety of the horses when they were off loaded. I was pleased for it showed that he thought of them as valuable as we did. They looked the worse for wear when they stepped ashore. Their legs shook and their coats were dull. It would take some time for them to regain their condition. When the mares came into season then we would begin to breed. Although we intended to use the horses we had bought for the bulk of our herd I intended to use Wolf with the mares we already had. The line would not be as good but his blood would make them all that much better. I would find horse masters just to watch over my most valuable of stallions.

We led the horses towards my fortress and the stables. We would base them here until they had foaled and then I would think about moving them close to the Narrows. The land there was better for horses.

As we approached the gates I saw Myrddyn waiting for me and, as the sun peered out from behind a cloud it shone on the half shaven head of Aileen. *Wyrd.*

Even before I had bathed I went with Llenlleog to see to the safety of the new horses. Myrddyn and Aileen followed us. I had just greeted them both with a smile. Neither seemed discomfited by my attitude and both smiled. It was eerie. Myrddyn had anticipated the needs of the stallion and the mares. There were two old warriors waiting in the stables. They had both served as equites but wounds had meant they could no longer fight. Both Griffith and Ban knew horses. I would impress upon them the need for security and care. They were guarding gold.

I went to the bath house and was joined by Pol. Our time in Constantinopolis had taught us the benefits of a bath. It was not just the cleansing of the body but the cleansing of the mind. Our kin across the waters used the Roman baths still and as we lay in the hot, steaming water of the caldarium I reflected on that kinship. How many others were there who were of our people? The Angles and the Saxons had succeeded because of their affinity. Had Morcant Bulc not betrayed King Urien all those years ago in the last great alliance who knows what might have happened?

We lay in the tepidarium and I felt more relaxed. "So we fight on even though we know that we will lose Warlord?"

"Do you remember those philosophers in the libraries when we lived in the east?"

"Aye."

"They spoke of the meaning of life."

Pol laughed, "They seemed to just talk about life rather than living it."

"You are right and we do live it. The woman in the cave has set me to thinking. My father could have died when the Saxons raided Stanwyck but he lived. His mother died but she spoke to him and guided him. Through my father Gawan and I were born to carry on the fight. I think that is a kind of victory. We ensure that our children live and through them we shall win."

"But we have no children."

I laughed, "Then let us make some!"

He looked at me and nodded, "You have chosen a woman?"

"I think she has been chosen for me. Think back to the cave; who did the woman remind you of?"

"Aileen."

"Aileen."

"And yet she hated you."

"I know but I feel that she was chosen for me and so I must win her."

"You could just take her."

"Pol, you of all people should know I would never do that."

"Others would."

"Others were not chosen to be the Warlord. Come we will dress. I would speak with Lann Aelle and Aelle. We have much to tell them."

Osgar and the others had all been talking of the island and our voyage. Poor Llenlleog was being inundated with questions as we entered the hall. There was silence as we walked in. I saw Aengus with a crutch and he was seated already at the table. He tried to rise. "No, my friend. You need not rise. I am no king. It is good to see you walking."

He laughed and shook his crutch, "Hobbling."

"And there are many who are in the Otherworld who would dream of hobbling. You have been spared and it is for a reason."

"Your healer is a mighty man. He lowered his voice. "Did I hear aright that he took out some poison from inside Aileen's head?"

"He took something but I know not what it was. She is well and that is all that matters."

The feast was a lively one. As I had expected my men embellished the story of our descent into the underworld and our meeting with a spirit. Only Pol, Pelas and I knew the truth. I would tell Myrddyn when time allowed. For the present I was just pleased that we had succeeded completely for once. We had sought a stallion and brood mares and we had them. We now needed the time to bring on the horses which might delay the inevitable.

After we had eaten Myrddyn caught my eye and I followed him to my solar. He was seated as I walked in. "You have much to tell me, Warlord."

I laughed, "And you know much already old man!"

He inclined his head to one side, "Perhaps but tell me anyway. It will reveal much to me."

I sighed and told him all from the first storms which had driven us south to the meeting with the woman in the cave.

"And you have chosen Aileen?"

"No, she was chosen for me and you know that."

He laughed, "I can see you have been with the spirits, however briefly. I told you that there was a connection between you and her."

"And you knew that we would lose."

"I have always known that. Since before I first met your father, the spirits told me that."

"And yet you still battle the Saxon."

"As you do." I was not so certain. He laughed, "If you were all alone and surrounded by your enemies, would you surrender?"

"No."

"Even though you know you cannot win?"

I laughed, "You are right."

He leaned forward, "But we can delay the inevitable. Your unborn children need time to grow. There are forces at work far across the sea and they will have an influence on what comes after us. Your decision to breed horses was a wise one and that will get us time but I fear our days on Mona are drawing to an end." Surprise must have shown on my face. "We both know that we cannot defend the island. It is low lying and vulnerable. We can defend the Narrows."

"I cannot live there again. The memories are too painful."

"Then live somewhere else. Build a new home. There are many sites between Deva and the Narrows which are suitable."

I went to the north facing window and peered out at Wyddfa. Myrddyn was silent as he allowed me to reach the conclusion, he wished me to. I know not how long I stood there but there was a knock on the door and Aileen stood there.

"You wished to see me, Warlord?"

I turned to Myrddyn who shrugged. "Are you well now?" I was struggling to make conversation. I was a man of war and flowery words did not come easily to me.

She touched her head, self-consciously, "I am, Warlord, and Myrddyn said you helped to save my life. Thank you."

"I merely held your head. But I am pleased you are well."

"And what will become of me now?"

She was blunt enough. I had not expected such a direct question. "Why you shall live here amongst my people. I promised Aengus that I would watch over all the Hibernians."

"I am the last of the women. All the rest died. Shall I fight with your men against those who killed my brother?"

"We do not use women to fight."

"Then I should work in your kitchens, preparing your food?"

I noticed the wry smile on Myrddyn's face. He was enjoying my discomfort. I wondered if he had primed her with these awkward questions. "Not if you do not wish to."

"Shall I lie with your warriors then and please them!"

"No! What a thought! Who has suggested that?"

Her voice became all sweetness, "You did, Warlord. I am a woman who is alone with neither father nor brother to watch over her."

"I would be as a father and a brother."

She paused and when she looked at me her green eyes bored into me. "And I would not have you for either, Warlord."

I looked at Myrddyn who shrugged, "I know what Aileen means Warlord and if you do not …. I shall leave you for I feel I am superfluous." He touched Aileen's shoulder as he left. "He is a warrior. He has no words but he has a heart as big as Wyddfa."

She nodded, "I know, I have spoken with Lann Aelle and Lord Aelle. I shall persevere with him. He has potential!"

We were married at Yule. The ceremony was held on the shortest day of the year. We stood on the edge of the cliff looking west and we were joined. I was happy. Aileen could read my mind just as Myrddyn had read my father's. Gawan approved for he too saw the seer in her. As we lay together, in my hall, I had told her what the woman in the cave has said and she did not seem surprised.

"I dreamed of the cave and I saw you there but I heard no words. The woman you spoke with looked like my mother. She died when I was but five summers old. She had the sight and the power. All the women in my family have."

"And you know then that we will lose?"

She laughed, "You men talk of war and killing. What of birth and living? We will have children and we will watch over them. We will teach them how to live and they will teach their children. We will not lose so long as our blood runs through their veins."

It was wyrd. Those were the words of the witch and of Myrddyn. I was just a play thing in the hands of the gods. I would do what I had always done and fight the enemies of my people.

Chapter 13

Aileen was soon with child and it seemed propitious for the mares came into season at the same time and Wolf was put to work. Soon we had twenty mares which had been serviced by the stallion. We would have to wait eleven months to see the result. As soon as the other mares from our existing herds came into season Wolf was in demand. I took Myrddyn at his word and left with Pol and Lann Aelle to find a new home for my family. I decided that I would just improve the castle close to the monastery of St. Asaph. The land there was just as good for horses as the island and with the fort at the head of the Clwyd Valley and Deva protecting the Dee we would be as secure there as anywhere. It had been deserted since the time of Asaph. We left the monastery untouched out of respect for the memory of our friend Bishop Asaph but there was little communication with the monks there.

I took my equites to the fort soon after the nights became a little shorter. Aileen insisted upon coming with us. I was learning that she was a strong minded woman. Where her husband went so would she. I had discovered many things about the new woman in my life. She was a fine archer and hunter. She could handle a blade too. As she told me, "If a Saxon tries to enslave me, then he will learn, the hard way, that I can fight for my own freedom.

There was a hall at the fort but the structure had fallen into disrepair since Gawan had moved to Deva. The walls were sound but the ditch needed deepening. While half of my men toiled there Pol and I began to build a much bigger hall. We demolished the old one. I remembered Castle Perilous and we used that as a model. The ground floor was to be the stables. The horses would be safe and it would provide heating for the living space above. Upstairs was where we had my eating hall and the bedrooms. A second hall for my oathsworn was attached to one end of the building.

All of my warriors joined in the building. We cut the huge timbers from the forests; choosing the straightest beams that we could find. The bark was stripped and they were each cut to the same length. Myrddyn oversaw the position of each wooden support as the hole was dug. Cobbles and rocks were brought to secure the wood in place. More rocks were found and Roman concrete used to build a wall between the beams which would support the roof. The skeleton of the hall looked a strange structure but once we had filled in the gaps with hazel, ash and lath it looked more like a home. It would take some days for the walls to dry but they would keep out the wind and the cold when they did so. The roof would not have the straw of the old houses but slate. Wyddfa had much slate and the gods had made it into usable pieces. With a slate rood we would be drier and safer from fire. We had learned lessons over the years. Finally the floors and internal walls were erected. They made it cosier and more like a home. Aileen supervised, along with Myrddyn and between their sharp eyes and tongues we produced a hall which satisfied them both.

When the hall was finished we built a new kitchen and smiths. The work took us until the first spring flowers risked the wrath of the weather. All the time my wife grew and blossomed. She kept working for she wanted a home. The inside was her domain. Gawan's wife, Gwyneth, came to help and I was happier. The two women would be good for each other. Gwyneth never complained about living on the border under constant threat from the Saxons. We were close enough now for the two women to visit.

King Cadwallon and my sister Nanna visited us during the feast of Eostre. Nanna was with child again and the three women, Aileen, Gwyneth and my sister were happy talking of babies. Gawan, Pol and myself took the king hunting. War would not be far off and we needed to begin to hone our skills again. Hunting was the best way.

"We have attacked their burghs and made life uncomfortable for the Northumbrians on our borders." I nodded. King Cadwallon had not been idle. "Penda sent me a message that King Edwin is massing an army in the south of his lands."

We had just managed to bring down a deer and Pol was skinning it. "That was inevitable once the threat to his northern borders disappeared. I am just pleased that he has not reinforced Manau yet."

"You fear for Mona?"

"It is not easy to defend."

"And that is why you have moved here to the Clwyd?"

"Partly and partly because I believe our horses will be of more use here than on Mona."

We watched as Pol and Pelas finished the skinning. We threw the carcass on the pack horse and headed back to my new home.

"I have done as you asked and built up my horsemen."

"Your archers can win any battle against King Edwin. They are the best archers I have seen. Pol and I saw many good archers in the east but they could not hold a candle against yours."

"Thank you, Warlord, I take that well coming from you." We came over a rise and saw our horse herd. There were ten guards dotted around. The horses were our future and we would not let them be taken easily. "How long before the new horses will be ready for combat?"

"Llenlleog thinks that it will take two to three years."

"He is a fine warrior. Why did he return with you? Was it to care for his horses?"

"He wished to see Wyddfa and meet Myrddyn. I believe that my brother and the wizard have promised that they will travel to the dream cave and take him with them."

"The witch's prophesy is still on your mind?"

"It is. She had no reason to lie and everything else of which she spoke has come true."

"You seem not to be worried about the end of your world."

"Aileen has given me a future again. I am content. I saw my grandmother's face when I dreamed. She looked like Nanna. It seems I cannot dream in Wyddfa but the Scillonia Insula allows me to get a brief glimpse into the world of the spirits. We all live again but we do it through our children. My descendant will drive the Saxon away. I am content."

"King Ceorl is unwilling to go to war with Edwin again although Penda is encouraging him."

"We hold what we have. Keep a close watch on the borderlands. If Edwin comes we can respond with our horsemen. Our mounted archers and our equites will slow down any attack and our border forts are well defended."

It was not until late summer that Edwin made his move. Perhaps we had hurt him more than we had thought. King Cadwallon's scouts reported many warbands heading towards the eastern borders of his kingdom. Penda brought his warband to help but

King Ceorl did nothing. We knew that we were largely alone. Penda's men aided us by giving a warband who would stand and face one of King Edwin's Northumbrians but it would be our archers and equites who would drive him hence. I wondered if Penda would take the throne of Mercia. King Ceorl was old and weak. Penda had the largest warband in Mercia. He could have usurped the old man had he chosen to do so.

King Cadwallon summoned his army and I gathered my equites and my archers. Riders were sent to Mona to warn them of the attacks. We would not be able to help Aelle. Being in the Clwyd helped for my men were just a few miles from the border. I had thirty spearmen who were left to guard my home. Gawan had more than three times that number at Deva. Although we had yet to reap the benefit of my stud, Wolf, we had horses which had rested well over the winter and enjoyed the lush grass of the Clwyd. Fifteen squires had become equites and twenty squires had joined our ranks. Sadly archers were harder to come by and Daffydd's numbers had only been swollen by a mere ten. This time, however, we would not be alone. We would have King Cadwallon and his men with us.

Pelas had grown over the winter. He had broadened out. He and Llenlleog had grown quite close. They were of an age and enjoyed each other's company. My new equite proved to be a good swordsman as well as one of the best horsemen I had known. He improved Pelas' skills as a swordsman. However, he found it difficult to come to terms with the stirrups we used. His people did not use them. They leapt on to the backs of the horses. Our enemies did not use them but they were one of the things Pol and I had brought back from the east. They enabled us to use the long spear.

Llenlleog acted as a sort of second squire for me. With Llewellyn holding my banner we were a knot of four warriors who would fight together. It allowed Pol the freedom to lead half of my equites should we need that option. In the months since he had arrived Llenlleog had grown on me. He was diligent and he was dedicated. Tuanthal, who trained my new warriors still, commented on the fact that the young man was the first for training and the last to leave the stables. Myrddyn had also commented on his propensity for knowledge and learning. He was, indeed, a perfect equite. That he had chosen to come with me was *wyrd*.

As we gathered on the Clwyd, ready to ride east Tuanthal returned to Mona. He would be there to train our new warriors. He had with him his two sons. As I saw him creak his way into his saddle I thought that it was right he should enjoy his old age. Of all of my father's warriors he was the one who had survived to become a greybeard and to father fine warriors. He would be a rock on which my uncle could depend. Myrddyn too went to Wyddfa. My father's tomb was still his dream world and he went there to talk with the dead. "You will not need me this summer, Warlord. Besides, last year, when you campaigned, you would have travelled faster without this old man to slow you down."

As the two left us I wondered if Myrddyn was letting me go. I felt like a young child being taught to walk. The father supports the first faltering steps and then releases the child to succeed or to learn from falling. Would I learn from this first encounter with the Saxons without my old mentor behind me?

Ardal son of Bors commanded my fort at the head of the valley. He only had thirty farmer warriors within his walls but that was all that he needed. It stood close to a narrow col. His men were all fine archers. Most had served my father in their youth. Now they farmed the uplands of the valley and guarded it from attack. We waved to them as we trotted over the col and into the land of King Cadwallon. He had arranged for us to meet at Wrecsam. It had been the court of his father and King Cadwallon had lived there but a growing family meant he wished the protection of the mountain and it was now the frontier and the garrison fortress of the border.

For once my scouts, now swollen to six, were not needed. Cadwallon had local riders who knew the land like the back of their hands. The Northumbrians had built burghs, crudely made but effective, along the edge of the ridge which marked the start of the high divide. They had learned from us. It would be foolish to assault them. We had not the man power to waste but we had to watch them. They would be the starting point for the king's raids and attacks. King Cadwallon had ensured that the burghs did not encroach into the lands of Gwynedd. They were well within the borders of Northumbria.

As we waited, in camps spreading out from Wrecsam, I felt a little guilty. Had we not been so successful raiding last summer then perhaps King Edwin would not need to raid the rich heartland of King Cadwallon. I also felt annoyed that King Ceorl was not with us. I could not see King Edwin leaving alone the lands of Mercia. They had not only fine farmland but also rich iron workings. With King Edwin's links to the East Angles then Mercia was a tasty morsel which might be devoured. I had come to respect King Edwin. He was, as my father had been, a thoughtful leader who did nothing without thinking it through.

By the time our baby was born this campaign would be over one way or the other. The animals upon which the Cymri depended would all be born and grown by that time and we would be collecting in the harvests on Mona. King Edwin would strike before Midsummer. Our job was to strike the moment that he did. We waited.

It was an idle and indolent wait. Each day one of my captains, Bors, Kay, Lann Aelle, Daffydd or Pol would lead out a patrol of ten equites and ten archers. We would ride as close to the burghs as we dared. The Northumbrians hurled insults but they fell on deaf ears. My men were counting heads. So long as the number on the ramparts remained the same then we knew that nothing had changed. We also kept a line of horsemen out each night patrolling the ground between us. We had assaulted enough forts at night to be wary of someone doing the same to us.

Each day that newly born animals were brought down from the hills was another day when we had won. They were the future. King Cadwallon and I watched as another shepherd brought his small flock past us towards the markets of Wrecsam. "When will he come, Warlord?"

"You have fought him as long as I have, King Cadwallon, but if I were to guess then I would say soon. He has an army to feed and the uplands are less fruitful than these plains. He will come for the grain which is ripening and for the lambs and calves which have been born and for the salt." To the north of us were the villages which produced such vast quantities of salt. It was how we preserved our food and was as valuable as gold. Little wonder that the Romans had given part of the payment to their legions in salt.

"Good, for my men become restless."

The men in the King's army were all warriors when they were needed. My equites were full time warriors. We had a smaller army than he did but they were a better army.

"Then why not give them a march along the front. It will make King Edwin think we are ready to attack and provide activity for your restless men. He might attack before he is ready."

He nodded, "This is where I miss your father and Myrddyn. I wish the old wizard was here for he could read the Saxon mind."

"Use Gawan. His skills are growing."

The thought had not occurred to the king. "I will. The two of you come to my hall tonight in Wrecsam and we will talk. I will tell my captains that we march tomorrow."

As he turned to go I said, "Do not tell them the reason for your march."

"Why not, Warlord?"

"If they think it is merely a walk for your men then they and your warriors will not be as alert as they need to be. Best make them believe they go to war."

"You do not trust my captains?"

"With respect, King Cadwallon, all of them are new. Dai and the other experienced captains fell. Let us view this as a test. It will be interesting to see how they cope with the threat of the Northumbrians."

That evening, as we ate, Gawan concurred with my ideas. We had met all of his captains before; there were six of them: Miach, Llewellyn ap Daffydd, Afron ap Dai, Terif the Bald, Garth ap Llewellyn and Griffith ap Daffydd. They all looked like experienced warriors. Each had scars and battle rings. I had fought with Miach and Garth before but the others were new to me. I had always found that it was hard to judge a warrior until you had fought alongside him. My father may have fought with some but I had spent my formative years with my equites in the borderlands.

Gawan studied them from across the table and spoke quietly with the king. "I have not looked into their hearts yet but looking at them now I do not feel a sense of confidence amongst them."

King Cadwallon looked a little worried, "You doubt them?"

"No but the spirits do not sing to me." He smiled at the King's puzzled expression, "When I look at my brother's captains I hear singing in my head. The spirits of our father and our dead comrades know their hearts and they sing. When Dai sings then I will be happier."

"Dai speaks with you?"

"He has spoken with me although not often. Since we have camped here in his land I have heard his voice more."

"Then tomorrow will be an interesting day for I will watch my captains even more closely than I might have done before."

"And we will also take our warriors out of camp and we will watch your northern flank. It will do my men good to manoeuvre on the plains before us."

Penda arrived as we were finishing. The King looked up in surprise. "Is there a problem, Penda?"

"There may be, King Cadwallon. My sentries spotted some movement on the ridge after dark this night. It may be nothing but this is the first sign of movement."

They both looked at me. "I would suggest, King Cadwallon, that you do as I have done. Have twenty or so of your equites patrol the land between us and Northumbria; just in case there is an attempt to take us at night by surprise."

The king nodded and waved over one of his captains. Penda took the beaker of beer offered by Gawan. He smiled, "I can see the benefit of horsemen. By the time my men reach anywhere the enemy could have gone."

"True but an army made up of horsemen is expensive to maintain. I hear that the Norse ride to battle and then fight on foot."

Penda nodded, "That would suit. I do not know how you can fight on the back of a horse. It takes me all my time just to sit safely!"

"It is practice only."

When the king returned we talked of the upcoming war and our strategies. I thought it strange that I could talk with Penda, even though he was a Saxon. He should have been an enemy but he never felt like one.

When we were returning to our camp Gawan said, "I have feelings of disquiet, brother." He shrugged, "I cannot be more specific. It is just that something does not feel right."

"Then we will heed them. Penda's words were a warning too. King Edwin has the initiative and we must be ready to react. The army has had plenty of rest. We will ride before dawn. We shall be the early bird."

Chapter 14

We would be much a smaller and compact army than that of King Cadwallon. The two hundred and ten men under my command all rode out whilst it was still dark. We had all loose tack wrapped so that we could ride silently and the dragon banner remained furled. Twenty squires and foot soldiers were left to guard the camp. My six scouts were spread out far ahead of us and we moved northwards towards the ridge and King Edwin's new burghs.

A faint sliver of light appeared in the east and we heard the hooves of two horses approaching. My men were too well trained to need a command and spears were pointed towards the approaching sounds and arrows were notched. It was Aed and Felan. I saw that they had something over the saddle of Aed's horse.

"We have caught a Saxon scout." He threw the unfortunate warrior to the floor. Gawan and I dismounted and lifted the semi-conscious youth to his feet. He looked terrified.

"You know who I am?"

"You are the Warlord."

"Good then you know my reputation. Speak truthfully and you might live. Lie and you will die piece by piece." I pointed to Gawan, "This is my brother Gawan, like Myrddyn, who trained him, he is a wizard and he can see into your heart, Northumbrian." He was almost shaking. Had I not been Warlord I might have felt pity for him but I was Warlord and I owed a duty to my people. "Where is your king?"

He pointed not to the north but to the east. "He is there; with his army."

"How many men does he have?"

He began to shake and to weep, "I am sorry Warlord, I do not know."

I understood. Counting was a skill which came naturally to me. This youth had never learned. "And which way does he come?"

"He comes west. He comes to attack King Cadwallon."

"You were sent to find us and report back." He nodded. I turned to Pelas, "Find two squires and have this youth taken to our camp.

Bind him but do not harm him. He has spoken the truth." I could see that the boy had not understood a word. I smiled and said, in Saxon, "You will be bound and taken to my camp. If you do not try to escape you will live and I will release you later."

As he was taken off Llenlleog said, "You did not kill him. Why not?"

"I had no need. The Allfather does not demand that we kill all of our enemies. He might have been Pelas here. Perhaps this act of kindness may make him less likely to fight us. It is worth the risk."

Llenlleog nodded as he considered my words.

"We will ride to King Cadwallon. He may need our help."

Riding now to the east Pol asked, "Why does King Edwin attack today of all days? Today King Cadwallon exercises his men and Edwin attacks? This seems strange."

"I thought so too Pol. I think that not all of King Cadwallon's men are as loyal as the king believes. The captains were told that King Cadwallon would be advancing this morning. By marching early King Edwin can strike before the Cymri are prepared. Felan, ride to King Cadwallon and warn him that the Northumbrians are advancing towards him."

"Felan will not reach him in time, brother."

"I know and we must ride hard to reach him before he is slaughtered."

As we rode Llenlleog asked, "How do you know that the Northumbrians will outnumber the Cymri?"

"We do not know the number of King Edwin's army but if there is a spy then we know that King Edwin will have the precise numbers of the Cymri. He will only attack if he knows he has superior numbers."

"This is not the way that we make war. My people have much to learn from you, Warlord."

Dawn broke brightly from the east. It promised to be a clear day. My archers would not have to worry about wet bow strings. We hurried through the lightening morning. Dai was the scout who found the Northumbrians.

"Warlord, the Saxons are five miles to the south. There are four warbands and each looks to be five hundred men strong. They are less than a mile from King Cadwallon. They will be there even now."

They would outnumber the Cymri by at least two to one. Even if Penda could bring his forces to their aid they would be at a disadvantage. The only hope was that the king's equites could keep the Northumbrians at bay until we reached them.

"Daffydd, take your archers and harry the rear of the Northumbrians. Approach from the north; it may throw them off. We will attack their flank. Do not risk your archers."

He grinned, "I will not."

The fifty or so archers could not hope to stop the warband but they could slow them up and make them look over their shoulders. As I raised my sword to lead my equites and squires forward I saw that although the land was flat it was dotted with streams and woods. We would have to wait until we were closer to the enemy to form lines. We cantered forward. It would not do to overtire the horses. I peered into the bright blue sky ahead. The battle, which I knew was underway, was hidden behind shallow folds in the land and the hedges and woods which abounded. When I heard the first clash of metal on wood I turned to Llewellyn. "Unfurl the banner. Let us give hope to our friends and bring fear to our foes!"

As soon as it was unfurled and the wind passed through it we heard the eerie wail which so terrified enemy warriors. If we could not see them then they could not see us but they could hear, on the breeze, the sound of their doom approaching. In their shield wall they would wonder when the Warlord would strike. Soon they would hear the thunder of our hooves and that would be like a death knell to them. Nor would they know our numbers; they would just know that we approached.

We crossed a shallow valley and the ground began to rise. I could hear the cries of the wounded and the dying. The battle was close. "Saxon Slayer!" My war cry was the signal for the equites to prepare their weapons. Spears were lowered, swords and maces readied. My captains began to spread the warriors out as we began to canter up the slope. As we crested the rise there were sixty equites in the front rank and seventy equites and squires in the second rank.

I saw the battle less than four hundred paces from us. I took the scene in quickly and assessed it. King Cadwallon had been caught. I could see to the north the bodies of horses and riders, showing where his men had bought him time. It had allowed him to form up on a slope. It meant the Saxons had to attack up hill. The glint of the morning light on mail told me that King Edwin had been busy over the winter and his men were well prepared.

I raised my sword. "Charge, for Rheged and for Cymru!" We hurtled forward. The gentle slope helped my horses to gather speed. I saw the shields ahead of me lock as the Saxons prepared to receive the charge. Arrows fell from the north as Daffydd and his archers caused small holes to appear. There were gaps which were filled from behind but, inevitably, they were not as tightly locked as they had been. I was the only one in the front rank without a spear and the equite to my side took out the warrior who faced Star. I crashed through the gap and brought Saxon Slayer down on the man to my left. His helmet crumpled as though it was piece of freshly baked pastry. His blood and his brains showered the man behind. Star was snapping his might jaws at the faces of the Saxons before him. His hooves flailed like war hammers and the Saxons fell back.

I was aware of Pelas to one side of me and Llenlleog to the other. Both had lost their spears but their swords carved a path of death into the centre of the warband. The deeper we went the more chaos we caused for the ones in the middle were pressed by their fellows and could not bring their weapons to bear. I slashed to the left and right of Star's head. I had practised the move until I could do it with my eyes closed. My long reach and my sharp blade brought death to the ones before us. The war band was like a bow pulled too tightly. The stress was too much and, as my second line struck, the warband disintegrated. The arrows from their rear and the relentless charge of our horses broke their spirit. It brought no relief for, as they turned their backs to flee, my men's maces and swords rained down on unprotected backs and skulls. Men who fell to the floor were trampled for the horses could not avoid stepping on them there were so many.

We were through and I yelled, "Reform!" The horses had ridden hard. They were blown and I needed to assess the situation. There were still three Northumbrian warbands ahead of us. I could see that King Edwin had halted his attack and turned one of them to face us. We had bought King Cadwallon time and I could see his men forming their own shield wall. We were still outnumbered but we had thwarted King Edwin's attempt at a surprise attack and victory.

When I heard the horn of Penda and his men approaching from the south east I knew that this battle was over. The Northumbrian horns sounded too and the warbands began the tricky task of marching backwards.

"Pelas, tell Daffydd to continue to harass the Saxons until he runs out of arrows."

My squire rode off and I hoped that King Cadwallon would do the same with his foot archers. I shouted to Pol and then Lann Aelle, "Keep your spears at them but no more charges. Let our archers whittle them down!" My two lieutenants waved their acknowledgement.

Gawan appeared at my side, "Did you lose many, brother?"

He shook his head. "Two men were wounded but we lost three horses. The Saxons have learned that they are as valuable as warriors."

I nodded, "What of our losses Llewellyn?"

I saw Luagh fall and we lost two horses," he grinned, "but I was too busy trying to keep up with you Warlord to pay too much attention."

We spent a long day pushing them back to their burghs. Their trail was marked by their dead. Their shields were covered in arrows showing that they had defended themselves but many had fallen to my bowmen. Had they not emptied their quivers then more would have joined them. As we marched wearily back to King Cadwallon my men stripped the bodies of weapons, helmets and booty. I saw that few of the warriors wearing mail had fallen. It had been the ones without armour who had died. We counted two hundred bodies as we headed south.

Sadly we saw that the Northumbrians had done great damage to the men of Cymru. Over two hundred lay dead and many more were wounded. Some of them would never fight again. Had Penda not arrived when he did then it would have been much worse. Our timely arrival too had helped.

King Cadwallon had been in the forefront of the fighting and he had suffered wounds. They were not life threatening but Gawan saw to them as Penda and I surveyed the field.

"We were lucky, Penda."

"I know. If you had not charged when you did then King Cadwallon would have been overrun." I had left Star with Pelas and I led Penda away from inquisitive ears. "There is a traitor amongst King Cadwallon's captains."

"Does he know yet?"

"No, I am letting Gawan heal him first. Find a prisoner, preferably one of rank and we will question him with the king present. Only your men and mine are above suspicion I will have my equites watch the captains. You are Saxon and they may tell you more than they tell me."

Nodding he left and I waved over my own leaders. I spoke quietly to them as though we were discussing the battle but I made my instructions clear. The traitor would not escape. We had dismounted to lead our horses back to the camp the king had made. It would only be temporary. Wrecsam was a safer place to rest. King Edwin still outnumbered us. Surprise had won the day for us and not for him.

Llenlleog was full of questions. He seemed filled with the joy of war. "Do your enemies always fight thus? They have neither horse nor bow?"

"Generally they do not use them."

"I can see why you win so often."

Pol snorted, "But did you not see the numbers that we fought?"

"Aye but you killed many."

"And the handful that we lost had taken us all winter to train. We cannot afford to lose any. I am just grateful that we lost none of the Warlord's archers."

Llenlleog was puzzled, "Then hire more. You must have gold for you paid Caradog in good coin."

I shook my head, "We fight with men whose hearts we know. We have used Hibernians before now but they fight like the Saxons. I think that our peoples are the only ones who use the horse and the bow."

He nodded. "Our enemies are harder to defeat for the Franks and Merovingians we fight ride their horses to battle and half of the warriors fight on them. We can never hope to defeat them. The best that we can do is to hold them at bay."

"You have seen our island home of Mona. It is vulnerable to attack from the sea. We can hold the land around Wyddfa for that is like your home but the rest…."

Some of the elation of battle was sucked from Llenlleog. I think he thought that we would ride gloriously through the Northumbrians and conquer the whole land.

"But you did well today young Llenlleog. My equites spoke of your skill. Had you used stirrups as we did then perhaps you could have used the lance."

"I will try them but I will need to practise for you use a different saddle."

"It makes it easier to fight on horseback and is essential if you are to use a spear."

When we reached the camp we saw just how many of the king's warriors had been wounded. They had been caught by the Saxons before they could form lines. Edwin's mailed warriors had caused devastating wounds in warriors wearing only leather armour.

King Cadwallon had had his wounds dressed and he greeted us. I pointed behind at the mail which we had collected. "I would use the mail you recover, your majesty, to protect the warriors in the front rank. It would save many casualties."

"You are right Warlord." He stood and clasped my arm. "Once again I am indebted to you. Penda and you saved the day." He looked around. "Where is my ally? He has not been injured has he?"

I took his arm, "No, King Cadwallon. He is on an errand for me. Come and I will tell you all." As we left I nodded to Pol. He and my equites were in position. If the traitor tried to flee then he would be stopped.

When we were out of earshot I said, "Do not look around and show nothing." He nodded. "You have a traitor amongst your captains. King Edwin was told that you were advancing today. He thought you meant to attack and did not know that you were merely manoeuvring."

He had his back to his captains which was just as well for his face paled, "Which one?"

"I know not but Penda is questioning a prisoner." Penda had done this for us before and he could be quite persuasive. Most of the warriors had returned from the battlefield and we were about to start back to nearby Wrecsam when we saw Penda and his oathsworn approach. They had a Northumbrian chief tethered and were leading him along. He had fine mail and a full face helmet. Penda had managed to persuade a high status captive to tell us all.

Miach attracted my attention, "Warlord, see yonder Penda brings a prisoner."

"Aye, Miach, I asked him to secure one who could tell us of Edwin and his plans. He has found a good one." I spoke loudly enough for the captains to hear me.

"That will indeed help us."

Already men were beginning to move west to Wrecsam and Miach joined the other captains who were waiting together for orders from their king.

My equites looked as though they were doing the same. In reality they were on guard.

Suddenly Terif whipped his horse's head around and burst away from the other captains. He galloped not west but east. I needed no command for Pol and Llenlleog hurtled after him. They were both experienced riders and, within two hundred paces, they had caught him. I watched as he raised his sword to strike at Pol. I could not believe my eyes as Llenlleog reached down and hoisted Terif's left leg up. The traitor tumbled to the ground. As he tried to rise he found Pol's sword in his throat.

Penda reached us as King Cadwallon said, "Terif! I would not have believed it. He was one of my father's oathsworn and was as loyal a warrior as I have in my army."

He pointed to the captured Saxon. "It seems we need not his testimony now."

Panda laughed and slit the bonds on the prisoner who threw off his helmet. "And that is fortunate for he is one of my men dressed up. We had to kill four prisoners and none would talk save to say that there was a traitor. It was a trick." He nodded towards me. "I am learning much from the Warlord."

When Terif was brought before us he looked angry. The king, in contrast, looked sad. "Terif, why?"

The former captain laughed sardonically, "You ask why? You pup! You could not defeat the Saxons. You have sat for the last few years cowering behind your walls. When the Warlord took the war to Edwin, I knew that you would not be the one for glory nor for riches." He shrugged, "I will be on the winning side and given the land that was formerly yours."

The king shook his head sadly, "The only land you shall have will be the earth in which we cast your body."

Penda said, "A simple death is too good for him, your majesty. Cast his body to the four corners of your land and leave his head on a spear to warn others of the punishment for treachery."

I think had Terif shown any remorse then the king might have given him a warrior's death. The king nodded. Penda said, "Get me four ropes!" He and his oathsworn pinned the warrior to the ground while ropes were attached to his legs and arms. He then divided his warband into four and each took hold of the rope.

I had never seen this done before but Terif must have realised what was coming for he began to scream. "King Cadwallon, I was oathsworn to your father!"

"And you are now foresworn. I can do no more. Warlord?" He nodded towards Terif's head.

I drew Saxon Slayer and stood next to the screaming Welshman. Penda's men took the strain and began to pull. I had heard of this being done by horses but that is quick. The limbs are torn from their sockets and the warrior dies quickly. I heard the crack as each limb was first dislocated and then torn. The flesh held it together and the screams were horrific. How he survived I knew not. King Cadwallon had had enough and he nodded to me. I sliced down with Saxon Slayer and his head was removed in a single blow. The silence was deafening. Then the Mercians gave one almighty heave and his body was torn asunder. I picked up the head by the hair and walked over to where his standard had been plunged into the ground. I jammed the head, the eyes still staring onto the standard of the traitor. That marked the site of the battle for many years. The birds picked the flesh clean and his whitening skull stood as a reminder of the payment for betrayal.

We spent a week in Wrecsam. Each day we had forty riders patrolling the burghs to see if King Edwin would make another move. Each day was one day closer to our survival. We knew that the Northumbrians had to ravage their own land for food. Their cereal crops were still to harvest and so they lived off the animals the farmers would need for the winter. Every time our scouts told us that the Saxons were preparing to move I led the combined equites of both of our armies, two hundred warriors and fifty mounted archers, to threaten them. Our attack at the battle of Wrecsam had shown them that they could not fight against us if they were caught in the open. When disease struck his burghs he departed north. I led the mounted warriors and we kept our spears in his back all the way to Lindum where they trudged the survivors to safety. We had followed the trail of sick and dying from their ridge of burghs. Remembering the effect of the plague on my family we rode around the bodies. Their weapons, armour and bodies were left for the carrion to devour. It was the borderlands and their bones would serve to warn them if they came west again. We had won.

Two months after midsummer's eve I led my army back to the Clwyd. The summer's campaign might not have had the ending we wished for, a complete victory over Edwin, but we had bloodied his nose. My new equites and archers had fought well and we had not suffered many losses. Our new foals would be born within a few months and we could build again, over the winter.

I arrived back to a wife who appeared to be ready to burst. Myrddyn was with her as were Gwyneth and her women. I was about to become a father again.

Chapter 15

As the father I was sent away from the birth. It would not be auspicious. Lann Aelle had returned to see his father; my uncle had not been well recently and so I sat by the river with Pol watching the Clwyd drift gently to the sea.

"Do you wish a son?"

"I do not know. I have changed over the last couple of years. If the spirits are right then it does not seem to matter if it is a boy or a girl so long as the blood is right."

"You are thinking of the dark days after we lose?"

I nodded, "If we lose and we are captured then death awaits us; we know that. However for the women, sometimes, often perhaps, they survive. They might become slaves but they do not die and in life there is hope. We need to teach my children to hang on to life dearly."

"Children? You plan more then, Warlord?"

I laughed, "Aileen is young and fecund. She will bear more children. She wishes to have many children. She is the last of her family and it weighs heavy upon her. Like me she is aware of blood. She is more like Gawan and Myrddyn than anyone I have ever known. She speaks with the spirits. She has not dreamed my death."

Pol shivered even though it was a warm day, "I would not wish to know the day I am to die. I would that it would just come and I would not like a lingering death such as your father suffered. I would have a quick death in battle."

"Do not rush such things, Pol. I have need of you yet."

Just then we heard the unmistakeable cry of a new born babe. "It seems you are a father, Warlord. Let us go and greet the child."

All had been cleaned by the time I entered Aileen's birthing room. Myrddyn nodded and smiled. He looked like a delighted grandfather. I though how sad it was that he had never fathered children. Aileen looked a little worried. Myrddyn shook his head, "It is a girl, Warlord and your wife worries that you might have sought a son."

I went to my wife and picked up the child. She was so small and yet appeared to be perfect. She had down the colour of my wife's hair upon her head and, as she opened her eyes to look on me she smiled.

"She smiled at me!"

"It is wind, Warlord! Every father takes wind for a smile. It is a common error."

"And what would you know old man?"

He chuckled as he left, "I know doting fathers, Warlord. You are just like your father. He was the same."

Pol followed Myrddyn with the others and then we were alone. I sat on the bed and gave the child to my wife to nurse. "She did smile."

"I know. She is happy to see her father. Have you thought to a name yet, husband?"

"I had thought to name her Radha after my mother but she is so pretty and small that I cannot get the name Myfanwy from my mind."

Aileen laughed, "And that was in my mind also. The spirits must have put it there. Myfanwy she shall be."

My child's eyes stared up at me as she fed. I stroked the top of her head. It was soft and felt like the silk I had seen in Constantinopolis. "And we shall teach you, my daughter, how to be as wise as your mother and how to survive in this world for you will grow in dangerous times."

Aileen put her hand on mine, "But the spirits will watch over you always, my child, and they will guide you and your children, long into the future."

After a week with my family I decided to visit my uncle Aelle. The fact that Lann Aelle had not returned made me fear that there was something more serious. I took Myrddyn with me. He would heal Aelle if that were at all possible.

The ride around Wyddfa made all of us silent. Llenlleog was looking forward to the winter solstice when Myrddyn had promised him he would take him to my father's tomb. Pelas was just in awe of the whole building. To Myrddyn it was even more special; he had had workmen building his own niche in the cave for his tomb. For me it just brought my father closer to me. I still regretted not saying goodbye to him. I know that events mean I could not have done so but the regrets remained. King Cadwallon was still at Wrecsam and his fort had the half deserted feel which I did not like. That was how it had been when I returned to find my family dead.

Once we reached Mona all of us talked more. I felt a little disquiet about the fort at the Narrows. It seemed sparsely defended. I would have to speak with King Cadwallon. My forces were stretched too thin and we needed his warriors to add to its defence. If it fell then his fortress would be in even greater danger. Rather than using the Roman Road across the centre of the island we rode along the northern coast. It was here that the Saxons would attack. Our towers stood yet but the walls of the forts seemed thinly defended. When we reached Ynys Mon I was already unhappy even before I met with my uncle.

I let Myrddyn go in to examine him before I did. The ride had made me too irritated and I needed to speak with Lann Aelle and Tuanthal.

Tuanthal looked old. "How goes it captain?"

He gave me a wan smile. "I grow old, Warlord, and I am no wizard who can heal himself."

"The warriors you trained fought well."

He nodded, "I have the next batch ready. They can travel back with you."

"Would they not be of more use here?"

He smiled, "Your father made me captain of the horse for he always preferred fighting on foot. We found that living, riding and working together made the horsemen better warriors. The sooner the new ones meet the experienced riders like Pol, Kay and Bors, the more rapid will be their improvement. Besides the land in the Clwyd suits horses better." He took a drink of wine. "And the ones who are recently trained tend to be disparaging about the new youths who have just started training."

"I bow to your wisdom. Lann Aelle, I know it is not your doing but, this fort apart, the island seems ill prepared. I saw few men in the towers and on the walls."

"It is harvest time, Warlord, and they are set in their ways. They have all been safe for many years. They think that you over react!"

I felt myself becoming angry. "I will show them when I over react! King Edwin and Aella are no fools. They will sense weakness and strike."

"Aengus is a good commander. He has taken charge here and this is like a rock now."

"Ynys Mon was always the easiest to defend but it is a barren isle. Mona has the grain. It will do us little good if this survives an attack and the rest of the island falls."

I felt a chill along my spine which I could not explain. I walked to the window which faced north. "When it is collected I want half of the grain taking to my new home on the Clwyd."

"Aye Warlord, as you command but why?"

I shrugged, "I know not but I am learning to use the feelings I cannot understand. And I would like a jetty building here, close to the fort."

"But it is not a sheltered anchorage. Caer Gybi is a much safer harbour."

"Humour me, cousin. I want an escape should the worst come to the worst."

He nodded. "I will arrange your accommodation."

Myrddyn came over to us and Lann Aelle halted. "Well?"

He looked at Lann Aelle. "Your father is dying."

"Can you not heal him?"

"It is something which grows inside of him."

"Cut it out as you did with Aileen!"

"I had read of that and knew what to do. I am only surmising that the hard lump I felt in his side is something unnatural. Besides," he put his hand on Lann Aelle's shoulder, "he is not young. Aileen was young and healthy. Your father is older than I am. He should be allowed to die peacefully."

I could see that Lann Aelle was upset, "How long has he, Myrddyn?"

"If he lasts until Yule then I will be surprised."

Lann Aelle nodded, "I will see to your accommodation."

"I will go to see him." I turned to Pelas, "Would you like to come and speak with your grandfather?"

"I would see him but I fear that if I try to speak then I will unman myself and weep."

I smiled, "That would not distress your grandfather but, as you will."

My uncle looked older and paler than I had remembered but I smiled as I entered. He shook his head and chuckled, "There is no need for illusion, nephew. I know I am dying. Myrddyn is an old friend and old friends do not lie to each other." He held his good hand out for his grandson. "And you, Pelas, shed no tears for I have lived a good life and I look forward to seeing my wife, Freja, and my brothers in the Otherworld." He looked up at me. "I am resting only. Myrddyn gave me something for the pain and it makes me sleepy but I will be up and about soon enough. I am well aware that I have let you down and not finished the defences."

"You need not worry about that, uncle. Your son will do all that is needed. Why not return with me to my home? I have a daughter now. Aileen would like you there."

"A kind offer but if I cannot die in Rheged then I will die here where I have lived for most of my life." He held up his hand as I began to speak. "Myrddyn thinks it for the best too. Let an old man go. It will not be soon but I am prepared."

The three of us spoke for some time. If you had asked me, as soon as I had left the chamber, what about, I would not have been able to tell you. We just spoke. Most of the time, I was remembering him as the rock on which my father had depended. He was my father's half brother but seemed closer than Raibeart had been. Perhaps that was *wyrd* for it had been Raibeart's son who had slain my father.

The next morning, I spoke first with Aengus and Lann Aelle. "We must make this into a citadel. When the Northumbrians come the islanders will flee here. Lay in food and make sure you have a good water supply. The well of Ffynnon y Wrach has never let us down but we need to build a cistern to catch the autumn rains. It cannot hurt."

"You think it will come to that?"

"I do cousin, and even if they do not come this year then they will the next so let us prepare for the worst and then we can be relieved when it does not come to pass."

I left and took Llenlleog and Pelas to the port. Old Gwynfor had died some years ago but Gwynfor ap Gwynfor, Daffydd's younger brother, was an able harbourmaster. As it happened Daffydd was in port. It was he who greeted me. "Warlord, I have just returned from the land of the Bro Waroc'h. I have four more mares for you. They were happy to trade them for the blue stones."

"Good. Next time you go take some gold and see if you can get a stallion. It does not need to be one of the better ones. A young one would be acceptable."

Llenlleog laughed. "You would not prise one from the horse master. You were granted one of the great sires. I would not expect more."

"I will Warlord." Daffydd knew me well and sensed that I had more than that on my mind. "What is it, Warlord?"

"We need to keep an eye on the Northumbrians. I fear an attack. I have asked for a jetty to be built close to the fort."

"It is not a good anchorage. Porthdafarch is better."

"I know but I need somewhere inside the defences. Have we a spare boat?"

Gwynfor said, "A couple of fishing smacks and the Saxon ship Aengus used."

"I want a good crew for the Saxon ship." I looked at Daffydd. "Did we name it?" He shook his head, "Then that might explain why we did not do better on Manau. The gods do not like such things."

"I know Warlord. We did not remember."

"Then name her '*Aelle*' after my uncle. I would have her crewed by good and reliable sailors. She is to be used to communicate with me on the Clwyd. I wish her to travel back and forth passing messages."

"Is that all?"

"It may be the most important task of all. Have the fishing smacks watch for the Saxons. When they begin to stir then let me know! And we will need another ship like '*Gwynfor*'. I would have more trade with our allies and a means of moving people from one part of our land to another."

I could see that they were both worried. Daffydd asked, "How is your uncle?"

I paused and glanced over to Wyddfa. "He is dying."

"That explains much. Fear not, Warlord, we will not let you down."

"And I would not have you two sacrificed. If things become desperate then get to the fort. I need both of you and your people. Take the mares to the Clwyd and tell Pol that I will be here for a little longer."

As we rode back Pelas asked, "Are things that bad, Warlord?"

"I do not know but I am Warlord and it is up to me to find solutions to problems that we have yet to meet."

I stayed another two weeks and I only left when I saw that the jetty and the cistern had been built. The farmers all came to see me to complain about my high handed attitude and the removal of half of their grain. I was not gentle with my words and I spoke to them as naughty children caught stealing cakes from the fire.

"If you had done as I commanded and improved your defences then I would not need to do so. You have done nothing! The Northumbrians could take this island with one warband. I am trying to save you by keeping one half of your grain safe. It is not for us. It is for you. If the Saxons have it then we suffer and they gain. Your crops are gathered. Prepare for the worst!"

"You are abandoning us?"

"No, but I am no longer close and even with my horsemen it will take some time to come to your aid. The Saxons will fall but it will take some time to bring that about. It will become darker before the sun rises once more."

Pelas was tearful as we parted from his grandfather. "You can stay here, you know. Llenlleog can be my squire until…."

He shook his head, "No Warlord. That would upset both my father and my grandfather. I am a man now and must bear it like a man."

By the time we reached home I had been away for a month and the weather was turning wintry. My daughter had changed. She cried when she saw me. I was upset until Aileen laughed and said, "You look like a bear! Trim your beard and tie your hair back. She will soon smile at you again!"

I had too much to do and I decided to wait until I had seen Pol. He was happier than I had seen him in sometime. "The horses have foaled! They look to be just like their sire. This is good, Warlord. And the new mares look to be fine too." He seemed to see that I was less than happy. "What ails you, Warlord?"

"I fear we may lose Mona."

"But it is well defended and the Northumbrians have been hurt."

"No, it is not well defended. We have one fort which can withstand an attack but the rest is like a ripe apple ready to be plucked from the tree. As for the Northumbrians; Edwin is cunning. He did not throw away his men when we fought him last summer. He took his losses and withdrew. Aella is undamaged. They will come. I want the new equites assimilating as soon as possible into the ranks. We divide them into banners under a leader: Kay, Bors, and Lann Aelle; each of them can lead a third of the horsemen. Llenlleog can lead the squires."

"But he is not of our people."

"But he is of our heart."

"And what of me?"

"You will command the equites. I am Warlord now. Visiting with my uncle has made me remember that. We need granaries building for the grain I sent over from Mona. As of now we are on a war footing." I rubbed my chin. "And now I will make myself look less frightening to my daughter. The beard will come off."

Chapter 16

The '*Aelle*' began her journeys back and forwards from Caer Gybi to the Clwyd. I think her captain, Dai ap Daffydd and her crew wondered if I had taken leave of my senses for they merely reported mundane events such as the arrival of trading ships or progress on the construction of our new ship. I was more than happy for such dull events to be the sole source of news. It meant that the Northumbrians were not yet ready to attack. If we could make it to Yule without an attack then I would breathe easier until spring. Yule was still many days hence.

We had discovered that the '*Aelle*' would return every three days. In an emergency they could have managed it sooner. On one of their visits I used the boat to sail to Deva and speak with Gawan. I needed to tell him about our uncle and my fears. Perhaps not surprisingly he was aware of the events. He did not know the specifics but his dreams had told him of danger. It reassured me and I returned to the Clwyd happier than I had been. I knew or I hoped that I had done all that I could to avert disaster.

When '*Aelle*' sailed into the estuary just one day after she had left us I knew that the Northumbrians had struck. I was alerted by my sentry as soon as she was sighted and I was by the small jetty before Dai even had the sail lowered.

"The Northumbrians, Warlord, they have taken the north coast of Mona! Caer Gybi is under siege."

"Have the boat readied. We sail for the fort as soon as I am dressed."

I ran back to my hall. "Pelas, Llenlleog get my weapons we sail now. Have Llewellyn join us."

Aileen looked up at me. I saw fear in her eyes but her voice was calm as she spoke. "What is it, husband?"

"Mona is under attack. I go to save what I can."

"I will have quarters prepared. You will leave Pol in command?"

I kissed her. "You know my mind better than I do."

Myrddyn was aware of the noise. I told him what had happened. He did not seem surprised. "This is *wyrd*. Aelle will die with a sword in his hand and will not waste away. Like your father he will be sacrificed to save his people." He put his hand on my arm. "Do not waste warriors. Save all that you can Warlord. This is not the end. I will watch over your family and Pol can defend your home. Return safely." He reached into the folds of his clothes. He handed me three small pots. "These may come in handy. You know how to use them?" I nodded.

The activity had alerted Pol. He met me as I went to meet Pelas and Llenlleog. "The Saxons have landed and Caer Gybi is under siege."

"Do you want the equites preparing?"

"Just one banner. Send Kay to the Narrows. Hopefully the people will flee there. Send Daffydd with twenty archers too but make ready here. This may be the opportunity for Edwin to launch a surprise attack. I want messages taking to Gawan and Cadwallon. They need to be made aware of the danger."

"And you? What will you do, Warlord?"

"I will organise the defence on the island. I know Lann Aelle is more than capable but the sight of my banner, sword and shield may help rally the people."

"But you think we have lost the island."

"We could hang on to Ynys Mon; of that I am certain, but what would be the point? The anchorage is unsafe and it is a barren rock." Pol nodded. "We knew this day might come once the Northumbrians gained Manau. At least we have half of the grain and hopefully we may have saved some more."

Daffydd joined us as we hurried down to the ship. "Give me ten archers to act as guards, Captain, Pol commands until I return."

"Aye Warlord." Daffydd was just like his father, Miach. Nothing ever upset him. He was always calm even in such testing situations.

As soon as we were aboard Dai set sail. "Shall we sail through the Narrows, Warlord?"

"No for I need to see the threat to Caer Gybi."

"There were many Saxon ships. We may be in danger."

"I am not meant to die at sea besides we are a Saxon ship and they may take us for one of their own." I could see he was not convinced. "Is this not better than ferrying empty messages back and forth?"

He laughed, "Aye Warlord."

I turned to the archers and my three companions. "Keep hidden until I tell you. When we are seen then we will show our teeth."

We were half way to our destination and the light was fading. One of the crew shouted, "Sail ho!" He pointed to the north.

Dai said, "Should we put on sail and try to lose them?"

"No, let us sail as though we were one of their own. Lower your sail a little and let them catch us."

I could see that they had enough men on the other ship to use oars and they were powering through the sea to reach us. They were suspicious.

"Archers ready your bows. When they close I want all of the men by their steering board killing. Then kill the rowers." The leader of the archers was Aidan. I handed him one of the pots. When we are close have this thrown and then use a fire arrow." He nodded, he had used one before. He began to prepare a fire arrow. Fire was dangerous on any ship but my men had practised this and knew what to do.

I turned to my three warriors. "Hopefully we will have nothing to do but have your weapons ready in case my plan fails."

Llenlleog looked confused, "What plan? We will loose arrows and hope to discourage them?"

Llewellyn laughed, "Watch young warrior and you will see the mind of the Warlord and the magic of Myrddyn."

I heard the Saxon captain shouting as he neared us. "Who are you and where are you bound?"

I wore no helmet and my cloak hid my distinctive mail. I had no beard now and I would not be recognised. "We are the '*Aelle*' and we are late."

It was a confusing answer and I saw the captain look at the warrior next to him. They were just a hundred paces from us. "Late for what?" I did not answer. "Lower your sail and let me see your face close up."

"Aye!" I turned to Dai and said, quietly, "Lower the sail but be ready to raise it as soon as I give the command."

I watched as the rowers on one side of the Saxon ship withdrew their oars. Obligingly they stood as they lowered them to the deck. "Now!"

My archers stood and loosed. They were so close that all six Saxons close to the stern fell as the twenty arrows struck them. My archers were so quick that they managed to hit some of the rowers before they dropped for their own weapons.

"Dai, hoist the sail. Aidan now."

One of his men hurled the pot of Greek fire towards their stern and then he and three of his archers loosed fire arrows. As the wind caught our sail and sent us west, the whole of the stern of the ship erupted in a sheet of flames. It caught the sail which also began to burn. I saw two men who had been unwounded close to the stern throw themselves overboard to try to douse their burning bodies. It would be in vain. By the time we were three hundred paces from the fire the Saxon ship was sinking beneath the waves. I saw the flailing arms of the handful of survivors. Soon they would drown.

Llenlleog came over to me. "What was that?"

"A little something which Myrddyn picked up in Constantinopolis."

Night fell but it brought us no solace for, as we passed Caer Gybi we could see, by the light of the burning buildings, that there were Saxons in the town. We were too late.

Dai said, sadly, for it had been his home, "Should I sail around the headland, to the fort?"

"No. Head to the beach to the south of the port. I have not finished with the Northumbrians."

The beach was hidden from the town but was just thirty paces from the anchorage of the Saxon ships. They had anchored away from the burning buildings and the ten ships were lashed together.

"Wait here, Dai. Aidan, bring your archers. Llewellyn, stay here. You may need to take charge."

"Aye Warlord."

We waded ashore. I had one more of the precious pots with me. My archers held their bows above their heads. Once we reached the beach I led ten of the archers while Aidan prepared his arrows. The dark of the east was behind us so that we were invisible. I saw the crews aboard the Saxon ships and they were busy watching the fighting which was still taking place. I had to steel myself for they were my people who were fighting and dying.

"Pelas and Llenlleog, I want one of you on each end of the line. We protect the archers."

"You are going to burn their ships?"

"I am. They may have the island but they will not be able to move from it."

Aidan came up with his arrows. I nodded to the ships. "I will get closer to the ships and I will throw the pot."

Aidan said, "Let one of my men do this, Warlord. It is dangerous."

I smiled, "I know but it is my choice."

I slipped down to the small wall which ran along the harbour. There was a coracle drawn up. I knew that there would be others close by. I had used one before. I sat in it and placed the pot in the bottom. Using my hands I began to paddle out to the nearest Saxon ship. I knew that I would be under observation from my men. I just had to remain unseen by the guards. They obliged by watching the fighting from the other side of the ship. I took out the stopper and then threw the pot high so that Aidan would see it.

As it clattered to the deck, and I began to paddle back to safety, one of the sentries came to look at the cause of the noise. Aidan's first arrow struck the mast. The sudden illumination shone on me. As the other arrows showered down and set fire to the ship two of the Saxons hurled themselves into the sea and set off in pursuit. I paddled as fast as I could. I had a good view of the ship as the fire took hold and flames raced up the mast and then leapt to the next ship. Already the other crews were desperately trying to free the others. I saw a hand grasp the coracle. I took my sword and slashed down. I struck the fingers and saw two of them drop into the coracle but the blow split the fragile boat and the coracle began to take on water.

The second man leapt into the boat and we overturned. My armour took me down. I was still some twenty paces from shore and safety. It was pitch black. I started to panic and then I heard my father's voice in my head. '*The sword came from the water. Trust in the sword.*' I remembered the story he had told of throwing the sword into the water and finding it without searching for it. I grasped the hilt tighter and lifted it. As I did so I felt it sink into the body of the man who was trying to reach me.

I began to walk. It was hard for I had my armour on but that, strangely kept me upright. I wondered if I was doomed to drown. I kept hold of the sword for my father's voice had told me to trust it. I took another three steps and felt my lungs were about to burst. I still held the sword aloft and that was what saved me. I felt the sword rising and pulling me with it. This was Myrddyn's magic! As my head broke through the surface I saw the flaming ships and the terrified faces of Aidan and his archers who were holding Saxon Slayer. As they dragged me ashore Aidan said, "We thought you were dead and then we saw Saxon Slayer rising from the water. It was a sign and we pulled it up. Thank the Allfather you were holding on to it!"

"Hurry, Warlord! They are sending warriors." Llenlleog's voice was filled with a mixture of awe and urgency.

By the time we were aboard our ship we could see that almost three quarters of the Saxon ships had been damaged or sunk. Aella now knew that we still had teeth. I hoped my people would know that they had not died in vain.

I scrambled back aboard our ship. My two companions helped me out of my armour and covered me with my cloak. I was lost in my thoughts. Saxon Slayer had saved me. That was *wyrd*. I now knew that my sword would return to water at the end. There was some satisfaction in that. I huddled in my cloak and I slept. As I slept images flashed before me. There were dragons and there were Saxons. I saw wolves and I saw swords. But each image ended with me falling down a long tunnel and then the next image came into view. I was shaken awake.

"Warlord, we are here!"

I stood, helped by Llewellyn. We were at the fort. I saw '***Gwynfor***' and the fishing smacks. I also saw that someone had put guards upon the jetty. We still had control. "Prepare to sail as soon as your ship is loaded. We will have to send the people to my home."

"Aye Warlord."

As we headed up to the hall I heard voices shouting, in the dark, "It is the Warlord, he has come! We are saved!"

I waved my arm but they were neither safe nor saved. Lann Aelle strode to meet with me. I saw that he was bloody. "It is good to see you, Warlord. You were right."

"I wish that I had been wrong, cousin. Is that your blood or have they attacked here already?"

"They did. It was early in the morning." He pointed to the east. "They came over the bridge and surprised the fort. If it was not for Captain Tuanthal we would have lost the last gate."

"He is a good warrior. Where is he?"

He shook his head. "He saved us but he is dead. He and his sons died defending the gate so that the others could reach the inner ward."

He was the last of my father's warriors. I closed my eyes and said, quietly, "Your last warrior comes to you now, Father; he served you to his dying breath."

Lann Aelle just nodded as I opened my eyes. "What do we do, Warlord?"

"How many farmers and islanders made it inside the walls?"

"Over a hundred."

I nodded, "I destroyed many of their ships. We must get them to the mainland as soon as we can. I have the Narrows protected. If any fled east they should be safe. Gather them near to the hall and I will speak with them."

As he hurried off I said, "Pelas, find Daffydd ap Gwynfor; I must speak with him. Llenlleog and Aiden take the archers and guard the gates. That is where they will attack."

When they had disappeared I began to work out what we would do. I strode to the hall and saw my uncle. He had on his mail and his helmet. "What are you doing uncle?"

He smiled, "What else should I do? I am defending my home and my land. I have spent my whole life doing so. You would not have me stop now would you?"

I knew then that I could not expect him to wait to die in his bed. He was my father's brother. "Of course not."

He nodded and swept his hand towards the people who were coming towards us. "And what of them?"

"What do you think?"

"I think that, despite their indolence, you will offer them salvation and that you and your warriors will die to buy them that time."

Daffydd trotted up to me, "I hear you have destroyed the Saxon ships?"

"Some of them."

He nodded, "Then my family is avenged."

"Your brother stayed?"

"He said he owed it to father." He shook his head. "I have no home now."

"You do, Daffydd. You shall make my home yours. Now go to your ship for we must ferry these folk back to the Clwyd."

"I cannot carry them all."

"You do not need to. We have *'Aelle'* and we can make as many voyages as it will take. Do not overload the ships I would have them safe. We will buy you time."

He bowed, "Aye, Warlord."

When the people arrived before me, they stood in silence. I saw some of the farmers who had moaned about having to defend their own land. Even Garth ap Griffith was silent now. I did not berate them for their earlier attitude. It would have done no good instead I spoke calmly and slowly so that they all understood what I was telling them.

"The Northumbrians are here. Your farms have been taken. I do not have enough men to take them back for you. I would just be throwing away the equites it has taken years to train. We will fight the invader. I will punish them but Mona cannot be defended by a hundred horsemen and fifty archers." Silence washed over them.

One woman said, querulously, "What can we do Warlord?"

"There is land along the Clwyd valley. There are few farmers there. The slopes of Wyddfa can be cleared and sheep raised but you cannot raise the grain that you raised here." I shook my head. "The land is wrong. There is better land to the north and the east of the Clwyd but you would have to fight for it."

The woman glared at her husband, "We will fight for it, Warlord! We have seen what results from indolence."

There was a collective cheer. "You are all agreed?"

There was a chorus of *'Ayes'*.

"There are two ships here. You will not all fit on them but they will return as many times as is needed to take you all to safety."

The woman, who had been speaking for the others, seemed to realise the import of her words. "And what of the Saxons? Will they just let us leave?"

"My men and the warriors will defend this place until you are safely away. You had best start now. Dawn will be upon us soon."

As families began to drift towards the jetty the woman came up and kissed my hand. "Thank you, Warlord. We should have heeded your words." I nodded.

I went to the ramparts. Lann Aelle was there with his father. I could see the burning in the distance which marked the end of Caer Gybi. The ditch before me showed where the first Northumbrians to attack had been slain. They would come again in the dawn. All the warriors who had come ashore in the boats we had burned would be eager to destroy this symbol of our world. Tuanthal and his sons had abandoned the outer ward. We now had the middle ward, which led to the jetty and the inner ward. It was a large area.

"How many men do we have?"

"Counting the twenty three you brought we have fifteen Hibernians and thirty warriors."

"Aengus is still here?"

"He is."

"We will need to hold the middle ward as long as we can. So long as they do not come from the west we can hold them." I suddenly remembered the stables. "Are the horses still here?"

Lann Aelle said, "Aye. "There are twenty of them."

"Good for I have a plan. Have all the men eat and then send whatever supplies are left to the jetty. I want this place burned to the ground before we go. Have the horses brought out to the middle ward. I want all the seal oil and pig fat we can find and I want it placed around the inner ward and the hall."

Aelle asked, "What do you plan?"

"We will be attacked today and we will repulse them. It will cost us many men but we will do it. The ships can be back tonight to take off the rest of the people. Before we leave we will fire the buildings and the walls. They will have to build anew if they are to use this ancient hill fort. Those who are left will either sail out on the fishing smacks or ride to glory with me."

Lann Aelle nodded his approval. His father shook his head, "Ride through the Saxons and across the island? It would be madness."

"Nonetheless that is what we shall do. Now go and attend to the tasks I have set up. Send Aengus to me." I looked at the hall. It was now surrounded by innocuous looking barrels and amphorae. It would be the last trick I would play.

I was left with my uncle. He stared to the east. Soon dawn would begin and we would see Wyddfa.

He leaned on my arm as we walked back to the hall. "The Saxons have driven me from every home I had. When my mother and I fled to Stanwyck and your father took us in I hoped that would be home and then we were driven from Stanwyck. My home at Wide Water was perfect and we were driven from there. You and your father saved us. I will not move from here." I nodded. "I know that you will watch over my son and my grandson." He smiled, "You are so much like your father it frightens me. When I see him in the Otherworld I will tell him that he can be proud of you." There were no words. "I will wait by the hall. Sound the buccina when you leave. I know what to do." He put his one good arm around me and hugged me.

He shuffled along the ramparts to the hall and I knew that he would help to buy us the time to escape. It was *wyrd*. He had been saved for this one moment. He was dying and yet, in his death, would come salvation for the men of Rheged.

Chapter 17

Dawn had broken by the time a weary Aengus joined me at the gate. Pelas, Llenlleog and Llewellyn stood with me. "Aengus, I want you to go back on the next ship. I need you in the Clwyd Valley."

He shook his head, "I swore an oath, Warlord, and I will stay by your side."

"No, you will not. You swore an oath and that means you obey me." I softened my voice. "When I leave I will be on a horse. If you are with us we will have to go more slowly. I need you in my fort for you will be the Steward and the protector of my family. This is *wyrd* for you abducted my wife and now you will be her guardian. I will be away from home more than I will be there and I need my family protecting. Lann Aelle and my uncle have told me how hard you work and I would use those skills."

He nodded, "I feel I have failed you; again."

"You have not. I will save as many of your men as I can and they will be on either the fishing smacks or the *'Aelle'*. Now go for you will need to help load the ship."

We watched as the Northumbrians began to move into position. They could not know that we had supplemented the garrison with twenty archers. They would be our surprise for them. They would expect that the farmers and islanders were still within the walls. His warriors would be anticipating slaughter and rape. I turned to my three companions. "We will be the last to leave, along with Lann Aelle. Pelas, your job will be to ensure that there are five horses for us. Stay by me until I send you for them. Llenlleog, bring the archers here but have them hide beneath the ramparts and Llewellyn prepare the dragon banner. When I bring out my shield they will know whom they fight and I hope to draw them here."

Lann Aelle brought the Hibernians to the walls and spread them out. The rest of the garrison was guarding the eastern wall of the middle ward. If that fell then all was lost. At least everyone had eaten and was full. There was not a scrap of food left within the walls and the last two boat loads of islanders and the food were waiting at the jetty. Six islanders who could sail were waiting by the fishing smacks to take off any of the warriors who survived. I did not think it would be many.

Lann Aelle said, "I did not think it would come to this, Warlord. It tastes like defeat."

"There is no defeat until every warrior of Rheged lies dead. So long as one walks away we are undefeated." Just then I heard the Northumbrian horns as they began their attack.

"Got to your places and remember we have to buy enough time for the boats to take off the rest of the islanders."

"Aye, Warlord."

The Saxons were using a wedge to advance across the uneven ground toward the gate. Their leader must have assumed that we had no arrows as the garrison had not used them the day before. I glanced down at Aidan and his men. "Are you ready, Aidan."

"I am."

"Llewellyn, the banner." As the banner was unfurled I swung my shield around so that they could see my wolf shield. I drew my sword and yelled, "Aella, I am the Warlord of Rheged! Behold Saxon Slayer. It has killed many kings, princes and champions. It will kill you. Will you meet me in single combat?"

As his men halted and turned around I knew that I had bought a little time. A heavy set figure in full mail with a war axe and a shield with three red legs painted upon it stepped forward. He raised his helmet so that I could see his face. "I need not fight you, Warlord, for you have no horsemen here. You just have the Hibernians I threw from my island. We will take this fort and decorate it with your heads."

His men began to laugh. "Aidan, now!"

The twenty archers stood and loosed their arrows. Even while the arrows were falling onto surprised faces a second and a third flight were released. The chief next to Aella fell with an arrow piercing his eye. Aella shouted, "Treachery!" And the whole warband lurched forward without any sense of order. Every warrior who did not have a bow had a sling and the Saxons were assailed by so many missiles that they all had to hide behind their shields. My uncle had ensured that every ditch was well sown with lillia and the Saxons screamed as they were impaled on them while trying to clear the ditch. A few made it to the wall where they were speared like stranded fish. The Northumbrian horn drew them back out of arrow range.

The ditch and the outer ward were filled with the dead and the wounded. We left the wounded to moan and to shout. It would make their fellows more reckless.

"Llenlleog, take ten archers and watch the west wall. Aella may try to attack from that direction although the cliffs are steep."

The Northumbrians regrouped. I saw Aella, now well out of arrow range as he spoke with his chiefs. "Well done Aidan. When you run out of arrows I want you down at the jetty."

"We would fight with you, Warlord."

"You are too valuable to lose and you will obey me."

"Aye, Warlord."

It was early afternoon by the time they were ready for their next attack. One of the boy slingers, who had remained, came racing to me. "Warlord, your equite says they are attacking the west wall."

"Are they being held?"

"Aye, Warlord."

"Then go back and help them. If they are in danger then come to me."

The attack on the west wall coincided with the next attack on the gate. This time they made a solid shield wall. My archers had to try to pick their targets. Fewer Saxons died but their progress was slow as they tried to maintain their lines of shields. Once they reached the ditch and began to clamber over the bodies of their dead comrades we managed to kill and wound a few more but there were still more than a hundred of them at the gate. They began to hack at the gate with their axes.

"Pelas, Llewellyn and Lann Aelle come with me. Aidan, take command here. When your arrows are finished then get to the ships. We will be safe."

As we readied ourselves behind the gate I heard a shout go up, "The ships are returned."

"Pelas go and secure the horses." I shouted up to Aidan. "The ships are here prepare to fall back on my command."

The Northumbrians were now attacking at all points around the walls. We held the advantage so long as we held the ramparts but once the gate fell then we would lose. I glanced behind me and saw my uncle leaning still against the hall. He was illuminated by the burning torch he was holding. He saw me and waved. Lann Aelle asked, "What is my father doing?"

"What he has always done; serving Rheged."

The gates were well made and it was not easy for the Saxons to break through. The archers and men with slings were cutting down those who wielded the axes and it slowed their progress. One of Daffydd's seamen ran to me. "Warlord we are boarded and we can take more men."

"How many?"

"Ten."

"Aidan, how many men are out of arrows?"

"Six."

"Send them to the ship and send four of the Hibernians with them."

"Aye, Warlord."

"Tell the captain to sail!"

The sailor ran off. The loss of ten men made the progress of destruction faster. "Aiden get the men from the walls. Have your archers join us. Send a messenger to tell Llenlleog to come here too."

As the men ran down to us I shouted to the garrison, "Sail the smacks. Save as many men as you can but do not wait for us. May the Allfather be with you!"

The Northumbrians broke through with a rush. Aidan's archers loosed their arrows and then the three of us ran forward with our swords swinging. I took the head of a chief who lost his balance close to me. Lann Aelle was fighting with a fury which terrified me and the Northumbrians were being forced back. The gate was wide enough for five men only and between the arrows and our blades no one could face us. When Llenlleog joined us we managed to push them back towards the ditch. I saw another wedge forming. "To the horses and the boats!"

We turned and ran. As we neared the hall I saw Aelle wave his torch in salute and then he plunged it into the hall. He drew his sword as flames suddenly leapt up the walls. A trail of fat and oil had been laid and it raced across the open ground towards the ramparts. The wooden walls burst into flames. We reached Pelas who looked in awe as the flames took hold. We grabbed our reins. Lann Aelle looked to his father and was about to race towards him when we saw him run towards the advancing warband and hurl himself into their midst. He slew two before he was hacked and cut down before our eyes.

I turned to my cousin. "He died well!" Lann Aelle nodded. "And now follow me." I turned and saw that the archers were mounted and the rest were on the jetty. The fishing smacks were being loaded. Even as I watched the jetty was set on fire and I saw the sails of the overloaded boats heading south. Before we were surrounded we needed to break through. I kicked hard and drew, from my tunic, the last pot of Greek fire. As we galloped towards the gate I hurled it to the right, where the flames had caught hold of one of the towers. A wall of flames erupted up and out. I saw Aella engulfed in flames. The men at the gate ran to douse the flames consuming their leader and his oathsworn. We barged through them with swords, spears and maces bringing death and destruction. Suddenly we were through and I led my tiny band of warriors towards the bridge which led to Mona proper. If the Northumbrians had left it we had a chance and if not we would all die when the Northumbrians saw that we were trapped.

I knew the land as well as any and we rode down the rocky valley which hid us from our enemies. We rode through groups of wounded warriors. They could nothing about us but just stare. When we reached the narrow neck of land I saw that the bridge remained and it was unguarded. We galloped across it. I halted the column. In the distance I saw the Northumbrians racing after us.

"Find kindling. Aidan, fire the bridge." It was a race against time. There was plenty of dead gorse and it burned well. Aidan's flint sparked and the gorse began to burn. Three of his archers still had arrows and they began to pick off those brave enough to step on to the bridge. As soon as the fire had taken hold of the wooden bridge we mounted and rode east. The bridge would fall and the Northumbrians would have to descend to the sea and cross the narrow straits. It would take time. Night was falling and I hoped to disappear. We would ride our horses until they fell and then we would run. Mona was no longer our island. It was Northumbrian.

I led us towards the Roman road. It was the quickest way off the island and it was the route with the least opportunity for ambush for it ran straight. Our problem was that the light was behind us and we were riding into darkness. Lann Aelle rode next to me.

When I glanced at him I saw that his face was a mask of fury. I remembered my anger when my father had died. I had taken my revenge on Morcar. I pitied any Saxon who had to face my cousin this night. After two hours of hard riding we halted.

"Llenlleog, ride up the road and see if it is clear."

He had proved to be reliable and calm. Lann Aelle was too upset as was Pelas who had just witnessed his grandfather being butchered.

Aidan approached me. "We lost three archers, Warlord."

"You and your men did well."

"All of them would have died for you."

I put my arm around him, "I would that they would live for me."

After we had rested and adjusted our girths we set off. I had no idea how many Saxons were on the island. I was counting on the fact that the bulk of them would have been attacking our fort. I knew that the fort at the Narrows would have been a target and as we neared the eastern end of the island I slowed us down to a walk. Suddenly my horse neighed. There was someone ahead. I silently drew my sword as did the others. I waved my arms to spread them out and we edged slowly forward.

"Warlord, is that you?"

It was Kay and my equites. We had reached safety.

"Is the fort held still?"

"Aye, Warlord. There are men of the Cymri there now."

"Then we had better warn them that they are all that remain on the island. It has fallen."

We rode to the pontoon raft which would ferry us to the mainland and safety. To many this would be a defeat for we had fled with our tails between our legs but to me it was a victory. We had saved the people and denied the Northumbrians the riches of Mona. They would have to begin anew and they would have a winter without food. We would begin again and try, once more to regain the land of Rheged. Mona had been a respite but that was all. Our life on Mona had been a brief but rich interlude. Soon it would change its name and become the Angle Sey.

I reached my home not long after my ships had disgorged both their passengers and their cargo. There were many people milling around as my wife organised their beds. There was a huge cheer as my band of heroes rode in. I saw the faces of the farmers who had questioned my request for warriors. Now there was gratitude.

As I dismounted Aileen came to me and hugged me. "I am proud of you husband, you have done well. The people speak of you as a king!"

"But I am just Warlord." I held her tightly and said, quietly, in her ear, "Aelle is dead."

She nodded as though she new and it was no surprise, "It is *wyrd*. He died well?"

"Aye he died well and it was not the sickness which took him. He had a sword in his hand and he is with his brother even now."

"Good." She took my arm and led me up the stairs to the hall, "A messenger came from King Cadwallon. He is on his way here to speak with you."

"That is timely for we need a counsel soon. The world has changed and we have lost the Holy Island."

She smiled, "But we still have Wyddfa and she protects us yet. Come, your daughter is keen to see you."

I quickly washed my bloody hands and face and followed my wife into my hall. The tables and chairs had been piled to one side and some of the refugees lay sleeping. We went into our chambers and there was the slave tending to Myfanwy. As soon as I entered she opened her eyes and began to gurgle. I picked her up. The smell of the fresh clean baby seemed to cleanse my heart. The deaths and the destruction disappeared as I held the child. I know not why but I felt tears coursing down my cheeks. Aileen hurried the slave from the room and sat with her arms around my shoulders as I wept.

"It is unmanly my wife, I am sorry."

"It is right that you grieve. Aelle was a fine man as well as being your uncle. You have also lost Tuanthal and I know how close you were to him."

I looked at her in surprise. "How do you know?"

"The spirits came to me and told me. And Myrddyn knew."

"Where is he?" I had missed being greeted by the old man.

"He is with Gawan and he too will be returning."

When I finally emerged from my hall, dressed and clean I felt much better. I had needed the love and the tears. I could face the world once more. Even though it was late afternoon I set the men who had not fought to chopping wood and clearing ground further up the valley for our refugees. They would need a home for the winter. The grain we had taken from them would now be returned and they would be fed for the winter. The next winter would be harder but we would cross that bridge when we came to it. After I had directed the men I spoke with Pol and told him of the fight.

"So you slew Aella. That is good. He was a wily general."

"There will be others, Pol, and do not forget Oswald and Oswiu. They have been quiet since we raided their lands. I would not expect them to allow us time to rebuild."

As we passed the field with the new horses and foals Pol stopped and pointed. "They are growing well and Wolf has serviced two more mares which came into season. He seems keen to mate."

"Good and we must choose the best young stallion from his line and use him to augment his father's work."

We turned our horses when we reached the top of the valley side and looked back to where the new halls and ramparts were being built. "This will be crowded soon, Warlord."

"It is temporary. We will improve the fort at the head of the valley and find another site along the Dee for a further fort. The Hibernians did well and I will use them to ring us in. Deva is isolated and it will not take Edwin long to realise that and to try to take it."

Over the next three days, visitors, in the shape of Cadwallon and Gawan arrived while the hall emptied as the new halls were thrown up and the families moved out. The women were keen to claim a roof for themselves. Aengus and his men built their own hall attached to our fort. We now had a healthy garrison and Aengus took his new responsibilities seriously. It was a load off my mind. I had larger problems to consider.

The snows came when we finally put the last roof on the last hall. The fort seemed emptier. We were seated around my table, restored to the centre of the hall. My leaders were gathered. Cadwallon sat next to Gawan while Pol and Lann Aelle flanked me. Myrddyn sat alone at the head of the table. Llenlleog and Pelas were the servants for the day and all else were absent at my request. This would be a day for planning.

I had the last amphora of the fortified Lusitanian wine. We had discovered it in the fort on Ynys Mon before we had fled. I had carried it in my bags and, miraculously, it had survived.

"Before we begin let us drink to those who have fallen and remember them. We are fewer in number now but stronger for our dead are with the spirits and they dwell 'neath Wyddfa. They protect us still."

I saw Myrddyn nodding his approval. We raised our beakers and each intoned his own prayer. As we sat Myrddyn said, to the table at large, "At Yule, Gawan and I will visit the tomb to dream." He looked at Lann Aelle, "If you wish to come, Lann Aelle then it would be a good thing."

"I will for I have some of my father's belongings I wish to leave." We waited for he had not finished. "The Warlord gave him a wolf charm as a symbol of his office. He gave it to me when he was ill. It should be returned to the tomb of the Wolf Warrior."

"Good."

"Can I come too?" We all looked around. It was Llenlleog who had spoken. Myrddyn inclined his head and my new equite continued. "In my land I dreamt of Wyddfa. It was why I begged to be allowed to come with the Warlord. All that I have witnessed since I came has confirmed the need to dream in Wyddfa."

There was silence and we all looked to Myrddyn who closed his eyes. When he opened them he smiled and he nodded, "It is *wyrd*. It was meant to be."

King Cadwallon said, "Now we must move on to more pressing matters." I saw the irritated look cross Myrddyn's face. To him the spirit world determined what we did in this mortal one. "What do we do about Mona?"

"Mona is lost. The men who hold the Narrows cannot hold it for long unless you reinforce it."

"But I need all of my men on the eastern border."

"Then you must think about extracting your men from the fort while there is time. If you destroy the pontoon bridge then the Northumbrians will not be able to attack your land."

The king's shoulders slumped. "And what of the grain which Mona produced?"

"We saved most of it and we can feed the people for this winter. As for next year... we need new farmlands which will support the grain."

He suddenly sat upright, "But our land is all upland! It is good for animals only!"

I sighed. We had thought all of this through already. Instead of discussing our strategy we were looking for farmland but I explained anyway. "The valley of the Dee and the Maeresea are both fertile. They are well watered and will support wheat, barley and oats."

"But they are in Northumbrians hands."

"Some are and some are under the control of Gawan. I intend to build another fort along the Dee and try to gain control of those lands with my horsemen. The land suits us and we frighten the Northumbrians."

"And what would you have me do?"

"You and Penda must convince King Ceorl of the need to attack Edwin and keep his focus there."

"But are we strong enough to bring him to battle?"

"With Penda and his men and the support of King Ceorl, I believe so."

"What if King Ceorl will not supply his warriors?"

"It matters not so long as King Edwin believes that they may come to our aid. Negotiate so that even if does not fight he agrees to respect and protect your borders. I believe we can trust his word."

"He has done that before."

"And he may do so again. We need a year to train our new horses and secure the border along the Dee. You need to buy a year. It will be a lean year, King Cadwallon. There will not be as much as there was this year but the Northumbrians will suffer as much. Your horsemen can raid Mona when the crops are sown and damage them or they can attack when they are harvested. But you must build up your army."

"We will but it costs money to arm them." I saw him chewing his lip. The loss of Mona had come as a surprise to him even though he had done little to save it. He would have to think more creatively about gaining gold and food.

"Take from the Northumbrians. They have gold enough to adorn Edwin's new churches and monasteries."

He smiled, "I am decided. We will do as you suggest Warlord. In two years' time my son, Cadfan, will be ready to ride to war and I hope he sees glory when we drive the Northumbrians hence."

"And I will be happy if we survive another year." The words of the witch still haunted me. She had said that the end was not imminent but how long did we have? I was running out of time. It was a luxury we did not have.

The counsel ended and the King and his son rode south to the Narrows. I had been tempted to offer to help but we had already lost many men in the defence of Mona. It was time for him to take responsibility. I had plans for the next months.

Chapter 18

It was *wyrd*. Even before we had reached our home news came that King Ceorl had died... in his bed. Penda was now king. We had our allies. We would have a much larger and stronger army. The Mercians hated the Northumbrians and Penda loathed and despised King Edwin; not least because he was a Christian and had abandoned the old ways.

Yule was just a week away and I was preparing for bed. Aileen had just put Myfanwy into her cot and, as she turned, she said, "Husband, I would go with Myrddyn and the others to visit the dream cave."

I nodded, "And Myfanwy?"

"I wish Myfanwy to come too. In fact the main reason for going is for her to visit the cave where her grandfather is buried."

"Will it be safe for her?"

She looked at me askance, "Safe?"

"It will be cold and she is young and fragile."

Laughing she said, "Babies are more resilient than you know. She will come to no harm. Trust me. It is important that she dreams there as soon as possible and I need to speak with my brother. He has come to me oft times since he died but Myrddyn tells me that the dream cave is the place where I shall see him." She paused, "And I am anxious for our daughter to see and hear her grandfather."

"Not that you need it but you have my blessing. I shall be with Aengus and his men. I am keen to begin work on the new fort."

"You have warriors who can do that for you."

"I know but it is important for me to see the fort erected." I smiled, "I have skills in that area."

She took my hand, "You have skills in many areas. Come."

I took half of my equites, half of Daffydd's archers and the Hibernians when we rode towards Deva. I took Kay with me while Pol watched over my home. Gawan would not be in Deva for he was journeying with the others to Wyddfa but I would call to reassure his wife, Gwyneth, that I was watching over my brother's lands. After speaking with her we followed the river. It turned sharply south and headed towards the land of King Cadwallon's lands. Aed and Dai were scouting ahead. We would not be surprised. We found the site for the castle just sixteen miles from Deva on the old Roman Road they had called Watling Street. There was a ford and a hill which would afford protection for the river crossing. Deva was well protected from the other directions. This was almost like the back door which I would now shut.

"Well Aengus, what think you to your new land?"

"I thought I was to be the steward of your fort on the Clwyd, Warlord?"

"This is a more important task for you. This is between Deva and Wrecsam. With this crossing of the Dee controlled we can hold back the Northumbrians." I pointed to the land before us. "You know the earth, Aengus. Does that not look like it will produce much grain?"

"Aye, Warlord."

"And we have the farmers from Mona who can make it so. We need you and your men to provide a refuge to which they can retire if threatened. My equites will patrol to the east but you will be the rock upon which the Saxons will be crushed."

"Then let us begin."

"Have your men cut down trees from yonder woods. We will work until dark and then return to Deva." He ordered his men to begin work. "Kay, leave ten equites here to watch over the Hibernians."

I led the rest to the east. We were heading into empty lands. The Cymri had fled to the west to avoid the Northumbrians and the land had yet to be settled. I needed to find the closest Northumbrian settlement. Midwinter was the best time for the people would be closeted within doors away from the cold and the damp. We were hardy folk and we would endure the elements.

We passed through one deserted village. Aed thought it was one called Tatenhale. It looked to have been prosperous at one time but all we saw were burnt out huts and discarded bones. There was an even smaller hamlet to the south. We thought that was the extent of Northumbrian settlement until Dai rode in and said that he had found a defended village. He led us through woods and across deserted fields until we found ourselves looking up at the ramparts of a small hill fort. Dai pointed to the north. "There is a river which runs from the north and passes along the other side of the fort."

"Can the river be forded?"

"Aye, Warlord. It is not deep."

"I wonder why the Northumbrians built it on this side then?"

"That is easy, Warlord; they have taken over a village of the Cymri and the land on the other side is flatter. There are salt pits there."

"Salt? Then it is valuable. Go with Aed and see if you can ascertain numbers."

When they had gone Pelas asked, "Will you take it?"

"I am thinking of that, squire. It is just sixteen or so miles from Aengus' Ford. The land here is good farmland and there is salt. We will wait until our scouts have reported."

That evening we rested at Deva where we provided the food for our hostess; my men had hunted on the way back and brought down two hinds. We ate well. We also discovered the name of the village which had salt pits; it was Namentwihc. That was valuable information.

I spoke with my leaders, "We will build the ramparts and dig the ditch on the morrow."

Aengus nodded, "The weather has yet to turn too cold to dig. We can work the earth. If we all work then we can have the walls and ditch finished in a few days."

I laughed, "You mean if my equites join you?"

He nodded, "I did not want to say, Warlord. I know that your equites are fine warriors."

"They are not afraid of hard work, neither is your Warlord."

He looked shocked, "I would not expect you to work Warlord."

"I will do. We will not be needed to attack the salt village until the weather improves. Aed says that they looked to be poor folk. It will not take much to capture it and I do not want Edwin to know of our presence on his borders. I want to have this fort built before we do anything. We will take that before we raid his lands to the north."

It took us seven days to finish the walls and cut the wood for the halls. I left Aengus with ten of my archers while we returned to my fort to send carts with the food and weapons they would need for the hard winter ahead. They would have plenty of time to improve the defences and make their home habitable. With luck the Saxons would not even know that they were there until the spring and by then we would be that much stronger.

The dreamers had returned by the time we reached the Clwyd and the weather had begun to turn. Aengus had been lucky. A delay of a few days would have meant the ground became too hard to put the posts in. As it was they had a roof over their heads and they had even built the fire pit so that they could cook. All of the ones who had been in the cave looked thoughtful; even Myrddyn. I knew why he had been affected; it would be his tomb when he went to the Otherworld. I did not press with questions. They would each tell me in their own way and their own time. I sent the carts of Aengus, protected by some squires and I played with my daughter. I would find out eventually what each had learned of themselves and the future.

As we ate in the hall it was Llenlleog who spoke first. "I will delay my return to my home, with your permission, Warlord."

"Of course but why?"

"I saw a war and I will be needed." He looked at Myrddyn who smiled.

I laughed, "I can see the effect that Myrddyn is having upon you."

Gawan was the next to speak. "I saw our father." I nodded for there was nothing that I could say to that comment. "He is pleased with you, Hogan Lann."

I saw a chorus of nods. "You all dreamt that?"

Aileen touched my hand, "His was the most powerful spirit in the cave. We all saw him and heard him. Even Myfanwy."

"How do you know?"

Aileen smiled, enigmatically, "The dreamers know."

Lann Aelle was the last to speak his thoughts and his voice was the saddest. "And I saw my father too. It was too brief but I am happier. He is in no pain now and he will watch over Pelas and me."

"Then the year has ended well."

"And what of your trip, Warlord?"

Although Myrddyn asked the question the answer was not for him. He already knew it. "We have a fort not far from Deva and it guards the ford over the Dee. The nearest Northumbrians are at

Namentwihc and in the spring I will capture that town. Then we can raid in the heart of Northumbria."

Llenlleog nodded, "That is good for it will bring the men of the north to battle."

"You saw the battle?"

"We did but not when."

Gawan said, "It was in the summer."

"And was I there?"

"And Cadwallon and Penda."

"Then I hope that it is next year for this year we will still be preparing our strength."

"If it is meant to be it will come whether we are ready or not." Myrddyn always believed that events were out of our control. I still believed that we could prepare ourselves for unknown events. Despite what they had all said and their confidence about the future I would rely upon my equites and archers."

We spent the winter watching the horses grow and sheltering from the cold. We even heard wolves that winter, in the high passes. They rarely came this close to humans and we knew that it had been a hard winter. When the weather allowed we travelled to visit with Aengus. He and his men were comfortable enough. We had swollen his garrison to twenty men. Although we sent them food they hunted for themselves too. His men were becoming useful archers. Even in winter he sent them out to explore the land around so that they knew it well.

We started training the first of the new horses as soon as the snows and hard frosts had finished. They would all be bigger than the ones we had already. It meant that some of us would have a spare horse. That would make us a formidable force once more.

King Cadwallon paid us a visit, the month before Eostre. It was a strangely ominous visit. He had lost the Narrows. His watch on the fort at the Narrows had not been careful enough and the Northumbrians had attacked at night; he had lost most of his garrison. Luckily the pontoon bridge had been destroyed but it meant that he would now have to leave more men guarding the straits. He seemed quite depressed.

I took him to the headland overlooking the estuary. From there we could watch both Wyddfa and Mona. "This is the year where we can make a difference, King Cadwallon."

"Perhaps but each time we try to best our enemies we suffer a setback."

"But we are never defeated. I will begin my raids in the next month. We did not manage to raid last year but I promise you that my banner will travel from one end of Northumbria to the other."

"Will you do as last time and head up the western side?"

"No, we will travel east through the heart of his land. I intend to push as far north as I can before he follows me and then I will draw him back to our border forts. Perhaps he will be angry enough to waste men trying to take them."

"Then Penda and I will prepare to repulse him. We will begin the muster of our armies. I know that King Penda is anxious to show King Edwin that he is the High King of the Saxons."

"Be careful of your new ally, my king. When he was the leader of a warband he had no ambitions. If we do defeat Edwin be wary of where he moves his gaze."

"I will heed your advice for, like your father's, it is always wise. When will you return so that we may be ready?

"I will be back by midsummer's eve. That will give our famers the chance to sow crops and harvest the young animals. We will be taking his men from their fields."

"Good. You have heartened me. I will send to Dyfed and to the other kingdoms. Perhaps they will send warriors too."

"I hope so. If we can defeat King Edwin this summer then that may end his threat for all time!"

Now that we had three garrisons guarding our eastern and northern borders I felt happier about leaving my wife. Once again we were mounted and we even managed to take with us fifteen boys who would be both messengers and slingers. Aed and his scouts numbered eight. I left half of Gawan's equites at Deva. They would be able to respond to an attack from Mona.

We passed the ford at Aengus' fort and pushed on to reach Namentwihc by the early afternoon. The gates were open. "Daffydd I am going to ride through the gates. Circle the town and stop any men from leaving."

I saw the question forming on his lips and then he thought better of it. Giving me a wry smile he said, "Aye Warlord."

Llenlleog was more open, "You will charge through the gates, Warlord?"

I shrugged, "It may work. I can see no guards on the ramparts and the gate is just two hundred paces from the trees. Even with these horses we should reach it but as you have the best horse you have my permission to try to hold the gates for us."

He suddenly grinned, "Why not pretend you are chasing me? Give me a start."

"Aye, we will try that."

He burst from the trees and galloped up the track to the gate. We left almost immediately for he had nearly reached the gates anyway. We thundered after him. I saw that there were men at the gates although there were none on the ramparts. Llenlleog's charge had confused them. For no one would be reckless enough to charge a fort on their own. Llenlleog laid about him with his blade and the two men at the gate were slain. He dismounted and stood in the doorway. As we galloped up a handful of warriors ran at him. As soon as they saw us they turned and fled before they even got close to Llenlleog. The eastern gate was soon jammed with those trying to escape from the fort. Horsemen in armour could only mean one thing; the equites of Rheged and the Warlord.

I turned to Kay and Bors. "Have the men search for carts that we can use and any horses. Osgar, find any food and load the carts when they are found."

Llenlleog stood looking pleased with himself. "Well done, warrior, your action was both clever and courageous."

"Why not chase after the warriors who fled?"

"It will merely tire the horses. They will not escape; Daffydd and his archers await them."

There was not a great deal of food but there were enormous quantities of salt. It was like white gold. "Osgar, tomorrow I want you and the squires to escort this booty to Aengus' Ford. He can distribute it to the other forts when he has the opportunity. We will head north east. You will follow us."

Daffydd returned as night was falling. "There were just twenty Saxon warriors and they all fell to our arrows. The women, children and the old we let pass."

The town was ours. We would have sheltered lodgings and we would eat well. That evening, as we ate, Pelas asked, "Why did you not enslave the women and children?"

"A number of reasons: we would have to escort them back to Deva and that would waste warriors. Slavery is not something I really like for you have enemies in your homes if they are taken from a neighbour but, most importantly, they will flee to other villages and tell them that we are coming."

Llenlleog's mouth dropped open, "You want them to know you are coming?"

I nodded for my mouth was full of food. When I had swallowed I said, "They will go in many directions and they will report a huge army far bigger than the numbers we actually have. It will cause panic and confusion. Many of the villages they flee to will also run and that will muddy the waters for they will all report different numbers. The Northumbrians will hole up in their burghs and send word to Edwin. He will not know where to go. Our scouts are the best and we will avoid his large army and swoop on his smaller warbands. Our aim is to spread terror, fear, and confusion in his land. That way he cannot attack the land of Cymru or our lands. When we do invade, we will do so swiftly and we will use surprise."

We left Namentwihc a burnt out shell when we had taken all that was of value. We headed north east through unfamiliar country. Our scouts kept us informed of the movements of the Northumbrians. We kept more east than north for the land was flatter and there were more farms for us to burn. We knew that King Edwin was mobilising his forces. Aed kept us well informed about what we were likely to encounter. I also knew that we were putting our head further into the jaws of the Northumbrians. I was counting on the speed of my army to withdraw just as quickly.

After another four days of rapid raids heading east I sent Dai and Felan to the north. I hoped that King Edwin and his leaders would be anticipating us continuing east. We would change direction. The move took us to the huge forest which seemed to fill the old land of Elmet. It went from the high divide almost to the coast and the marshy swampy land. The Roman Road went through the middle of it and, as we had never travelled in the area we risked the ride along the road through the forest. It proved to be a disastrous deviation. We were just five miles along the road when Dai came galloping back bleeding from his arm. There was no Felan with him, just his horse. "Turn and flee, Warlord. The forest is filled with Northumbrians. We ran into an ambush!"

I wondered how this had happened for we had moved quickly. They could not have known we were coming. Something was not right. There was little point in trying to work out why and so we turned and galloped back down the road. Had we not been on the road then we would have been slaughtered. The Northumbrians had moved swiftly through the trees along the side of the road as well as on it. Their mailed warriors were running down the road. It suited them for they could fill the road from ditch to ditch. We could be trapped if we tried to attack them. The lightly armed fyrd used the trees. They were able to run easily. They moved almost as quickly as we did for they had no armour. They attacked the squires at the rear of our column. They had caught us quicker than I had anticipated. I heard their screams as the young warriors fell and were butchered.

. "Pol, take command. Lead the men from the forest and wait for us. Bors, turn your men around. We will charge them."

My men were the best trained. They knew that a delay in following orders could be the difference between success and failure.

I whipped Star's head around and rode back through the squires. "Squires, follow Captain Pol!" I saw five riderless horses showing that the Northumbrians had had success. As soon as the last squire had ridden past us I charged the shield wall which formed on the road. I had a long spear with me. Rather than using it to punch I threw it when I was just ten paces from the wall. They were not expecting it and the spear head went into the open mouth of a mailed warrior. He fell and, as Star went through the gap I swung the mace which had been hanging from my saddle and smashed it into the face of the next Saxon. They had not expected me to go on the offensive and the shield wall was only three warriors deep. Star trampled the last warrior and I jerked his head around to the right.

Speed was of the essence. "Destroy the shield wall!"

A shield wall only works with locked shields. We were inside a disordered shield wall. My mace fell upon helmets and leather skullcaps. It was soon covered in blood, brains and gore. The warriors who remained fled into the forest and back along the road.

I reined in Star. We needed to reform. I saw that three of my equites had either been killed or wounded. Even as Bors went to the aid of one the lifeless body of the equite fell from the saddle.

I knew that the road would be filled with the lightly armed warriors we had passed through and they would be ready for us. There was just one alternative; we had to use the forest. "Follow me through the forest."

It was a risk but I guessed that they would gather by the road and expect us to use it for speed. If we rode individually, we could be almost as swift in the forest. I was aware that Lann Aelle was with me along with Pelas. I hoped that Llenlleog had not fallen; he was a good equite. Star picked his way through the forest. You needed quick reactions for Northumbrians would leap from behind trees. I had hung my mace from my saddle and unsheathed Saxon Slayer. It was a faster weapon.

I saw a spear head as it came from behind a tree. I leaned forward and anticipated where the warrior would be. As his head came around I swung my sword and felt it bite into flesh. I swerved to avoid a tree root and went to the left. It saved my life for an axe swung at the empty space I had occupied. I heard a scream as Lann Aelle ended the life of the warrior.

We had only ventured a few miles into the forest and yet the ride south seemed to take forever. When I saw the brightening light ahead I knew that we had made it. We burst from the trees. Daffydd's men were watching for us and they launched a shower of arrows. I heard the shouts as the pursuing Northumbrians fell. We reined in behind the line of spears of Pol and my equites.

The Northumbrians stayed in the forest. To have ventured out would have invited slaughter. Pol said, "Head south, Warlord, and we will cover you!"

It was my turn to obey orders and I led my column of equites to the last village we had attacked. We halted there. Pol and the rest arrived a short time later. He dismounted and joined me. "I set Dai and Aed to watch them," he waved to a warrior who had a bundle on his saddle. It was Osgar. "We have a prisoner."

Osgar dropped the unconscious Saxon to the ground. I saw that he was probably a farmer for he had no mail and just a leather skull cap. He was no warrior. I went to him and began to slap his face.

He awoke and stared in fear at me. I took off my helmet. "You know who I am?"

"You are the Warlord."

"Then know this, I keep my word. If you answer my questions truthfully then you shall live. If not we will open your guts and let the animals of the forest feed on your flesh. Understand?" He nodded. I could see that he was barely fifteen. "How did you come upon us?"

"Warriors reached Caer Daun and said that you were raiding. Eorl Eadfrith led us south to catch you. We were to meet with Eanforth and trap you between us."

"What were you doing at Caer Daun? There were a large number of you. Were you seeking us?"

He hesitated and then said, "We were ordered there after the spring sowing. We were told that King Edwin wanted us mustered. We did not know it was the Warlord we faced." I heard the fear and awe in his voice.

That was ominous and I stored that information but the most important fact was that Eanforth also had warriors. "Where is Eanforth?"

He hesitated, "Life or a slow death- it is your choice."

"He is in the east. That is all I know; I swear."

I nodded, "I believe you now go." I pointed up the road. He ran as fast as he could. I had no doubt that Eanforth and Eadfrith would question him but he could tell them little more than they already knew. The Warlord and his equites were raiding.

When he had gone I said, "We were unlucky. They were gathering ahead of us. They did not know where we were going it was just *wyrd*. It means that King Edwin is gathering his army. He is heading south to face King Cadwallon. Once again he has anticipated us."

Pol said, "What now?"

"We cannot travel either east or north. There are enemies there that we know of. Both would be too dangerous for we would be trapped." I rubbed my chin. "They will expect us to go west. Therefore, we will head south and make our way to Mercia and the lands of King Penda. It will also mean that we can draw them towards the armies that we know are preparing for war."

"Is that safe?"

I shrugged, "I know not but it appears to be the only chance we have. I just hope that the two kings have prepared their armies. I said I would be back by Midsummer's day and it is past that now. Send for Aed, we will ride and put distance between us. Send riders to warn the two kings of the invasion."

Chapter 19

The land to the south had been the land of the Angles. It had been settled for a long time. Here there were more cleared areas and fewer trees. After hours of hard riding we passed through a smaller wood and my scouts found a small Northumbrian burgh. A river ran around one side of it. There were many farms whose smoke we could see as we approached. Our wounded warriors needed somewhere to rest so that we could heal them and our horses just needed time to recover from their exertions. We had ridden further on their backs in mail than was good for them. Only Llenlleog's horse looked fresh. It was a risk but we needed to capture this burgh and hold it. Hopefully Penda and Cadwallon would reach us sooner rather than later. I knew that the Northumbrians would take some time to catch up with us. Dai reported that the gates were closed and that there were sentries upon the wall. That was unusual for it was still daylight.

"We will attack this evening. Daffydd, take your men to the south and prevent reinforcement from that direction. Kay we will use your equites and squires to attack."

Lann Aelle asked, "Who will lead the attack?"

"I will."

"No cousin. You are always putting yourself in harm's way. You are not invincible and we should share the load. There is your brother, Pol and myself. Do you have no faith in us? Do we merely follow?"

I could see from the looks on their faces that they had discussed this and were unhappy. "I cannot help my nature. I trust you all but I would put myself at the fore rather than you."

Gawan said, "Brother, when you had no family and you had the death wish, we understood your reckless bravery." I looked up, startled. My brother had known of the darkness within me. "Now you have a wife and a child. Hopefully your next child will be a boy."

"My next child?"

Gawan smiled, "We are dreamers." He nodded, "And so let one of us lead. It is a small burgh. There will be little danger."

"Then why should I not lead?"

"Because your body is tired. You fought hard the other day and we did not."

He was right. My shoulders slumped, "Very well Lann Aelle, you lead."

Leaving Bors and his men to guard the road to the north we swam the river upstream and headed to the burgh keeping out of sight. We found a wood just half a mile or so from the walls. Lann Aelle led the ten archers and twenty equites who would assault the walls. We would wait until the gates were taken and then enter the burgh. It is harder to wait than to do. Time seemed to drag. We watched the black shadows as they flitted forward. My men were well trained in using cover and moving so that their motion would not be detected. When they reached the ditch I found myself holding my breath. Gawan said, quietly, "Trust Lann Aelle brother. If you were there would you fear the guards and the walls?"

I shook my head, "The guards will have little armour and they are not as well trained as my men."

"Then breathe."

I laughed. He was becoming more like Myrddyn each day. I heard a cry from the burgh. "Ready your weapons." When I heard the clash of steel I shouted, "We ride."

I counted on the fact that my men would capture the gate. When we were half way to the gate, I saw a light as it was opened. Pol pointedly led my warriors through the gate and past the dead sentries. The rear gate had opened and I could see many of the inhabitants fleeing. I left Saxon Slayer in my scabbard. It would not be needed.

"Aed, send for Daffydd and Bors. We have secured the burgh." It was not quite true for there were pockets of fighting going on. The Northumbrians were fighting harder than they normally did and I wondered why.

Lann Aelle strode towards me, his blade bloody and his face grinning. "There cousin, we have captured the burgh and we had just four equites wounded."

"Well done. You were right to chastise me."

"Call it counselling! I sound less like a wife then."

Daffydd and Bors returned with the same news. The handful of women, children and a few men had fled north. "We could have chased them, Warlord but I was aware that our horses needed rest."

"You did right Bors. We will hold up here for a day or so. I would have us recover our strength."

We went to the warrior hall. It had been recently built as had the walls. This was King Edwin consolidating his lands. There was a pot of food on the fire and we ate. Osgar came in and interrupted us, "I am sorry, Warlord, for the interruption, but we have made a great discovery."

Osgar would not have disturbed us for nothing and we all followed him. What I had taken for houses turned out to be four small halls. Osgar opened one of the doors and I was lost for words. It was jammed full of supplies. There were barrels and amphorae from floor to ceiling. "I know, Warlord and the other three have the same within them."

Gawan nodded, "These are for an army, brother. That explains this new burgh and why there were just warriors guarding it. The prisoner told us of a muster. They must be heading south. This clever Saxon is making sure that his men are well fed and supplied."

"But the prisoner did not mention King Edwin's name."

I suddenly saw it all clearly. "He did not Lann Aelle because he is still to arrive. It is the fyrd and the men of this area who have reached here first. He has further to travel with his main army. They will have needed to sow their crops and gather their new born animals. We have stumbled upon an invasion."

I turned to my cousin. "Lann Aelle, take five squires and ride to King Penda and King Cadwallon. Tell them that the Northumbrians are heading south and that we have found their supplies." I had had no word from the first riders I had sent and I feared the worst.

"What will you do, cousin?"

I laughed, "Irritate them and slow them down. They will try to get to their supplies and we will stop them."

Lann Aelle took off his armour. It was speed he would need and not armour. After they had left I issued my orders. "We make this more defensible. The squires, slingers and half of the archers will guard its walls. Tonight, we rest but tomorrow we begin. We will ride north again but this time we know where the Northumbrians will be. They will not ambush us again."

As I lay in the hall I could not sleep. This was *wyrd*. The Northumbrians would have caught both kings unprepared had we not ventured north and yet the forest would cause them problems too. I knew that they had a large burgh at Caer Daun. I needed to scout that out. I needed to find Edwin. It would take many days for the two armies to reach us. Lann Aelle would reach them by tomorrow and they had begun the muster but the Mercians were, like the Northumbrians, foot warriors. It would take at least three days to reach us. The decision made, I slept.

"Llenlleog and Pelas, find Aed. You will not need your armour today." I could see that they were intrigued but they left to do as I had bid.

Gawan saw me talking to them. "What are you up to brother? Where is your mail?"

"I will not need my mail today. I am going to take the scouts north and find Caer Daun. You and Pol command in my absence."

"Others can do this brother."

"I know but only I can decide the best strategy to defeat Edwin. I need to know his defences and anticipate what he will do." I could see that he was not convinced. "We have a great opportunity here. King Edwin thinks that we are the only force between him and Mercia. This is like the attack last year. He does not know that King Penda and King Cadwallon have mustered their armies. We have surprise on our side. I am not going to fight. I am going to watch. I wear no armour for I will be swift."

When my men were ready I mounted Star. There were just eight of us. We were all armed with bows. "I may be away for two or three days. Your task is to keep the equites at the edge of the forest and harass the Northumbrians if they come. Do not enter the forest."

Pol shook his head, "This is madness. You will be entering the forest."

"We will be nowhere near the road. Caer Daun is not in the forest. It is to the north of it. We will move swiftly."

We rode out of the north gate and I headed north west. The forest was not like the ones in the Land of the Lakes where the trees were close together. Here they were oak, birch, elm and ash. There was little undergrowth and there was light.

I kept the scouts with me and we rode in single file. Aed was the most experienced and he led. I used Llenlleog at the rear for he had a calm head and made wise decisions. We stopped at noon when we found a clearing with a small stream. We saw no signs that anyone had visited it recently. There were only animal tracks. When we set off again, I headed slightly east for the land began to fall away slightly and I knew that Caer Daun lay on a bend in the river. It was a short while later that the forest began to thin. We stopped when we saw the stumps of felled trees. The Saxons had been here.

Aed and Dai dismounted and examined the land around the stumps. "The stumps are weathered. This is not recent." He pointed to the north east. "There is a track way there and I think they took the trees that way." I could see the furrows cut in the soil.

"From now on we use hand signals. Keep your bows ready and silence any Northumbrian that we see."

The forest ended suddenly. Once again there was evidence of tree felling and we looked down on the river valley. "Ced keep hidden. Aed check the ground for footprints."

I crouched behind the stump of an oak. It must have been a mighty tree for the bole was as wide as I was tall. I saw that there were many men camped by the river. The burgh itself was busy with warriors coming and going. Here was Edwin's army. The ground before us was hidden by a depression in the ground but it mattered not for we were well above the river. There was a bridge and more and more warriors were marching from the north. I felt we had seen enough. I was about to order my men to mount when two dozen warriors leapt up towards us. They had advanced unseen from the depression.

Pelas and Llenlleog had their bows in their hands and two arrows were loosed to strike two warriors. My bow was hanging from Star's saddle and I pulled my sword and ran towards the advancing Northumbrians. I felt naked for I had no helmet, no shield and no armour. I did have my gauntlets and I grabbed the spear head and brought Saxon Slayer down to bite into the neck of one warrior. I felt a blow to my side which made me gasp in pain and I punched with the hilt of my sword. I heard a grunt. As another spear jabbed towards me I spun and, still retaining the spear head, swung the haft to smash into the side of the warrior's head. He fell stunned and I plunged my sword into his throat.

"Come, Warlord, we are mounted and I have Star." I turned and ran towards the sound of Pelas' voice. Two arrows flew dangerously close to my head and I heard screams behind me as my pursuers were struck. As I mounted, I saw that two of the scouts lay dead but the Saxons had lost eight warriors. Even as I turned Star to wheel away another Saxon fell to Llenlleog's arrow. Aidan and Dai had saved the two horses from their dead scouts and we saw the eaves of the forest looming up. The horses had rested and we began to increase our lead. We did not stop for half an hour and then we halted to rest and to see if we were being pursued.

It was only when I stopped to adjust the girth that Pelas shouted, "Warlord, you are bleeding!"

I looked down. The blow I had felt had been a sword and it had sliced along my side. I was bleeding freely. Llenlleog took charge. "Aidan and Dai, watch the trail for pursuit. Aed, find the trail home. He lifted my tunic. "Pelas, there is a flask in my saddlebags and some bandages bring them." He examined the wound. "This is deep, Warlord. You have lost much blood. Do you feel unsteady?"

"A little tired, that is all."

"Then sit."

I did as I was told. Pelas brought the flask and bandages. "This will sting, Warlord." He poured some of the liquid on my wound. It burned. I knew what it was. It was the spirit his people made from apples. "Pelas, hold the two edges of the wound together." As he did so, Llenlleog poured a little of the spirit into my mouth. It too burned but I felt warmth inside of me. He took out a bone needle from the pouch he had on his waist and some cat gut. This will not be pretty Warlord, but it will slow down the bleeding." He threaded the bone needle and began to sew. It did not hurt as much as I had thought for the spirit had numbed it somewhat. I did, however, begin to feel faint. This is what came of fighting without the protection of armour. Llenlleog worked quickly. "Pelas, the bandage." He wrapped the bandage so tightly that I felt it hard to breathe.

By the time I had my tunic on once more Aidan and Dai had returned. "They are following but they are more than a mile behind." Aiden grinned, "We hit two more with arrows. They will be more cautious now."

"Find Aed, I sent him ahead. Pelas, let us help the Warlord on to Star."

Once I was mounted Llenlleog used a piece of rope to tie me to the saddle. "I am not a piece of meat!"

"Until we get you back to Gawan and have the wound seen to properly, you are. Pelas, lead the Warlord's mount."

We set off and I was placed, like a piece of baggage, in the middle. Pelas kept giving me anxious looks as we made our way south. I had no doubt that the Northumbrians would have heard my men call me Warlord. They would pursue and I became increasingly tired. I felt my wound begin to stiffen as the spirit wore off. The dull pain became a throbbing pain. It served to keep me awake. It began to draw on to late afternoon. I found that I was thirsty but I would not ask my men to stop. It was too dangerous. I hoped that Aed and Llenlleog could find the way back to the captured burgh. A night in the woods which would soon be crawling with Edwin's men did not appeal.

I briefly closed my eyes and felt immense relief. I panicked and opened them again but I was tiring and I closed them once more. I enjoyed the experience and I kept them closed. Suddenly I felt hands on my legs and we were stopped.

"Watch him Pelas! There are men ahead."

My eyes jerked open and it was night time. Pelas looked up at me anxiously. He looked relieved when I spoke, "Any water?"

He handed me a water skin, "You had me worried, Warlord. If Llenlleog had not tied you to the horse you would have fallen."

"Where is he?"

"Aed heard men ahead and they have gone to see if there is a way around them."

I knew that if I was anyone other than the Warlord I would have been left for I was endangering the rest and the news we bore was vital. I heard the leaves move and I went for my sword. The pain was too much. I felt like Myfanwy; helpless.

Aed appeared. "There are some Northumbrians ahead, Warlord."

"Are they searching for us?"

"Llenlleog thinks not. He has the other men with him. It looks like they are a band of hunters but it may mean there is a warband camping in the woods around here. We are close to where we were ambushed."

There was a sudden scream and then the noise of combat followed by total silence. Despite the pain I pulled my sword from my scabbard and we watched for whoever came out of the dark. It was Llenlleog and my scouts. They had a hind over the saddle of one of the spare horses. "They are dead but we had best hurry in case others heard their cries."

Although I felt more awake I allowed Pelas to lead me. It would not do to fall from my horse. When we reached the edge of the forest it was hard to tell for the night was so black that it all looked the same. By the time we reached the burgh even the others were almost as tired as we were. It was just a relief to see the lights from the hall as the gates were opened. I saw Pol and as I opened my mouth to speak blackness enveloped me.

Chapter 20

When I came to, I stared up into the anxious faces of my brother and Pol. "You had us worried, brother. That was a serious wound although our new equite made a good job of stopping the bleeding. He could make a healer if he chose."

I tried to sit up but Gawan restrained me. "You rest. It is barely morning."

"What of the Northumbrians?"

"Pol here has kept his patrols out and they have killed the few scouts sent by Edwin."

"They have a huge army. If he heads this way we will not be able to hold him." I waved my left hand around the hall. "Not in this burgh anyway."

"It will take him some time to make his way through the forest. And we can bloody his nose. At the very least we can deny him his supplies. This hall and the stores will burn well."

I sank back, "Very well. I will rest but I want waking the moment that the Northumbrians appear."

When I was woken it was after noon. Pelas brought me some water. "Thank you Pelas for last night. I would not have made it home without you."

He seemed embarrassed. "I am your squire, Warlord. How would it have looked had I returned without you?"

I drank. The wound did not feel as bad and, when I lifted my tunic, I saw clean bandages. Gawan had obviously used some of Myrddyn's herbs. "Are the Northumbrians close?"

"Captain Pol is still out with the equites. We do not know."

"Then help me to dress and I will speak with Gawan." He looked at me dubiously, "I need to make water in any case. Come, Pelas."

He reluctantly aided me. I strapped on my sword even though it felt uncomfortable against the bandages and the wound. Men's faces looked worried as they saw me emerge but I waved and smiled; it reassured them. I climbed the stairs to the gate. Gawan glanced around and shook his head. "You cannot obey instructions, can you?"

"I feel fine. I am not certain I could fight yet but I can walk and I can look. Tell me what has happened."

"We had a messenger from Lann Aelle. The Mercians and the Cymri are on their way. He said they should be here in three of four days."

"Will we be granted that time?"

He shrugged. "We had put traps in the ditch and deepened them a little. If they attack at night we will be warned and I have men detailed to fire the halls if they get too close."

"I would like those supplies for our men."

"I know but sometimes we cannot have what we want."

The light was fading in the east. I caught a movement from the forest and I pointed. It was Pol. I had no idea how many equites he had taken but I saw no empty saddles. He glanced up and shook his head as he rode through the gate.

I made my way, slowly, down to meet him. "Well?"

He shook his head. "We killed their scouts again but they are getting closer. I think they will be here by noon tomorrow."

"Good. Come, I am hungry as you will be and we can plan. There is plenty of food for us, at any rate."

The archers and squires who had not been on patrol had prepared a feast and we ate in the hall. I was not lying; I was ravenous. As we ate, I gave them my thoughts. "This burgh is small and we have an advantage for we have more warriors than the garrison. We will keep the archers and the squires within the walls. I will command here." I held up my hand to silence their arguments. "The two of you will be needed to lead your men." I waved my knife in the direction of the forest beyond the walls. "Split the men into two groups. You will each lead one. Before dawn you lead them to the east and the west and you hide them from the Northumbrians. I will keep Llewellyn and the buccina. Pol, you take the dragon banner. I will sound the buccina when the time is right and you can sweep down on their rear."

"When will the time be right, brother?"

"When they have seen me here and know I command and have committed an attack on the walls. If they see me in here they will believe that my horsemen are here too."

They looked at each other and Pol asked, "And if we fail?"

"Then I will fire the burgh and we will escape."

"You are taking a risk."

I sighed, "What else can we do? Should I lie in my bed and wait for them to come?"

"No, brother, but we could fire the burgh and flee south to meet with our allies."

"This way is better. King Edwin cannot know that Penda and Cadwallon are coming. Do we want him to bolt again and hide in his burghs? This is our chance to end this, once and for all." I smiled, "I am awake now and I can make the decisions again. When I am in the Otherworld, brother, then the choices will be yours."

He laughed, "You are incorrigible and just like father!"

I smiled, "Compliments are always welcome."

The horsemen left before dawn. Despite his protests I had Pelas help me into my armour. Llenlleog understood. "Your uncle is a warrior. It is what we do."

As I went to the walls I could smell the effect of the horses. We had no stables and the horses had soiled a large area of the burgh. It could not be helped but it was not pleasant. One advantage of having the horses outside the walls was the fact that they did not add to the effluent within. I frowned; that was not our only problem. Once we were besieged we would have to husband our water. When the day was over I would send the squires to gather in as much water as they could manage.

I only had four mailed warriors within the burgh. All of the rest were either archers or squires without mail. Any with mail had gone with my brother and Pol. I was gambling that King Edwin would send just a vanguard to the burgh. He might know that we had taken it but his people would have reported a force of equites. He would be confident that his warriors could defeat us. I hoped that he would never contemplate that I would put my handful of equites outside of the walls. As he had shown before King Edwin was a cautious commander. He took no risks. For my part it was not much of a risk. I knew that we had many men hurrying up the road. We could run at any time but I wanted his men hurting and softening up for the Mercians and the Cymri.

The scouts had been accurate. It was late afternoon when the first Saxons emerged from the forest. The cautious King Edwin brought out over five hundred of his men and formed them into a wedge. On the flanks he had the same number of lightly armed men. Some were the fyrd; they were the farmers who went to war when needed with whatever weapons they had to hand. They guarded the flanks and I could see that King Edwin regarded them as expendable. They would buy time for his elite warriors who wore mail. I knew then that I had the measure of this Saxon.

They moved forward cautiously so as not to break ranks. The burgh was Saxon built and they would know their own design. Pol and Gawan had added to the defences: they would not expect that.

"Daffydd do not release your arrows until I tell you. Let us make it a surprise."

My plan was to wait until they tried to cross the ditch. The bridge over the ditch was now behind the gate as an added defence. The shields were locked and the heads hidden behind them. With their mail they were almost impossible to hurt. I knew that the enemy would be supremely confident. When our foes were just twenty paces from the ditch, I took off my helmet. "I am the Warlord of Rheged! Go back to your king and tell him not to waste the lives of his brave warriors. If I chose, I could come amongst you with my squire alone and destroy you."

As I had expected that infuriated the warriors and they began to bang their shields and chant. I nodded to Daffydd. His men could send flights over and shower them but that would waste arrows. Instead his best archers looked for the tiny chinks in the shield wall when men lowered them slightly as they banged. An arrow flew and struck a warrior on the face. The arrow pierced his cheek. The feathers looked strange sticking from the side of his face. A second who had turned to look at his neighbour died when the arrow came in at an angle, hit his cheek and continued into his shoulder. A flurry of arrows thudded into mail and bodies. Another warrior fell before they regained their solid line. They came forward slightly faster than they had hitherto. The arrows had made them wary and they kept their shields up. As they descended into the ditch more warriors fell to my archers. However it was the traps at the bottom of the ditch which caused the most damage.

Pol and Gawan had concealed them with branches and twigs. As soon as they stepped onto the sharpened stakes all their discipline went. They screamed in pain and their cohesion went. My archers could not release their arrows fast enough to hit all of them. Once enough had died the traps were hidden by the bodies of the fallen and they locked their shields once more. I looked to the warbands. They were now all committed. Their attention was on the burgh and on me.

"Llewellyn, sound the buccina!"

As soon as the strident note of the Roman horn sounded the Northumbrians in the ditch paused. They looked for danger. They saw just the archers and the slingers who were now close enough to hit helmets. A lead ball at thirty paces can render a warrior unconscious and my boy slingers were keen to impress the Warlord. When there was no change in what they could see they began to attack the wooden walls with their axes and swords. The wailing of the dragon banner was the first warning that not all was well. As Pol and Gawan's equites hit the lightly armed fyrd, a human wail went up. The unarmoured men were slaughtered. The cries of the dying made the armoured men look around and more died as Daffydd's arrows struck them. The circle of horsemen closed with the rear ranks of the shield wall, for the fyrd were either dead or fled.

Many were too slow to react and were speared by the deadly lances. I saw that King Edwin was trying to get reinforcements into the fray but it would be too late. The shield wall broke assaulted as it was from two different directions, and they ran. I saw some of the younger equites chasing after the fleeing Northumbrians. "Sound the buccina!" As it sounded most turned and returned to the walls; slaying the wounded as they did so. Two equites, caught up in the moment, chased after the Northumbrians and they were butchered by Edwin's reinforcements. We had done better than I had hoped but I hated the waste of two young equites. We opened the gate and my men entered. We had bought another day. We also had good news, for an hour after my men had returned Lann Aelle and his scouts returned. "The men of Mercia are two days behind me."

"That is good news. We need to buy two more days then."

That evening as we stood on the gate and saw the fires which ringed the edge of the forest to the north, Lann Aelle said, "That will not work a second time."

"No. But I wonder if the Allfather will work some magic for us?" I looked at Gawan. He was as enigmatic as Myrddyn at times. "This Edwin is a Christian now. He will want his people burying.

Perhaps we negotiate a truce tomorrow so that he can collect his dead."

Pol laughed, "Would he be so foolish when his main army is as close as it is?"

"It is only the risk for the rider who goes to negotiate the truce. I believe they will honour it. After all they are Christians now." I could hear the sarcasm in his voice.

"I agree with my brother. Even if they do not agree to the truce then the negotiations can eat up some time and bring Penda and Cadwallon ever closer."

"Then we choose someone with a silver tongue."

I laughed, "We choose no one; for the speaker is chosen already. It is me."

"Why you?"

"There will be no fighting tomorrow and they will be more likely to send for the king if the Warlord comes to negotiate."

Gawan nodded, "You are relying on your reputation."

"I am and that is why I will just take Llewellyn and Pelas with me. I want to show them that we are not afraid."

Pol and Lann Aelle spent the rest of the evening trying to persuade me not to go. Gawan came to my aid. "Neither Myrddyn nor I had dreamt his death yet."

Pol snorted, "Did you dream the wound the other day, Dreamer?" Gawan shook his head, "We cannot afford to fight the Northumbrians without the Warlord. Even if we have Penda and Cadwallon with us it is your brother that the warriors on both sides will look to. Today they hurled themselves at the wall to get to grips with him. Young boys in Northumbria dream of becoming the hero who slays the Warlord. It was your father and now it is your brother. The warrior matters little it is the title and the reputation which draws them."

I put my hand on Pol's arm. "And you have argued wonderfully for me to be the one. Thank you, old friend. And now I am tired. We will leave at dawn. Lann Aelle, inform your son and Llewellyn that I need them."

Kay waved as the last of the water carriers returned. We had every container we could muster filled with water. We were prepared.

I regretted my decision as I began to don my armour. Raising my arms for the leather byrnie was painful enough but when I lowered them after the mail shirt was lowered was agony. It would take a few days for me to be able to fight. It did, however, gleam as did my helmet. Pelas had polished them well. He must have been up all night for Star gleamed as we left the burgh.

My men were stood to on the walls and we rode slowly across the field of battle. The bodies still lay where they had fallen. The smell was already beginning to fill the air and I could see where rats had begun to gnaw at them. "Remember Pelas, keep your hands from your weapons."

"Aye, Warlord." I heard the doubt in his voice. We halted half way between the burgh and the Northumbrian camp. I opened my palms and put my hands to the side in the sign for peace.

I saw a warband forming up and then five warriors detached themselves and rode their ponies towards us. They were heavily mailed warriors and I saw many battle rings adorning their bare arms.

They dismounted as did I. It was not easy but I gritted my teeth. I could afford to show no weakness.

"I am Eadfrith of Caer Daun. I command here."

"And I am the Warlord of Rheged."

Eadfrith took off his helmet and I did the same. These were the rituals of negotiation. It showed peaceful intent on both sides and I could almost feel the relief from the burgh behind me.

Eadfrith was younger than I was with a blond beard and a scar running down one cheek. He had done well to command at such an early age. He smiled, "You are here to surrender?"

I laughed, "Why should we? Your king was kind enough to lay in such supplies that we may never choose to leave such a lovely spot."

Anger briefly flitted across his face and then he smiled again. "When the rest of our army arrives we will have your surrounded and you will have to surrender."

"You have such little faith in the walls which your men built. How sad."

This time he allowed his irritation to show. He had already revealed his lack of experience by giving me too much information. "We shall see, Welshman! What is it that you do want?"

I spread my arm around the battlefield. "Your men fought and died bravely. Now that you follow the White Christ we thought you might like to bury them."

A frown crossed his face. "Why would you do that?"

I shook my head, "Such suspicion. Leave them there then for the beasts of the night to devour and despoil. My holy men thought that your priests might like to bury them and send them to their new god. My men died well with swords in their hands and they are already in the Otherworld but you are Christians are you not?"

I could see from the faces of them all that they were not all committed Christians. King Edwin might have been converted but some of his men still adhered to the old ways.

"Very well then."

"We will have a truce until noon."

Eadfrith shook his head, "That is not enough time to collect the dead and to bury them."

I shrugged as though it did not matter, "Until nightfall then."

"Until nightfall."

He nodded and we remounted. It took me all my time to do so. He grinned as he looked up at me on my magnificent mount, "And the next time I see you, horse lover, my sword will bring you down to my level and I will wear that fine armour."

"Many men have promised that Eadfrith of Caer Daun and yet I still wear it." I wheeled Star's head around and we rode back to the fort.

When we were out of earshot Pelas asked, "Warlord, why did you say the truce would be until noon? Surely we needed as much time as possible."

"And that is why. If I suggested night fall then he would have been suspicious. I made him suggest that which I desired."

Llewellyn chuckled, "And that is why he is the Warlord, young squire. He uses his mind as well as his sword."

"There will be a truce until nightfall. Have Aed and the other scouts collect our dead. Have them listen to the Northumbrians. Do not let on that they speak Saxon and I want other Saxon speakers on this wall to listen to the Northumbrians as they collect the bodies. We can gain valuable intelligence." Pol nodded and ran off to find the men. As I stepped down I said, quietly to Gawan, "My wound feels damp."

He nodded, "I will look at it. I feared this."

In the hall Pelas and Llewellyn helped me to take off my armour. The wound looked angry but there was not as much blood as I had feared. My brother sniffed it and seemed satisfied. He took a clean cloth and dipped it in a mixture of vinegar and herbs. He wiped at the wound which stung but I knew it would help the healing process. He took out his balms and salves. "It is healing but you need to rest more. No more armour for a day or two."

I laughed and regretted it for it hurt. "Tell the Northumbrians that, brother. I have, at least, bought us a day. I will try to avoid becoming involved in the fighting."

Pelas said, "Fighting? Surely you have bought us a day and a night, Warlord."

"No, Pelas. They will come tonight. They will take their dead away and then this Eadfrith will try to capture the burgh before King Edwin gets here. He is young and I think he is keen to impress. As soon as it is dark I want the ditch sowing with lillia. Llewellyn, you can go now and have the ditch to the south sown for tonight they will surround us. We will have a ring of fire by morning."

"How do you know?"

Pelas was inquisitive and that was good but I did not have the time to explain every decision I made. "Eadfrith told me when he asked for a truce until nightfall. He also said that King Edwin would surround us. It was a slip of the tongue. They will come and we will be ready."

Chapter 21

As the last Saxon left the field I ordered the squires and the boy slingers to collect every piece of horse manure they could and throw it into the ditches. Some was already dry but even the fresh would soon dry. It would make the interior of the burgh slightly sweeter smelling but, more importantly it would disguise the lillia and make any slight wounds potentially mortal.

"Daffydd, as soon as it is dark, tell the squires and the boys to throw down kindling and faggots into the ditches. Not too many but enough for you to start a fire. Have spare faggots ready to keep the fire going. I will give the command when you are to release fire arrows. Have your best archers around the walls to make sure they take hold. " It took skill to use a fire arrow effectively. There were only five or six of my men who could do so easily although I would have as many as possible sent into the ditch.

"Aye Warlord."

"Bors, have any pig fat and oil poured down the sides of the ditch. I want it slippery and I want it to burn."

"Aye Warlord."

Of course the pig fat and the oil would also burn. I risked it igniting the walls of the burgh but the fort was made of new wood and would not burn as easily as an older fort.

I went to the hall with my warriors and ate well. Pol looked at me as we ate and said, "You will not fight tonight!"

"If they break through then I will have no choice will I?"

"Then we will make sure that they will not break through."

"They will come at us from all sides. I will stand at the north gate with Pelas and Llenlleog. Lann Aelle, take the south gate. Pol and Gawan I think they will attack the hardest at the east and the west for there are no gates there. You each take one. I want the men evenly spread around: an equite, a slinger, a squire, an archer and so on. I would that we all had equal protection. Daffydd, you take charge of the fire arrows. When they have suffered wounds in the ditch we fire it and we feed the fire. The dung in the bottom will help to keep the fire going."

I caught Pelas looking south. "Fear not, squire, King Penda will come. He has already won the support of the Saxon kings to the south. He will want to defeat King Edwin for that will make him high king of the Saxons in this land."

"And then we will have to defeat him."

I smiled at Gawan. "You are right brother but that is in the future. *Wyrd* puts one obstacle in the way at a time. Who knows what might happen between now and then? We did not expect the help from the Hibernians but that helped us." I pointed to Llenlleog. "We did not know we had kin across the sea but we do now." I shrugged, "Who knows, at some time in the future our kin may come across the waters and conquer the Saxons, eh Llenlleog?"

He grinned, "Aye my lord. For I now see that this is a land worth fighting for. We have a toe hold in Frankia but we are like you, a hardy and resilient people. Do not rule it out, Pelas!"

I donned my armour despite the pain. I would not fight but I could not risk an accidental wound because I was not wearing armour. I knew, from Pol, that the warriors felt better when they saw me amongst them. I smiled and spoke to each one as I passed. I had learned the names of each of the slingers too. I had known many of their fathers. My own father had taught me the value of knowing the warriors with whom I fought. The number of my warriors was small and everyone was as valuable to me as any other.

We stood silently awaiting the enemy. I did not wear my helmet. Although well made, it did dampen sounds a little and I needed sharp ears that night. I scanned the forest. It blended into the land but there was a darker shadow there. I began to wonder if I had mis-read Eadfrith for all we heard was the sounds of the night. My warriors knew better than to talk and to move. By standing silently we made it hard for an approaching warrior to spot us.

I became aware that there was total silence. The animals of the night were still. The Northumbrians were coming. I slowly picked up my bow and took out an arrow. I was not certain if my wound would allow me to pull the string but it felt better having a weapon in my hand. I saw moving shadows making their way from the forest. I did not need to speak for my men would have spotted them too. The boy slingers had especially good eyes. Every equite had either a bow or a javelin. They were all ready. This was the hard part as we waited for them to come. We had to remain still to create the illusion that we were not ready. This was where I missed Myrddyn for he would have had some magic up his sleeve. I had not had time to speak with Gawan but I hoped he had something too. If I had but one pot of Greek fire it would make all the difference.

I saw that the shadows had stopped some twenty paces from the ditch. They had learned from their earlier attack and would not come forward blindly this time. It mattered not. I turned to see if Llewellyn had the buccina to hand and I saw that he had. I could make out the Northumbrians now. They were slithering like serpents towards the ditch. That was clever. They would feel the stakes. Of course it would not be pleasant for them as they would have the horse dung to go through first. Eventually they would need to stand and when they slipped they would be impaled anyway.

The Northumbrians disappeared into the bottom of the ditch; it was all shadow. I saw one of them. He had not blackened his helmet and I saw a reflection. He began to pull himself up the side of the ditch. He had a sword in his hand and that was his undoing. His foot slipped on the slippery bank and his one free hand was not enough to save him. He fell backwards knocking over a companion and, more importantly, impaling his foot on a dung covered stake. He screamed. We were all ready and arrows, lead shot and javelins were accurately hurled at the men we had watched for some time. Llewellyn sounded the buccina. It seemed to be answered by Saxon horns and we saw more shadows running from the forest to join the attack.

The initial attack had been thwarted but now more Northumbrians ran to join their beleaguered comrades. The ones in the ditch had shields above their heads for protection but they could not ascend the slippery sides nor the wooden walls. They would wait for their comrades. The technique had been mastered by us. They would use two men to hold a shield and make a platform for a warrior to use. They would either scale the walls or fight the defenders from the top of the shield. It worked. Our forts had higher walls but the Northumbrian's burgh had walls which could be scaled.

We were causing fewer casualties. My men were waiting for a certain target rather than wasting precious missiles. It emboldened the Northumbrians; perhaps they thought we were running out of arrows and stone. I was waiting until the ditch was filled. My eyes were so accustomed to the dark by this time that I could make out faces. When I saw the ditch filled with faces I yelled, "Now, Daffydd!"

There were only four or five fire arrows along each wall and they were not aimed at men. They plunged into the faggots and the brush. The faggots began to burn. There were not many of them and the Northumbrians ignored them. They had light now to see the walls and the defenders. They began to hurl spears at their tormentors. Daffydd and his archers began to spread out their fire arrows and more of the faggots flamed. Suddenly some of the pig fat ignited and then the oil. There were spurts of flames and some of the warriors lying wounded in the ditch found themselves on fire and unable to move. The dried dung burned and began to send ripples of flames along the ditch. Now the Saxons could not ignore the flames and they tried to throw the faggots from the ditch towards the walls. To do so they had to use two hands and more warriors fell to stones and arrows. They were brave. I saw a leader exhorting his men to attack once more. Llenlleog's arrow silenced him.

"Throw more faggots into the fire Daffydd!"

Faggots were thrown in to join the inferno. We fed it as the Northumbrians gamely tried to climb the walls. Eventually we heard the Saxon horns and the living left the ditch. The air was filled with the shouts and the screams of the wounded and the smell of burning hair and flesh. It was not pleasant. I saw some of the slingers being sick at the sight and the smell. They now knew war.

Dawn brought us the grisly sight of blackened bodies lying in our ditch. The dung and the bodies smouldered still. We would be trapped within the walls for the rest of the day but the Saxons would have to lick their wounds and decide what to do next. Daylight also brought us the size of the problem we faced. The Northumbrian army had arrived and now stretched all around us. We were ringed in by warriors. The supplies we held were vital to King Edwin. He would have to keep attacking us if only to reclaim his own supplies.

"Have the men eat and sleep in shifts. They will not attack for a while and we might as well rest and eat."

"And you, brother, will you rest?"

"I would have to descend and to climb the steps to return here. I think I will watch for King Edwin."

At noon I was rewarded for my patience by King Edwin and his leaders coming towards us, their hands held out in the sign for peace. I recognised Eadfrith, Osric, Oswiu and Oswald. The sixth I did not recognise but as he looked much like the brothers I took him to be the elder, Eanforth.

They halted out of bow range. That, in itself, was discourteous. The king took off his helmet. I noticed the huge cross of the White Christ which he wore now that he was a Christian. I waited for him to speak. He had sought this conversation.

"Warlord, I see that you are up to your usual tricks, burning warriors because you fear to fight them."

I laughed, "Your warriors are like fleas on a dog Edwin, you get rid of them any way you can for there is no honour in getting rid of lice."

I saw that I had struck a nerve with the three brothers. The lack of a title would also have irritated the king. He held out his hands to quieten the brothers. "You are now completely surrounded and you must be running short of firewood. Surrender and I will allow you to leave the burgh unharmed."

From their reaction I could see that he had not discussed this with the sons of Aethelfrith. None of them appeared happy: I was their Nemesis.

"We are comfortable and, as you have been so kind as to lay in supplies for us, we will stay here until they are gone."

This time I had got to him. "Then there will be no quarter given and you will all be put to the sword. Even the boys."

"Good for I would hate them to be the slaves of Northumbrians!"

They turned and rode their ponies away.

I turned to Pol, "They will attack soon. Bring all the men back to the walls."

Daffydd said, "Should I throw the last of the faggots in the fire, Warlord?"

"No Daffydd, save those for tonight. If we are still here."

I donned my helmet for I knew that I would need it. I looked at my quiver. There were ten arrows left and then I would have to rely on Saxon Slayer. I estimated that the Northumbrians were in their hundreds. I could see at least eight hundred before me and we were surrounded. I had to assume there were others in the forest too. The odds were more than twenty five to one against us.

King Edwin organised four wedges to attack us. He had more than enough men to divide our forces and he would be able to outnumber us on every wall. The attack the previous night had, effectively, filled in the ditches with his dead warriors. The Northumbrians did not have many archers but they would be able to target our men on the walls and they could afford to lose twenty five men just to kill one of us.

Each wedge was led by a chief and mailed warriors. Further back they were lightly armed. Between the wedges came the fyrd. They had an assortment of weapons and would fight individually. They were useful in dividing our attack.

"Daffydd, concentrate your archers on the men without armour. The slingers can deal with the mailed warriors." We had a limited number of arrows and I wanted the maximum casualties.

The advancing wedges chanted their Saxon war cries. It was meant to intimidate. It did not affect my equites and archers but I saw some worried looks amongst my slingers. "I will give a silver coin to any slinger who brings down a warrior in mail!"

The cost was immaterial; I wanted them to forget their fears and try to win the silver coin. I heard the lead balls as they cracked against the shields of the warriors. One suddenly pitched backward as the lead ball struck his helmet. He might not have been killed but he was out of the attack and the gap enabled Kay to hurl a javelin into the chest of the warrior in the second rank. The wedges slowed up. The archers began to hit the warriors at the rear of the wedges. It was like the effect of dripping water; it was slow but eventually it would cause the dam to break. I just hoped we had both the arrows and the time.

"Ready the javelins!"

As soon as the warriors stepped into the ditch their line of shields would not be continuous. That was the time to strike. I had three arrows left. When the leading warrior stepped down on to the crisply blackened bodies I loosed an arrow at the warrior behind him. Although he kept his shield up I struck his knee with the barbed missile. He dropped to his good knee and Llenlleog sent an arrow into the shoulder of the warrior next to him. We were not killing warriors but these were their best and they were being wounded.

By the time the wedge reached the gate there were handfuls of wounded warriors lying sheltering beneath their shields. Some tried to drag themselves back towards safety; that was easier said than done with their fellows trying to get to grips with us.

"Pelas, go to the other walls and report on how they are doing."

I hoped they were doing as well as we were for their main thrust would be towards me. I could see King Edwin and the brothers, less than two hundred paces away staring intently at the gate. Eadfrith was already readying a second warband of two hundred men to exploit any weaknesses. I heard the axes as they smashed against the wooden walls. It was ironical that they were destroying their own burgh. Although not well made, it was new and the wood resisted the blows better than an older fort. The slingers were now causing the most damage as their lead balls struck at very close range. Warriors were dying. Even as I watched a shot struck the arm of an unarmoured warrior and I heard the sharp crack as the bone broke. Had Myrddyn been with us then I am sure he would have had some device to cause more casualties but we were without his assistance.

While some hacked at the walls others were being raised on shields. I saw Llenlleog fighting a grizzled veteran who wielded an axe as though he had been born with it. He whirled it over his head and I watched Llenlleog time his thrust. It took great courage as well as skill to duck beneath the axe head and stab forward. The warrior was mailed and had a full face helmet. The gap was small but the tip tore into the throat and, as he twisted it free, the men supporting him were covered in his spraying blood. His body crashed into the new warriors coming to their aid.

We were slowing them but I heard a cry from below. "They are almost through!"

"Llenlleog, take half of the equites from the walls and attack whoever comes through the gate."

The walls looked half empty as the huge, mailed warriors descended. I was left, largely with archers and slingers. Pelas raced back. "They are holding them back, Warlord, but my father has spied another Saxon warband marching from the south!"

I wondered if our luck had run out. It mattered not. We would fight on until we were all dead. We knew that there would be no quarter given but we would damage the Northumbrians with our sacrifice.

Eadfrith and his warband were close to the ditch now. I loosed my last arrow. Perhaps my father's hand guided it for it flew unerringly straight and went through the eye piece of the warrior protecting Eadfrith's sword side. The Northumbrian looked up in surprise as his oathsworn fell. I put down my bow and took out Saxon Slayer. Pulling my shield around I prepared to sell my life dearly. A hand appeared over the top of the rampart and I swung down hard severing it half way across the palm. I sensed, rather than saw, the warrior who stepped behind me. Holding my shield up, I swung my sword in a wide arc. It went beneath his shield and I felt it strike his mail shirt and bite into it. The force of the blow made him over balance and he fell, bleeding to his death inside the burgh below.

Pelas was suddenly felled by a mighty blow to his shield. As he fell to the floor I roared a challenge and leapt at the warrior. The fighting platform was not wide and, as he turned to face me I dropped to one knee and stabbed upwards. My sword went beneath his mail shirt and ripped into his abdomen. I twisted and pulled out a mass of white and pink worms. He, too, fell to the floor. I held out my hand for Pelas. "Come squire, your work is not yet done."

Just then I heard the sound of a horn from the south and a cheer from Lann Aelle's men. As I looked over the ramparts I saw the fyrd fleeing. Then there was a horn from King Edwin and his men and the mailed warbands fell back, too. Llenlleog shouted up. "It is King Penda, he has come!"

The Allfather and the spirits watched over us still. We had held.

Chapter 22

Despite the timely arrival of the Mercians we had lost too many men and boys. I was happy to pay the silver coins to the brave survivors. I saw equites and archers, whom I had fought alongside, lying dead. It did not help the fact that we had killed many more of the Northumbrians. As my squires went into the ditches to ease the suffering of the dead and to get their byrnies, I made my way, gingerly, to the southern gate. Although I had not opened the wound I was in some pain. On the positive side, I knew that I could fight, once more. My body was recovering.

"We had better put the horses beyond the walls; I dare say King Penda may want to stay in this burgh. Have the equites and squires set up a camp to the south of the burgh by the river."

"Aye Warlord." Pol grinned, "I think the horses are also getting sick of the smell."

"Llewellyn and Llenlleog, keep watch on the Northumbrians and tell me what they are doing."

I went to the southern gate to meet with Penda. He clasped my arm in the warrior's grip. "Well done, Warlord. Edwin has, indeed, brought all of his army. He intended to defeat us once and for all. It is good that you found him."

"Come to the hall, there are supplies for all of your men."

He lowered his voice and spoke to me urgently, "You and I must talk alone."

There were three squires in the hall. "Go and help Pol move the horses to the pasture."

"Aye, Warlord."

As they were leaving Penda asked, "Is there any ale? I have a thirst on me."

I found him a horn of ale and I poured myself one too. "Thank you for your timely arrival."

He quaffed his in one. "It is King Cadwallon. He has become Christian." I was stunned. He had served with father and with me. He had been to the dream cave. Why would he become Christian? "There is more." He put his hand on my arm. "Your sister has died."

"How?"

"She and their son Cadfan had the sleeping sickness. Cadwallon sent for Myrddyn but before he could reach Wrecsam a priest of the White Christ arrived. Cadwallon asked him to intercede but his wife, you sister, died. The priest made the king promise that if his son was saved then the king and his kingdom would become Christian."

I nodded. I began to see it. "And Cadfan was saved." He nodded as he poured himself another horn of ale. "Tell me, did this priest have a name?"

"I believe he was called Paulinus of Eboracum."

That confirmed it. "He was the priest with King Edwin. I see a Northumbrian plot here. The sooner the king arrives, the better."

"If the Cymri do not fight alongside us we cannot defeat Edwin."

"I will persuade him."

I took Lann Aelle, Pol and Gawan across the battlefield, ostensibly to look for the Northumbrian leaders who might have fallen, but actually to talk about King Cadwallon away from the warriors.

When I told them Gawan nodded, "I had strange dreams last week and I saw our mother dying again but now I see that was our sister."

I nodded. "I see a plot here. It cannot be a coincidence that this priest was at the wedding of King Edwin and then turns up at the court of Cadwallon when there is sickness."

Lann Aelle suddenly started, "You mean the priest caused the sickness?"

"I would not put it past them. I am the ultimate pagan and Nanna was my sister. It makes sense that they would punish me through her and inveigle their way into the heart of the king by saving his son."

"But how would they do that?"

Gawan said, "There are ways. Myrddyn would know them."

"Does this mean that the men of Cymru will not fight?"

"I think, Pol, that the intention of the priests and Edwin was for that to happen but the fact that they are on their way gives me a kind of hope. I cannot believe that his warriors will have embraced the White Christ." I looked to the south, "This is where we need Myrddyn. He has the power to reverse such things."

Gawan shook his head, "I am sorry, brother. I am a pale imitation."

"No, for we all walk in the footsteps of giants. I try to be our father and you try to be Myrddyn. I doubt that we will ever achieve what they did but that does not mean we give up. I will speak with Cadwallon. Gawan, you can deal with the priest."

He nodded, "And tonight I will dream." I looked at him. "There are some herbs and potions which we can use to help us enter the dream world when we are not in the cave of Wyddfa. I will try to send a message to Myrddyn."

Lann Aelle said, "Perhaps he knows already."

"That would be my thought too but we plan as though he will not be here. Speak not of this to our men. To them we must have a common front. Dissension only helps Edwin and our foes."

We were all in good cheer that night as we celebrated. The Northumbrian fires still lined the forest and we were still outnumbered but so long as we held the burgh then Edwin could not attack. The next day we discovered that the bodies which lay before the burgh had been collected and buried during the night; we had not needed a truce.

I felt better when I woke and I mounted the equites for a show of force. We rode towards the Northumbrian camp. I needed to ascertain their numbers and to show them that we had no intention of leaving. We rode along the length of their camp just out of bow range. We rode with our left side towards the Northumbrian camp. If they did loose arrows then our shields were there to protect us. I noticed, as we rode, that there were men of Dál Riata there too. Edwin had allied with the men who had also chosen the White Christ. It made me even more suspicious of this Paulinus.

When we were approaching the burgh riders were at the gate. "King Cadwallon comes!"

Pelas led my horse away and I went to speak with King Penda. "They have Hibernians with them and they outnumber us still."

"Then the arrival of King Cadwallon may swing the numbers in our favour."

I told the king of my suspicions about the priest and he concurred. "What do we do, Warlord? You know him better than any."

"I thought I did. He was like a brother to me but I will try. Gawan dreamed last night. I hope that Myrddyn can come."

King Penda smiled, "Perhaps he can fly here as he did when he killed Morcant Bulc."

"Perhaps. But however he gets here I would it were soon." I paused, "Suppose this Paulinus has already poisoned the mind of our friend. We would be trapped between two armies."

I could see that the thought had not occurred to the Mercian. "Surely he will not have fallen that far so soon."

"The priests of the White Christ hate us. They would do anything to eliminate us and make the world worship their White Christ."

We watched the army of the Cymri as they wound their way north. I saw the priest riding next to the King with Cadfan between them. Neither Penda nor I bowed as King Cadwallon dismounted and, for the first time since I had known him, he looked unhappy about the lack of deference. I saw the cross hanging around his neck. I ignored the priest.

"It is good to see you, brother." As he dismounted, I embraced him. He did not respond. "I am sorry for your loss but my sister is in the Otherworld with my father."

He almost recoiled. He held the cross before him. "I follow the cross now, Warlord, as do my warriors. We are Christians."

I looked beyond him. His leaders, with whom I had fought, did not look happy and I saw no crosses. I nodded, "There are many supplies within. Come and we will talk," I looked pointedly at the priest, "the three of us."

King Cadwallon said, "Brother Paulinus can offer sage advice, Warlord."

"Unless he has stood in a shield wall he cannot." I stared at the king, "I am Warlord still, King Cadwallon."

The priest said, "And he is king!"

I turned on the white clad servant of the White Christ and put my face close to his. "The last I heard you were at the wedding of King Edwin and now you are here. If I were you priest I would stay beyond the reach of my sword."

He paled and clutched his own cross. "You would threaten a man of the church?"

I laughed, "Of course I would! It is not my church. My church is the world and we need no white clad priests to instruct us." I turned to the king, "Come Cadwallon, it is too hot to debate in the sun. Come to the hall with Penda and me. We have things to say to you. Pelas, watch over Prince Cadfan."

I had them bemused. The priest was not happy but he could do little about it and the king had been listening to me for his whole life and so he followed me. Pol and Lann Aelle would speak with the leaders of Cadwallon's army and find out their intent. Penda and I needed to undo the work of the poisoned tongue of the priest. Gawan watched the priest.

Once in the hall I sent the warriors to join the others outside. King Cadwallon looked unhappy, "That was not well done, Hogan Lann."

"What was not well done, my friend, was changing your religion because of *wyrd*. My sister died; these things happen. My wife, child and step mother died." I let the words hang in the air.

"Brother Paulinus says that there is no such thing. It is God's will which determines our lives."

Penda spat into the fire, "Then Brother Paulinus is talking out of his arse! We all know that *wyrd* makes the impossible possible. How does your priest explain that?"

"Enough! We are not here to debate religion we are here to plan how to defeat Edwin."

"Brother Paulinus says that it is a sin to make war on a fellow Christian!"

I could see Penda's anger and I held up my hand. "Did you know that your priest was at the wedding of King Edwin and saved his life when the men from Wessex tried to kill him?"

I could see that he did not but he tried to bluster, "It matters not. The message is the same. King Edwin is a Christian king."

"A Christian king who was set to invade your lands!" I waved my arm in the direction of the other halls. "He had enough supplies here to feed his army all summer."

"Brother Paulinus said that Edwin was just coming to punish the Mercians for their pagan ways."

I laughed for I saw the flaw in the priest's argument. "And when Edwin set out did he not believe that you were a pagan too? You were the target."

"But I am Christian now."

He was blind and could not see that he had been duped. Penda caught my eye and shook his head. I changed my tack. "Cadwallon, my father was your friend and he helped you to gain your throne. I have fought for you. Have I ever lied to you or told you an untruth?" He shook his head. "Have I ever advised you badly?" Again, he shook his head. "My whole life has been fighting for you and for Rheged; will you not trust me again? Let us drive Edwin back to his own lands. Let us inflict such a defeat upon him that he never dares head south again."

I could see him wavering, "But I have been baptised!"

I laughed, "And I have fallen in the water before now too. Will your men fight?" He looked up sharply. His men wanted to fight. His shoulders slumped and he nodded. "Then let us take our armies to the field."

"You would fight now?"

"We will not have to fight now. I wondered why King Edwin waited here and now I know. The serpent in priest's clothes was meant to subvert you so that we would be defeated and he would have a free rein in Mercia and Cymru. As soon as he sees our banners arrayed he will melt into the forest." I was guessing now but it all made sense inside my head and my father had always taught me to trust my inner feelings. "What have you to lose? If he melts away then I am right and if not then, perhaps, your priest was speaking the truth." He nodded and I put my arms around them both. "I will speak with them as I am Warlord still."

When we emerged from the hall all of my leaders, Penda's and King Cadwallon's were waiting and I could see the questions on their faces. I noted that the priest was there and was being closely watched by Gawan.

"We go to show the Northumbrians that the Great Alliance is still alive and we are still brothers in arms!" The cheer from all of them was so loud that I felt King Cadwallon recoil beneath my arm. Even if he wished to his men would not back away from the fight. I saw the priest try to speak but he was silenced by Gawan.

"Let us array our men before the burgh and see if this Edwin wishes to fight or to flee."

The gates at both sides of the burgh were opened. Pelas brought Cadfan and my horse. There was much confusion as leaders sent orders to their men. If we were to fight today it would be without order but I felt that there would be no fight. As I mounted, I looked around and felt pride that the leaders of the warriors still chose to fight for me. Any doubts I may have had about being Warlord disappeared. Suddenly a figure on a horse galloped past, almost knocking Cadfan to the ground. I saw the white robes and knew that it was the priest.

"Stop him!"

There were just a few slingers on the walls and they tried their best. I saw one lead ball strike the priest on the shoulder but he kept his saddle and headed north to the waiting Northumbrians. King Cadwallon ran and picked up his son. I pointed to the fleeing priest, "If you wanted confirmation of what I said, King Cadwallon, then look at Edwin's man racing to his master!"

"You were right, Warlord. How could I have been so blind?"

"You were trying to save your son."

We had not even arrayed in our battle lines when the Northumbrians began to break camp and head into the forest. We had more men than he did and he had no surprise. The priest had told him that the game was up and the cautious king was retreating. With the backs of his warriors to the forest he was inviting disaster if he stayed to face us.

"Pol, Lann Aelle, have Daffydd and his archers join us." They galloped off. "King Penda and King Cadwallon, Edwin has a large burgh at Caer Daun on the other side of this forest. He has more men there. We need to stop him from gaining reinforcements from the north. Take your armies and keep your swords in his back. Do not try to bring him to battle for the forests will suit his lightly armed men. Give him no rest. We have fed well and he has not."

"What will you do, Warlord?"

"I will take your equites and mine and we will get ahead of him. I will take my men through the forest and we will be waiting before Caer Daun for him. We will end this there."

Cadwallon nodded and waved forward Dai ap Dai. "Go with the Warlord!"

The leader of the equites of Cymru nodded. I could see the smile on his lips. He was one of us yet.

Chapter 23

It was a mighty force of horse which I gathered. "Aed, take your scouts and find us a way through the forest. Head to the west for I would avoid King Edwin and his army."

"Aye Warlord."

I saw Gawan looking annoyed, "What ails you brother?"

"That priest struck me and knocked me from my horse. I will pay him back before too long."

I laughed, "It does not matter. He knows nothing. He can do us no more harm. Kay, have your banner as the rearguard."

"What of the slingers, Warlord?"

"They can guard the burgh with the wounded. They will eat well at any rate." Although many of the supplies had been divided amongst us there was still a hall full at the burgh. "Dai, you can ride with me for I would speak with you."

We headed west in case there were any Northumbrian spies watching us. We would enter the forests where the land began to rise. I had no doubt that we would move as fast, if not faster than the Northumbrians.

"Tell me what happened to my sister, the Queen. Had she been ill for long?"

"No, Warlord. She was in good health for a day or so before she and the Prince began to feel drowsy. We thought nothing of it but then a day later they just slept. It was then that the priest arrived. He spoke with the king and he sat, alone, with the Queen and her son. A day later and the Prince awoke but the Queen did not." He hesitated, "The priest said it was because she was a pagan and did not believe but Prince Cadfan did."

"And what do you believe?"

"I believe in the old ways as the Queen did."

"Did anyone leave the town at about this time?"

He looked at me in surprise. "How did you know?"

Gawan, who was behind us, laughed sardonically, "Perhaps my big brother is getting the second sight."

"No but you have worked out what I have, Gawan."

He nodded and Dai looked from one to the other, "What am I missing, Warlord?"

"Who left?"

"The Queen's handmaidens were all upset by her death and there was much weeping and rending of clothes. The king ordered us to let them grieve and two of them disappeared. The others said that they were so upset by the Queen's death that they took their own lives."

"But you did not find their bodies?"

"No, Warlord, we searched but..." his shoulders slumped, "The Queen was murdered."

I nodded, "Edwin must have planted the women some time ago. The priest was sent to finish the deed."

"But he is a priest of the White Christ!"

I remembered when I had been in Llenlleog's country and I had seen the look of pure hate on the bishop there. He had been capable of murder in the name of his church. I had no doubt that Paulinus would have done so in the name of the Pope. If I saw him again he would die. As events turned out I did not. He fled back to Rome where he was lauded as a hero of the church for having converted two heathen kings. He would beg forgiveness for the murder and be absolved. That was the difference between our worlds.

Now that I knew the truth I could concentrate on the matters at hand. King Edwin had a well built stronghold and I had no doubt that the cautious king had left it well garrisoned. He would expect us to come after him and he would be prepared to defend and let us waste our strength on his shield wall. I hoped to be the surprise he had not anticipated.

Summer was on the wane but the leaves were still heavy upon the trees. We rode through dappled sunlight. We kept a steady rather than fast pace. I did not think we would have to fight when we emerged but it paid to be ready. It took the rest of the day to pass through the oak and birch trees of Bilhaugh Forest. It was still light when we emerged well to the west of Caer Daun.

"Pol and Dai rest the men here. I will ride with the scouts to spy out the burgh."

"You cannot go alone."

"No Pol. My brother and cousin will escort my squires and myself. Fear not I was not meant to fall before Edwin dies." I had no idea what put that thought into my head but I was learning to trust these feelings which had recently come into my head. I wondered if Nanna's death had aught to do with it. As dusk descended we approached the river north of Caer Daun. I was going to head south when I saw that the Northumbrians had arrived and they were setting up camp in the bed of the river.

I was curious. There was a perfectly good burgh some two miles away and yet the king had chosen the bend of the river for his men to camp and, presumably, fight. Why?

"Dai, ride to Pol and have him bring the equites here. We will camp on this high ground. There is shelter from the eyes of the Northumbrians but tell him no fires."

He rode off. "And what do you intend, brother?"

"I intend to go down and inspect his camp after dark. This Edwin is cautious. Why has he chosen here to defend?" I pointed to the forest to the south. "If we had followed him north then when we came from the forest we would not see where he has camped. It is in a hollow and hidden. Why does he hide?"

There were six scouts with us. As darkness fell they led us down the slope towards the camp. The Northumbrians had lit fires and were cooking. We halted half a mile from the camp and leaving Llewellyn and two scouts to watch the horses we made our way toward the river. We had not gone far when I discovered why he had chosen this site. The ground was swampy and although we did not sink into it I knew that horses with mailed warriors upon them would struggle. They would, at best, go so slowly as to be rendered ineffective and, at worst, they would sink into the swamp.

Suddenly we heard the sound of hammering ahead. We crept closer. The fires of the Northumbrians lit them and the darkness hid us. I saw, just fifty paces away, the warriors hammering sharpened wooden stakes into the soft swamp. They were there to catch our horses. I had seen enough. I led my men back to the horses. We waited until we were well clear from the Northumbrian camp before I spoke.

"He has chosen this so that he can slaughter our equites. If we tried to charge then our horses would sink in the mud or be impaled upon the stakes. Even the fyrd would be amongst us and their knives would make short work of heavily mailed warriors floundering in the swamp. He is a cunning opponent."

"Then what can we do?"

"I will sleep on it, brother."

We were awake before dawn. I sent two of Aed's scouts with the news of the Northumbrian's dispositions. The two kings would have to bring their army further north. I led the equites to the north of the camp and positioned my warriors across and along the road. We waited.

Dai asked, "Warlord, why do we wait here?"

"Your king and King Penda will take most of the day to reach here. I am waiting for King Edwin to send a rider north for reinforcements."

"But he will see us!"

"I know. I wish him to."

It was mid morning when the five riders crested the rise. They saw a mighty host of horsemen. We had well over a hundred equites and with the twenty squires and sixty archers we filled the road between the trees. They turned and fled.

"Good, now we can advance on the Northumbrians."

Gawan rode next to me as we trotted south down the old Roman Road. "You have closed your mind to me brother. I cannot read your thoughts."

"I am sorry, Gawan. I did not know I had. Perhaps I am gaining powers I did not know I could possess. I seem to be able to read Edwin and his purposes."

"You have a plan to deal with the swamp?"

"I have. He is counting on the fact that the river will protect him. I intend to use that misplaced confidence. He also thinks my horsemen cannot attack him or if we do then it will be a disaster. I will have my horsemen ride at him as though we are meaning to attack and then pull back."

"How will that help?" I smiled and told him. He nodded appreciatively. "A cunning plan."

"Not an original one. I read of this when I was in Constantinopolis. I was not certain how I would manage to use it but Edwin has given me the opportunity."

I called for Daffydd and gave him his instructions. He rode north along the Roman Road. I knew he could be relied upon. He would not act rashly. The buccina and the dragon standard were all that he needed.

We reined in a mile from the Northumbrian lines. It was impossible to see the strakes and the swamp. It looked like a grass covered bend in the river. The area just behind was covered in warriors. They watched us but made no move to form a shield wall. He could see that our numbers were too few to attack. King Edwin was waiting for our foot to arrive.

"We will camp here. Let us rest the horses. Tomorrow we will begin our attack."

Aed's scouts returned. "King Penda and King Cadwallon will be here by dark."

"Good." We had already laid out the camp for our allies. The slightly higher ground meant we could peer down upon them. I went with Lann Aelle and Pol for a closer inspection of the Saxon defences. We halted just four hundred paces from them. I knew that they could ride at us if they chose but we could easily outrun their ponies. They would have to watch us and grind their teeth in anger.

We sought the banners. I spotted King Edwin's and his two sons. They were in the bend of the river. To the south were the men of Eadfrith. I also saw the banners of Eabald of Kent. On the extreme southern flank were the men of Dál Riata. To the north were Aethelfrith's sons. They were a formidable army. The fyrd was spread out in a long line in front of the housecarls of the leaders. We would have to cut our way through them first. King Edwin was hoping that I would be foolish enough to attack my heavy horses and then his wild fyrd would deal with us.

We returned to our lines and I lay down to sleep. My side still ached and I would need to have all of my strength for the battle to come.

King Penda and King Cadwallon came ahead of the long column of warriors and joined me to view the Northumbrians. I told them of the trap which Edwin had planned.

"And what will you do, Warlord?"

"Why I will charge him as he expects me to!" Penda looked at me as though I had taken leave of my senses. King Cadwallon was more like his old self and he smiled. "Trust me I will not fall into his trap but I want him to commit his men to attack me. They will allow your warriors to cut their way through Eadfrith's men. We will have him between us." As with Gawan I took them into my confidence and gave them the details of my plan. They were both happier when they knew that I had thought this through thoroughly.

That evening we gathered the Mercian archers, of whom there were just a handful, and the Welsh archers who numbered more than a hundred together to give them their instructions. As the Northumbrians' fires burned the archers crept close to the swamp. Llenlleog led them for he had been there with me. We watched from the hillside although there was little to see. We could hear, however. The archers began to loose flight after flight of arrows into their camp. We heard the screams and shouts as warriors were struck. After ten flights of arrows I heard Llewellyn sound the buccina and they withdrew. Three hours later, as the moon rose, they returned to send another ten flights over. Once that was done they enjoyed a rest. The Northumbrians had no rest for they expected to have their sleep shattered by a further rain of deadly arrows.

When dawn broke we saw the bodies huddled in little groups. The Northumbrians began to clear them and we prepared for battle. We left the squires with the horses and we joined the equites of Dai ap Dai. Llewellyn was the only one of my men who was horsed for he carried the dragon banner. Dai's squire carried my shield and I held his stirrup. The hard part would be reaching the battlefield.

Dai led his men from the north so that we, running on the right of the horses, were hidden. At the same time King Penda and King Cadwallon led their men in a long line to the south of us. The horses cantered but we had to run hard to keep up with them. I heard the Northumbrians horns as the men were called to arms. The fyrd would already be moving close to the stakes. We were just thirty paces from the stakes and the swamp when Llewellyn halted. The squire handed me my shield. The well trained Welshmen halted as one. With the exception of Llewellyn they turned and rode back up the hill. We ran towards the fyrd. They were well in front of the shield wall. Llewellyn rode his horse up and down making the dragon standard wail. We ran forward. The fyrd suddenly saw not horsemen charging them but mailed men on foot. The stakes could easily be seen and avoided. I lowered my sword and the buccina sounded. I could see, from the other side of the river, Daffydd and my archers as they rode to the eastern bank of the Daun where they would soon begin to rain death on the warbands of Aethelfrith's sons.

The fyrd were caught in two minds. Did they do as they had been ordered and come towards us or retreat because their plan had failed? They panicked and looked for instructions. I brought Saxon Slayer around in a wide arc and decapitated the first warrior. I punched a second with my shield and, stepping forward stabbed down on his middle. We had to get as close to the shield wall as possible. The farmers who faced us stood no chance and they did what any sensible man would do in that situation, they ran. They hurtled towards the shield wall which was advancing towards us. Oswald and Oswiu's men would not let them through. To do so would invite us to close with them. They all knew how good my equites were. Some of the fyrd perished at the hands of their own countrymen. They began to tear their way through the shield wall to reach the safety of the river.

It was not as though the river was any safer either for Daffydd and his archers could not be reached and already I could see the rear ranks of the shield wall turning their shields to protect themselves from the new danger.

Pol, Lann Aelle and Llenlleog were with me and Pelas guarded my back. The five of us headed directly for the large housecarl of Oswald who hacked down one of his own men trying to get past him. I brought my sword from behind my head. It came down so fast that it was a blur. The warrior held up his shield for protection but my blade ripped through the wood and carried on down to slice through the metal of the helmet as though it was the skin of an apple. He sank to the ground and I punched with my shield to get inside the shield wall.

A spear head darted at my face and I turned my head slightly so that the edge slid down my helmet. I brought Saxon Slayer up and watched warrior's horrified face as the sharp tip entered his body and ripped upwards. He screamed as he tried to catch his intestines and I pushed him backwards. He was a big warrior and his tumbling, writhing body knocked two more warriors to the ground. I stamped on one and stabbed the other. The shield wall was broken and my warriors were laying about them. Pol was using his mace to great effect. I shouted, "Saxon Slayer!" for the joy of battle was upon me and the Northumbrians closest to me fell backwards.

I had breathing space at last. I spied Oswald and Oswiu. I pointed my sword at them and began to run towards them. Pol, Lann Aelle and Gawan followed me. My wolf shield was covered in the blood of my enemies. My helmet and mail were similarly draped with the remains of men. I knew how terrifying I looked. The Northumbrians of Oswald and Oswiu ran. They hurtled towards Edwin and the standard of Northumbria. Daffydd moved his archers even closer to the edge of the river and the arrows no longer rained, they were aimed with purpose. At less than forty paces the arrows were deadly. The helmets of the Saxons and the mail could not stop them. The retreat became a rout and even Oswald and Oswiu joined their brother to run south. Behind me I heard the hooves of Dai ap Dai who had brought his equites and our squires into the fray. The sight of reinforcements had been too much.

"Reform! Wedge!"

King Penda and King Cadwallon were pushing hard at Eadfrith and the Hibernians but they were holding their own against the attack. The battle was in the balance. In my head I heard my father's voice urging me to get to Edwin. If he fell then the battle would be over.

I turned to my men. I could see that we had lost some but more than sixty equites were with me. "We end this war today. We go for Edwin. Are you with me?"

I could see the light of battle shone in their eyes and they all yelled, "Aye Warlord!" It was so loud that I saw warriors on the other side of the battlefield stop and look. I sheathed Saxon Slayer and picked up a Saxon spear. I was the point of the arrow. We began to march. The men banged their shields and chanted as we marched, "Saxon Slayer! Saxon Slayer! Saxon Slayer! Saxon Slayer!" It was not only terrifying it helped us to march in time. I saw Edwin organising his shield wall to take us. His sons Osfrith and Eadfrith stood before their father and the banner.

As we drew closer the men chanted faster as we picked up speed. The last few paces would be at a run. It took skill to run and strike at the same time but we were well trained and they knew me.

I watched the Northumbrians brace themselves for the shock. I pulled back my right arm and punched as we were one pace from the shield wall. My spear went through Osfrith's head and emerged out of the back. As he fell the head broke from the spear and I whipped it sideways into Eadfrith's helmet. As I punched with my shield, I drew Saxon Slayer and stabbed blindly ahead of me. I felt Lann Aelle's presence as he swung his mace at Eadfrith who, already stunned, fell unconscious at our feet.

Those two blows seemed to enrage the oathsworn of King Edwin. A knot of them suddenly lurched at us. I was already tired; I was not used to fighting on foot. My wound was now aching and two warriors came at me at once. Lann Aelle was fending off an attack from my right and, although I took the two blows on my shield and my sword I was forced to my knees. I saw the look of triumph on the faces of the two warriors. I felt like a fish stranded on a beach. I could barely get my breath. As the swords were raised to end my days Gawan thrust his shield in the way of one blow. I managed to protect myself with my shield but the warrior facing Gawan was a mighty one and he punched Gawan in the face with his own shield. My brother fell next to me.

Perhaps that was the spur I needed for I found new energy. I brought my right hand back and punched up as hard as I could. The tip of Saxon Slayer peered out from the neck of the surprised warrior. As I stood I pushed my shield and he tumbled from my blade. The huge warrior had his sword raised to strike the recumbent Gawan. I leapt at him with my shield and my whole body weight behind it. We crashed to the ground. Had I been on the bottom I fear I would never have risen but it was he who had the wind knocked from him. We were too close for a blow with the blade of Saxon Slayer and so I raised my hand and brought down the jewelled pommel into his eye. I kept punching until his face was a bloody mess and he moved no more.

I was aware of Llenlleog, Pelas, Lann Aelle and Pol standing around the bodies of my brother and myself. I raised myself to my knees and lifted Gawan's helmet. His eyes opened. "Thank the Allfather you are alive!"

He gave a pained smile, "And you, brother."

I stood. We had broken the charge of the oathsworn but the banner still stood. I could see that Eanfrith and the Hibernians were holding against Penda and Cadwallon. I knew that the battle could turn in an instant. We had to get to Edwin. Once his banner fell then the heart would go from the enemy.

The Northumbrians were also tired but they stood in steel ring around their king. My men looked anxiously over their shoulders at me. Pol inclined his head and I said, "I am ready, Pol, one last push. We take the banner and the king." They nodded and took their places around me. Gawan got to his feet although he was somewhat unsteady. "Pelas, watch my brother!" I raised my sword, "Saxon Slayer!"

The brief rest had given my legs and arm some respite and we ran at the ring of shields. The spears had been shattered and it was sword against sword. Perhaps we had already slain their best warriors but the four of us fell upon the shield wall like furies. Bors, Kay and Osgar followed the sword and all along the Northumbrian line my equites crashed into the Saxon shields.

I stabbed forward with Saxon Slayer and the blade went towards the head of a warrior who moved his head out of the way. The warrior behind did not see the sword which ripped into his shoulder. He was no longer pushing and supporting the warrior before me. Gawan and Pelas pushed my back and the warrior was forced to step back. The warrior behind had sunk to his knees and my opponent tumbled to the ground. He could not avoid the sword which pinned him to the swampy earth.

There was no one between me and Edwin. "Surrender Northumbrian, for you have lost!"

"I will never surrender to a pagan and a devil worshipper. God is on my side this day and you will die."

I swung my sword high behind me and brought it down towards Edwin's head. He brought his shield up. I was the first man he had fought this day. He did not brace himself for the blow. He recoiled and struggled to keep his feet. I too was tiring but I knew that he was mine for the taking I brought the sword around in an arc to my right and King Edwin struggled to lower his shield in time. He was pushed back again. The ground was slippery with mud, blood and bodies. I could see that his face was now filled with fear. He managed to stab forward with his sword but it was a weak blow and I deflected it easily. It opened him up and I stabbed forward. Had this been the start of the battle then it would have ended there but my sword was not as sharp as it had been. It tore through a few of the links and scraped a tear in the leather byrnie but he lived still.

I heard a roar behind me as the banner fell when the bearer was killed. The cheer went up along our lines. "Surrender! You have lost!"

"Jesus will not abandon me. I will overcome you, heathen!"

He was a brave man for he was facing a warrior who was at the peak of his powers. I feinted with the sword; aiming at his helmet. He brought the shield up and I punched mine at the same time. He tumbled to the ground and made the cardinal mistake of breaking his fall with his arms. He lay like a beached fish on the ground at my feet. As I stuck my sword through his throat I thought it ironical that he died in the same pose as the cross which hung around his neck.

The wail from his men seemed to spread along and down the river. His men fled. The ones without armour hurled themselves into the river while many others ran north through my exhausted warriors who could not catch them. I pushed my helmet back and turned. My equites had taken losses but my captains, brother, cousin and squire lived still. They began to bang their shields and to chant, "Warlord! Warlord!" King Edwin was dead and Northumbria was no more. We had won. *Wyrd*!

Epilogue

The pursuit of the survivors of the battle of Hatfield was left to King Cadwallon and his men. Perhaps that was why the books they wrote spoke of it as King Cadwallon's victory. The warriors who were there knew that it was my victory. I had lost over thirty of my equites but we had slain King Edwin's oathsworn. King Penda asked me for Eadfrith as a hostage for the sons of Aethelfrith had caused Penda great loss. As it was Oswald and Oswiu whom I sought, I concurred. The pyre from the burning Northumbrians was so large that it burned for three days. They say that the ground was blackened for a generation. The priests of the White Christ took the manner of the death of their king as a sign from their God and he was made into a saint. I have no idea what a saint is; perhaps it was to commemorate that he fought as a warrior and died with a sword in his hand. I wondered if that meant he would be in the Otherworld.

Two days after the battle we mounted our horses and headed north. King Cadwallon seemed to enjoy the adulation of being a hero. It was at that time that he began to believe that he had won the battle. King Penda was less than complimentary about him saying that he had ridden behind his oathsworn and let them do the fighting. I could understand that; he was merely a king but I was Warlord.

We reached the old Roman fort of Eboracum. Autumn was upon us and we could travel no further. While King Cadwallon continued to rampage through the north the warriors I had led from Mona and the Clwyd valley wintered in the fortress. The Northumbrians had largely fled and left only the slaves. I freed them and they stayed to be our servants.

As we walked the old Roman paths and marvelled at the buildings I was reminded of Civitas Carvetiorum. We had left that town many years ago. We had fought in the wilderness and the wilds of Wales for many years but now we were within touching distance of a final victory. King Penda went back to Mercia and the warriors of Rheged rested before we would finally rid our old land of the Northumbrian stain. We had felled the Saxon and the Warlord had won. The Kingdom of Northumbria was ended.

The End

Glossary

Name-Explanation
Abbatis Villa- Abbeville –Northern France
Aengus Finn mac Fergus Dubdétach-Irish mercenary
Aelfere-Northallerton
Aelle-Monca's son and Hogan Lann's uncle
Aileen- Fergus' sister, a mystic
Alavna-Maryport
Artorius-King Arthur
Banna-Birdoswald
Belatu-Cadros -God of war
Belerion-Land's End (Cornwall)
Bilhaugh Forest –Sherwood Forest
Bone fire- the burning of the waste material after the slaughter of the animals at the end of October. (Bonfire night)
Bors- son of Mungo
Bro Waroc'h- one of the Brythionic tribes who settled in Brittany
Byrnie – mail shirt
Caedwalestate-Cadishead near Salford
Caer Daun- Doncaster
Caergybi-Holyhead
Cadwallon ap Cadfan- King of Gwynedd
Caldarium- the hot room in a Roman bathhouse
Civitas Carvetiorum-Carlisle
Constantinopolis-Constantinople (modern Istanbul)
Cymri-Wales
Cynfarch Oer-Descendant of Coel Hen (King Cole)
Daffydd ap Gwynfor-Lann's chief sea captain
Daffydd ap Miach-Miach's son
Dai ap Gruffyd-King Cadfan's squire
Delbchaem Lann-Lann's daughter
Din Guardi-Bamburgh Castle
Dunum-River Tees
Dux Britannica-The Roman British leader after the Romans left (King Arthur?)
Edwin-King of Bernicia, Deira and Northumbria

Erecura-Goddess of the earth
Fanum Cocidii-Bewcastle
Fiachnae mac Báetáin- King of Strathclyde
Fiachnae mac Demmáin King of the Dál Fiatach
Freja-Saxon captive and Aelle's wife
Gareth-Harbour master Caergybi
Gallóglaigh-Irish mercenary
Gawan Lann-Lann's son
Glanibanta- Ambleside
Gwynfor-Headman at Caergybi
Gwyr-The land close to Swansea
Halvelyn- Helvellyn
Haordine-Hawarden Cheshire
Hen Ogledd-Northern England and Southern Scotland
Hogan Lann-Lann's son and Warlord
Icaunus-River god
King Ywain Rheged-Eldest son of King Urien
Lann- First Warlord of Rheged and Dux Britannica
Llenlleog- 'Leaping one' (Lancelot)
Loge-God of trickery
Loidis-Leeds
Maeresea-River Mersey
Mare Nostrum-Mediterranean Sea
Metcauld- Lindisfarne)
Myfanwy-the Warlord's stepmother
Myrddyn-Welsh wizard fighting for Rheged
Nanna Lann-Lann's daughter, wife to King Cadwallon
Namentwihc –Nantwich, Cheshire
Nithing-A man without honour
Nodens-God of hunting
Oppidum- hill fort
Oswald-Priest
Paulinus of Eboracum- The Pope's representative in Britannia
Penrhyd- Penrith, Cumbria
Penrhyn Llŷn- Llŷn Peninsula
pharos- lighthouse
Pol-Equite and strategos
Prestune-Preston Lancashire
Roman Bridge-Piercebridge (Durham)

Roman Soldiers- the mountains around Scafell Pike
Scillonia Insula-Scilly Isles
Solar-West facing room in a castle
Spæwīfe- Old English for witch
Sucellos-God of love and time
Táin Bó- Irish for cattle raid
Tatenhale-Tattenhall near Chester
Tepidarium- the warm room in a Roman Bath house
The Narrows-The Menaii Straits
Treffynnon-Holywell (North Wales)
Tuanthal-Leader of the Warlord's horse warriors
Vectis-Isle of Wight
Vindonnus-God of hunting
Wachanglen-Wakefield
Wrecsam- Wrexham
wapentake- Muster of an army
Wide Water-Windermere
Wyddfa-Snowdon
Wyrd-Fate
Y Fflint-Flint (North Wales)
Ynys Enlli-Bardsey Island
Yr Wyddgrug-Mold (North Wales)
Zatrikion- an early form of Greek chess

Historical note

There is evidence that the Saxons withdrew from Rheged in the early years of the seventh century and never dominated that land again. It seems that warriors from Wales reclaimed that land. I have used Lord Lann as that instrument. King Edwin did usurp Aethelfrith. Edwin was allied to both Mercia and East Anglia.

There is a cave in North Yorkshire called Mother Shipton's cave. It has a petrifying well within. Objects left there become covered, over time, with a stone exterior. In the seventeenth century a witch was reputed to live there. I created an earlier witch to allow the Roman sword to be discovered and to create a link with my earlier Roman series.

The Saxons and Britons all valued swords and cherished them. They were passed from father to son. The use of rings on the hilts of great swords was a common practice and showed the prowess of the warrior in battle. I do not subscribe to Brian Sykes' theory that the Saxons merely assimilated into the existing people. One only has to look at the place names and listen to the language of the north and north western part of England. You can still hear anomalies. Perhaps that is because I come from the north but all of my reading leads me to believe that the Anglo-Saxons were intent upon conquest. The Norse invaders were different and they did assimilate but the Saxons were fighting for their lives and it did not pay to be kind. The people of Rheged were the last survivors of Roman Britain and I have given them all of the characteristics they would have had. They were educated and ingenious. The Dark Ages was the time when much knowledge was lost and would not reappear until Constantinople fell. This period was also the time when the old ways changed and Britain became Christian. This was a source of conflict as well as growth.

It was at the beginning of the sixth century that King Aethelfrith was killed in battle. His sons, Eanforth, Oswiu and Oswald became famous and outshone both their father and King Edwin. Although Edwin became king he did not have the three brothers killed and they had an uneasy alliance.

King Cadwallon became the last great British leader until modern times. Alfred ruled the Saxons but no one held such sway over the country from Scotland to Cornwall in the same way that King Cadwallon did. He did this not by feat of arms alone but by using alliances. He even allied with the Mercians to ensure security for his land. His death saw the end of the hopes of the native Britons. They would survive but they would never reconquer their land. I have invented a Warlord to aid him but that is backed up by the few writings we have. Dux Britannicus and Arthur are both shadowy figures who crop up in what we now term, the Dark Ages.

King Edwin's life was saved by Bishop Paulinus who had been sent by the Pope to convert the Northumbrians to Christianity. The act made King Edwin order all of his people to convert. I have used Paulinus as a sort of villain. I have no doubt that the Church at the time thought they were doing good work but like the Spanish Inquisition a thousand years later they were not averse to suing any means possible when dealing with what they deemed pagans. King Cadwallon did convert to Christianity but still fought King Edwin. Bede, the Northumbrian propagandist, portrayed Cadwallon as a cruel man who destroyed the Christian kingdom of Northumbria. Perhaps that was because King Edwin became an early Christian martyr. History is written by the winners and the Anglo-Saxons did win, albeit briefly before the Norse and the Bretons combined to reconquer England in 1066.

The people of Brittany did arrive there as stated in the novel. I have obviously invented both names and events to suit my story but the background is accurate. They spoke a variation of Welsh/Cornish. There was a famous witch who lived on one of the islands of Scilly. Although this was in the Viking age a century or so later I can see no reason why mystics did not choose to live there.

The horses used by William the Conqueror at Hastings were about fifteen and a half hands high. The largest contingent of non-Norman knights who accompanies him were the Bretons and their horses were marginally bigger. It is ironical that the people of Britain came back to defeat the Saxons. It was a mixture of Briton and Viking (Norman) who finally conquered Britain. (*Wyrd*!)

The battle of Hatfield took place on the River Don close to Doncaster. It was fought on a swamp in a bend of the river. It was in the early 630s. King Edwin was killed at the battle and the leaders of the victorious armies were named as Penda and Cadwallon. It marked a reversal in fortunes for the Saxons. They were forced to retreat further north and Eanfrith, the eldest of Aethelfrith's children became king of Deira. He was also killed by Cadwallon and Oswald became king. The kingdom of Northumbria would never be as powerful again until the Vikings conquered it in the ninth century. Bernicia and Deira emerged as minor kingdoms. King Cadwallon had a brief year of glory when he rampaged through the land of Bernicia. It was not to last.

I used many books to research the material. The first was the excellent Michael Wood's book "***In Search of the Dark Ages***" and the second was "***The Middle Ages***" Edited by Robert Fossier. The third was the Osprey Book- "***Saxon, Viking and Norman***" by Terence Wise. I also used Brian Sykes book, "***Blood of the Isles***" for reference. "***Arthur and the Anglo-Saxon Wars***" by David Nicholle was also useful. In addition, I searched on line for more obscure information. All the place names are accurate, as far as I know, and I have researched the names of the characters to reflect the period. My apologies if I have made a mistake.

The Warlord and King Cadwallon will return and they will meet the Saxons once more on the field of battle.

Griff Hosker December 2014

Other books by Griff Hosker

If you enjoyed reading this book, then why not read another one by the author?

Ancient History
The Sword of Cartimandua Series
(Germania and Britannia 50– 128 A.D.)
Ulpius Felix- Roman Warrior (prequel)
Book 1 The Sword of Cartimandua
Book 2 The Horse Warriors
Book 3 Invasion Caledonia
Book 4 Roman Retreat
Book 5 Revolt of the Red Witch
Book 6 Druid's Gold
Book 7 Trajan's Hunters
Book 8 The Last Frontier
Book 9 Hero of Rome
Book 10 Roman Hawk
Book 11 Roman Treachery
Book 12 Roman Wall
Book 13 Roman Courage

The Aelfraed Series
(Britain and Byzantium 1050 A.D. - 1085 A.D.)
Book 1 Housecarl
Book 2 Outlaw
Book 3 Varangian

The Wolf Warrior series
(Britain in the late 6th Century)
Book 1 Saxon Dawn
Book 2 Saxon Revenge
Book 3 Saxon England
Book 4 Saxon Blood
Book 5 Saxon Slayer
Book 6 Saxon Slaughter

Book 7 Saxon Bane
Book 8 Saxon Fall: Rise of the Warlord
Book 9 Saxon Throne
Book 10 Saxon Sword

The Dragon Heart Series
Book 1 Viking Slave
Book 2 Viking Warrior
Book 3 Viking Jarl
Book 4 Viking Kingdom
Book 5 Viking Wolf
Book 6 Viking War
Book 7 Viking Sword
Book 8 Viking Wrath
Book 9 Viking Raid
Book 10 Viking Legend
Book 11 Viking Vengeance
Book 12 Viking Dragon
Book 13 Viking Treasure
Book 14 Viking Enemy
Book 15 Viking Witch
Book 16 Viking Blood
Book 17 Viking Weregeld
Book 18 Viking Storm
Book 19 Viking Warband
Book 20 Viking Shadow
Book 21 Viking Legacy
Book 22 Viking Clan

The Norman Genesis Series
Hrolf the Viking
Horseman
The Battle for a Home
Revenge of the Franks
The Land of the Northmen
Ragnvald Hrolfsson
Brothers in Blood
Lord of Rouen
Drekar in the Seine

Duke of Normandy

New World Series
(Iceland and America- 10th-11th Century)
Blood on the Blade

The Anarchy Series
(England 1120-1180)
English Knight
Knight of the Empress
Northern Knight
Baron of the North
Earl
King Henry's Champion
The King is Dead
Warlord of the North
Enemy at the Gate
The Fallen Crown
Warlord's War
Kingmaker
Henry II
Crusader
The Welsh Marches
Irish War
Poisonous Plots
Prince's Revolt
Earl Marshal

Border Knight
1182-1300
Sword for Hire
Return of the Knight
Baron's War
Magna Carta
Welsh War
Henry III

Struggle for a Crown
1360- 1485

Blood on the Crown
To Murder a King

Modern History

The Napoleonic Horseman Series
Book 1 Chasseur a Cheval
Book 2 Napoleon's Guard
Book 3 British Light Dragoon
Book 4 Soldier Spy
Book 5 1808: The Road to Corunna
Waterloo

The Lucky Jack American Civil War series
Rebel Raiders
Confederate Rangers
The Road to Gettysburg

The British Ace Series
1914
1915 Fokker Scourge
1916 Angels over the Somme
1917 Eagles Fall
1918 We will remember them
From Arctic Snow to Desert Sand
Wings over Persia

Combined Operations series 1940-1945
Commando
Raider
Behind Enemy Lines
Dieppe
Toehold in Europe
Sword Beach
Breakout
The Battle for Antwerp
King Tiger
Beyond the Rhine

Korea

Other Books
Carnage at Cannes (a thriller)
Great Granny's Ghost (Aimed at 9-14-year-old young people)
Adventure at 63-Backpacking to Istanbul

For more information on all of the books then please visit the author's web site at http://www.griffhosker.com where there is a link to contact him.

Made in United States
Orlando, FL
05 April 2022